Match wits with bestselling crime writers as they
dare you to solve cases of . . .

DEADLY DOINGS

Other mystery anthologies Edited by Martin Greenberg and Bill Pronzini
Published by Ivy Books:

DEADLY DOINGS

EDITED BY MARTIN H. GREENBERG

IVY BOOKS • NEW YORK

Ivy Books
Published by Ballantine Books
Copyright © 1989 by Martin H. Greenberg

Library of Congress Catalog Card Number: 89-91318

ISBN 0-8041-0296-1

Manufactured in the United States of America

First Ballantine Books Edition: November 1989

Acknowledgments

"Sylvia," by Ira Levin. Copyright 1955 by Flying Eagle Publications, Inc.; copyright renewed 1983 by Ira Levin. First published in *Manhunt*. Reprinted by permission of Harold Ober Associates Incorporated.

"Murder, 1986," by P.D. James. Copyright © 1970 by P.D. James. First published in *Ellery Queen's Mystery Magazine*. Reprinted by permission of Roberta Pryor, Inc., and Elaine Greene, Ltd.

"It Wouldn't Be Fair," by Jack Finney. Copyright 1948 by Jack Finney; copyright renewed 1976 by Jack Finney. First published in *Collier's*. Reprinted by permission of Don Congdon Associates, Inc.

"The Parker Shotgun," by Sue Grafton. Copyright © 1986 by Sue Grafton. First published in the PWA anthology *Mean Streets*, Mysterious Press, 1986. Reprinted by permission of the author.

"Never Marry Murder," by William Campbell Gault. Copyright 1949 by Popular Publications, Inc. First published in *Dime Mystery*, December 1949, under the pseudonym "Roney Scott." Reprinted by permission of the author.

"The Case of the Emerald Sky," by Eric Ambler. Copyright 1940 by Eric Ambler. Reprinted by permission of the author and Campbell, Thomson & McLaughlin, Ltd.

"Woman Missing," by Helen Nielsen. Copyright © 1960 by H.S.D. Publications, Inc. First published in *Alfred Hitchcock's Mystery Magazine*. Reprinted by permission of the author and the author's agents, Scott Meredith Literary Agency, Inc., 845 Third Avenue, New York, N.Y. 10022

Contents

Introduction

The crime story has undergone numerous refinements and updatings during this century. It reflects its times perhaps better than any other form of popular writing, and therefore has not only flourished but has taken its rightful place as a major facet of world literature. Today its popularity is at such an all-time high this may be termed the "New Golden Age of Crime Fiction," owing in no small part to the growing number of innovative writers working to stretch the once-confining limits of the genre.

Deadly Doings is the sixth in a series of anthologies designed to bring the modern reader some of the most unusual, finely crafted, and entertaining stories by today's crime-fiction specialists, as well as by important figures in other areas of popular and mainstream fiction. The first five volumes—*Prime Suspects*, *Suspicious Characters*, *Criminal Elements*, *Homicidal Acts*, and *Felonious Assaults*—contain the work of such luminaries as Stephen King, Ruth Rendell, Loren D. Estleman, Donald E. Westlake, John Jakes, P.D. James, John D. MacDonald, Lawrence Block, Ed McBain, Isaac Asimov, Robert Bloch, Edward D. Hoch, William Campbell Gault, Marcia Muller, Brian Garfield, Jonathan Gash, John Lutz, Sue Grafton, Simon Brett, Tony Hillerman, Joseph Hansen, Edward Gorman, Norman Mailer, Leslie Charteris, Ray Bradbury, Margaret Millar, Arthur C. Clarke, Stephen Greenleaf, Jesse Hill Ford, Stuart M. Kaminsky, Harry Kemelman, Michael Collins, and Dorothy B. Hughes. In this volume you'll find wholly different stories by some of the above, plus first-rate efforts by Ira Levin, Jack Finney, Eric Ambler, Helen Nielsen, and Robert J. Randisi—most if

INTRODUCTION

not all of the very best writers producing contemporary mystery and suspense fiction.

Good reading.

Martin H. Greenberg

Sylvia

•

Ira Levin

One of the finest pure suspense novels of the past fifty-odd years is Ira Levin's A Kiss Before Dying *(1953)—an amazing piece of work not only for its quality but because it was published when Levin was just twenty-four years old. Since that auspicious debut, he has authored four other novels, most notably the bestselling* Rosemary's Baby *(1967), and numerous successful Broadway plays, among them* Deathtrap *(1978). "Sylvia" is Levin's only criminous short story, published in the hard-boiled magazine* Manhunt *two years after the appearance of* A Kiss Before Dying. *It, too, is a tale of suspense, with a savage sting in its tail.*

Shortly before noon on the day of his scheduled departure for the Italian Riviera, Lewis Melton searched his daughter's room for a letter she had received a few hours earlier. This secret violation of Sylvia's privacy was performed with reluctance. Like every act it was the result of a somewhat involved set of circumstances and motivations.

A month before, Sylvia had been granted a divorce. Her husband, Lyle Waterman, had been a fortune hunter—a fact which, though obvious to everyone else, had not been demonstrable to Sylvia until he was caught red-handed tracing her endorsement onto an intercepted dividend check. When this happened Melton made a bargain with his son-in-law; Melton would not press a charge of forgery and Waterman would not contest a Nevada mental cruelty divorce. Melton, who was retired, then accompanied Sylvia to a dude ranch

1

outside Reno, where in the usual six weeks the divorce was accomplished.

Back again in Connecticut Melton succumbed to the idea of a few weeks on the Riviera, a suggestion of Sylvia's. The year before, returning from two months abroad to find Sylvia married to Waterman, Melton had been forced to recognize that despite her thirty-two years it was unwise to leave her alone for long periods of time, and he had resolved to avoid doing so in the future. But his relief at Sylvia's freedom, coupled with her expressed desire for solitude, had erased his resolution and lulled him into booking air passage, renewing his passport, contacting acquaintances in San Remo—and now, on the very day of departure, Mrs. Redden, bringing the coffee into his bedroom, had said, "Redden thinks I should tell you, sir, that Miss Sylvia just got a letter addressed in Mr. Waterman's handwriting"—and immediately the whole trip was subject to cancellation.

A letter from Lyle might be harmless; a request, perhaps, for the forwarding of some clothes he had left behind. But it might also be the first step in a brazen campaign to reestablish his influence over Sylvia, undertaken in the knowledge of Melton's planned absence. If that were the case the trip was certainly out of the question, for Sylvia was as easily led as a child's pony. Furthermore, Melton suddenly realized, her habitual demeanor of withdrawn silence, which had deepened since the moment when she learned the truth about Lyle, had effectually masked what emotions might lie within her, and he really had no way of knowing whether her love for Lyle had turned to bitterness, as he had assumed, or whether there might not linger an inclination to forgive, an eagerness to accept any explanation. . . .

Desultorily he began his packing, almost certain that the suitcases would have to be unpacked before the day was over. At eleven-thirty, when Sylvia retired to her garden at the rear of the estate, Melton entered her room and began to search for the letter.

In the course of the search he came upon a gun. He had opened a quilted satin box in the top drawer of her dresser and had riffled the edges of the handkerchiefs stacked within it. They parted in mid-pile. He lifted off the upper stack and there it was; a small nickel-plated pistol with a black bakelite grip, incredible upon the soft cushion of Sylvia's flowered handkerchiefs. Melton looked at it, his right hand blindly depositing handkerchiefs on the dresser, thinking: *It must be a joke or a cigarette lighter or something.*

He picked it up. It was heavier than it looked; certainly no cigarette lighter. He held it disbelievingly on the flat of his palm. The bakelite grip was milled in a pattern of tiny diamonds. The short barrel gleamed with an oily sheen, smooth to the fingertips, the whole having an indefinable smell of newness. Where had she gotten it? Reno? The fool! A gun . . . Events of the past month suddenly sprang into a new and frightening significance. "You really do need a rest," she had said. "The Mallinsons are still in San Remo, aren't they?"

"Well . . . yes. I suppose we *could* leave on the—"

"Not we. You go alone. Honestly, I think being here by myself for a while would be the best thing."

And he had let her talk him into it!

"About the Reddens," she had said later. "We might as well give them their vacation while you're away. I can fend for myself, and then you won't have to put up with a few weeks of canned food later on. I really think that being completely by myself . . ."

Knowing that each of his previous absences had been the occasion for some sort of irresponsible behavior on her part, he had still let her talk him into it! So lulled, so blind!

He found the way to open the gun; the bakelite plaque on the right side swung clockwise, revealing within the handle a vertical metal rack holding five small bullets ready to be pushed up in turn into the firing chamber. Melton shuddered and swung the plaque back down, wishing he could as easily replace Sylvia's mask of stolidity which, penetrated, had disclosed such unsuspected depth of feeling, love warped into such pathetically intense hatred.

The letter from Lyle . . . Melton set the gun carefully

upon the dresser and, with an aggrieved headshake, returned his attention to the handkerchief box. He found the letter almost immediately; it was beneath the uppermost handkerchief, the one on which the gun had lain. The envelope, ripped open at one end, was addressed to Sylvia in Lyle's bold, affectedly masculine hand.

Melton drew out a single sheet of paper and unfolded it. It was the stationery of an unfamiliar hotel on West 54th Street in New York. Dated the day before, it read:

Syl darling,

How can I tell you how happy your sweet letter has made me? I can't—not on paper. But when I see you, darling!

Lewis's plane leaves at midnight, so I suppose the train you are driving him to will be the 9:01. I will take the 8:00 from N.Y. which will get me into New Haven at 9:35, so you will only have to wait in the station half an hour.

Until tomorrow night, darling—

Always your loving
Lyle

Melton read the letter twice, then folded it back into its envelope. He picked up the gun and stood with the letter in one hand and the gun in the other, staring at them, thinking that Lyle, poor Lyle, with his scheming and conniving, wasn't truly dangerous at all; but Sylvia, slow, quiet Sylvia . . .

He put the letter back on the handkerchiefs in the box, covered it with the single one, and put the gun on top of that. He replaced the other handkerchiefs, closed the box and closed the drawer. With his hands braced on the top of the dresser, he leaned forward, resting his suddenly tired weight upon them. Slow, quiet Sylvia . . .

He straightened up and stared unseeingly at his reflection in the mirror. After a moment he turned and walked quickly from the room.

He went back into his own room and to the telephone beside the bed. A call to Information supplied him with the number of the hotel on West 54th Street. He relayed it to the operator along with his own number and stood waiting, his eyes on Sylvia's photograph on the bedside table, until a female voice small in his ear slurred the name of the hotel into an unintelligible syllable.

"Lyle Waterman, please," Melton said. Again he waited, searching for words that would not sound melodramatic. After a moment there was the sound of a receiver being lifted and Lyle's voice said, "Hello?"—thick, cut out of a yawn.

"Lyle? This is Lewis."

"Well. What a *lovely* way to start the day."

"Lyle, I have to speak to you." There was a moment of silence. "You mustn't come up here tonight. Sylvia—"

Angrily Lyle said, "Been reading Sylvia's mail?"

"Lyle, she's—"

"Let me speak to Sylvia."

"She isn't in the house. She—"

Lyle hung up.

Melton jiggled the crossbar and got the operator back. He told her he had been disconnected and she put the call through again.

"Mr. Waterman doesn't answer," the girl in the hotel said.

"This is a matter of life and death," Melton said. "Literally of life and death."

"I'll try again," the girl said nervously.

She tried again, but there was no response. "Should I send one of the boys up?"

"No. Never mind." Melton hung up.

He rang for Redden and took off his sport shirt. He put on a white shirt and was knotting his tie when Redden came in. Melton told him to bring the Lincoln around front. He ran a comb through his white hair and took a tweed jacket from the closet.

When he descended the stairs into the hall, Mrs. Redden was on a stepladder polishing the mirror with a ball of wadded newspaper. Melton said, "Tell Sylvia I was called into New York on some business. I'll be back at five or so." He straightened his tie in the mirror. "I want you to take all the phone calls this afternoon, Mrs. Redden," he said. "If Mr. Waterman calls—you'll know his voice, won't you?"

"Yes, sir."

"Tell him that Sylvia's in New Haven. He's been bothering her."

"Yes, sir," Mrs. Redden said.

Melton went briskly out into the graveled drive, where Redden was holding open the driver's door of the Lincoln.

At a quarter past two Melton parked the car in a lot on West 53rd Street and walked around the block to Lyle's hotel. It was a shabby building with a blue neon sign—*Transients*—glowing dispiritedly in the bright sunlight. The lobby was dim, with sagging leather chairs and the smell of rubber floormats. There was a quarter-circle desk in one corner and behind it, in a nest of pigeonholes, a round-faced man with no facial hair whatsoever and an embarrassingly obvious wig. Melton asked him for Lyle Waterman.

"He's out," the man said.

"What room is he in?"

"Three-fourteen, but he's out. You can't go up."

"Did he tell you to say he was out?"

"He's out," the man said. He pointed to the 314 pigeon-hole; a brick-colored key tag hung from it. "He went out about an hour ago."

"Did he leave any word as to when he'd be back?"

"No word," the man said. "He just went out."

Melton sat down in one of the leather club chairs, across from two dark-skinned men speaking machine gun Spanish. The chair was too deep for comfort and there was a fetid cigar butt in the pot of sand beside it. After a few minutes Melton pulled himself up, went to the newsstand and bought a *Journal-American*. In a different chair, which was just as bad, he sat skimming the newspaper, glancing up at each sibilant push of the revolving door.

Lyle came in at twenty after three, his finger hooking a paper-sheathed clothes hanger over his shoulder. Melton stood up. Lyle paused for a moment, staring at him, and then

6

he continued on his way toward the desk, his lips clamped and his thick-lashed eyes narrowed, like a spoiled child going up to bed without his dinner. Melton intercepted him and caught his free arm, gripping it tight in a sudden burst of hatred. "Let go of me!" Lyle whispered.

Melton took a deep breath and, with urgent emphasis, said, "I have to speak to you."

"Let *go* of me."

Melton released his arm.

"Go on," Lyle said, not looking at Melton, "speak. I can hardly wait."

"Not here," Melton said.

"Look, if you—"

"I drove all the way for this, Lyle. Not for my sake; for yours."

Lyle's mouth worked peevishly, and finally he said, "Oh, hell," and went resignedly to the desk to collect his key. Melton followed him. Waiting for the elevator Melton saw that Lyle had just had a haircut; bits of black hair clung to the back of his shirt collar.

They rode up to the third floor and walked along a narrow corridor whose floor creaked under thin carpet. Lyle unlocked 314. "The presidential suite," he said wryly, pushing open the door and going in. Melton followed him and closed the door. Lyle hooked the clothes hanger on a partially opened closet door. "*House Beautiful* is taking pictures next Tuesday," he said.

The room was small and crowded. There were a bureau, a writing table and a sink squeezed together against one wall, and jutting at them from the wall opposite, twin beds separated by a night table with a spindly white lamp. The single window, in the central wall, had a buff shade and a green one, but no curtains. The beds were metal, painted to look like wood. On the one nearer the window lay a gray leather suitcase with white whipcord stitching and L.W. in small gold letters.

Lyle sat down on the other bed, then swung himself out full length, his hands cupping his head on the pillow, his

7

heels pushing ripples into the faded peach bedspread. He lay looking at the ceiling, blinking occasionally, as though he were completely alone.

Melton drew a chair from the writing table, turned it to face the beds, and sat down.

"Before I tell you what I have to tell you," he said, "I want you to bear in mind that Sylvia is thirty-three years old, that she was thirty-two when you married her, and that she had never been in love before."

Lyle closed his eyes.

"You should also know," Melton said, "that her face, when she was shown your little penmanship exercise on the back of her check, was not a very pleasant face to behold. It was like watching a human being turn into a statue. And she's remained that way. She holds a book in front of her but she doesn't read. Or she goes into her garden and presses earth around flowers that are already dead."

A deep breath lifted Lyle's chest and sighed out from his nostrils.

"I think she has it in her mind to kill you tonight," Melton said. "There's a gun in the top drawer of her dresser."

Lyle's eyes opened.

"I assume she bought it in Reno."

Lyle raised himself on his elbows and looked at Melton. After a moment he said, "You're making this up."

Sharply Melton said, "Oh, yes. I go around telling people that my daughter is contemplating murder." He stared contemptuously at Lyle, and then sank back in his chair. "This trip of mine," he said. "It was Sylvia's idea. And the Reddens are leaving for Vermont tonight. Immediately after dinner. That was Sylvia's idea too."

Lyle said, "She didn't tell me the Reddens would be away. . . ." He swung his legs off the bed and sat leaning forward, his elbows on his knees and his hands clasped in space.

"What *did* she tell you?"

Lyle rubbed the heels of his clasped hands together.

Melton said, "For pity's sake, there's a *gun* in her dresser!"

8

Lyle unclasped his hands and sat up straight, palming his thighs rigidly. "I got a letter the day before yesterday," he said. He was trying to sound brisk and businesslike, but he sounded frightened. "She said she wanted to see me. She was driving you to New Haven and she wanted me to come up and meet her at the station after you left. Tonight. She wanted to give me a chance to explain. She told me—" his voice wavered— "she told me not to tell anyone where I was going because it might get back to you somehow and you might call off your trip."

Melton put his hands to his face and rubbed his eyelids with his fingertips. "Oh Lord," he said, "can you conceive of her plotting, planning. . . ." He stood up and turned his chair back under the writing table. "It's my fault," he said. "I never should have let her talk me into taking the trip." He turned to the window and stared out into a gray courtyard. "Did she ever tell you about the gypsies?"

"Gypsies?"

"Eight, no, ten years ago. My wife was alive then. We went to South America for a couple of months. You would think you could leave a girl of twenty-three alone for two months, wouldn't you? With a houseful of servants? Well, we came back to find the servants gone—she'd paid them off and given them a holiday—and the house full of gypsies. Gypsies! She'd invited them in for tea, like a girl in a fairy tale." He shook his head dolefully. "There were two goats in the garage."

"Gypsies," Lyle said, smiling thinly.

"There are some people," Melton said, "who grow up without ever attaining a firm grasp on reality."

They fell silent for a moment.

"What are you going to do?" Lyle asked.

"I'm not sure," Melton said. "My trip is canceled, of course. I'll tell her that there's been some trouble with my passport or something. I'd like to avoid humiliating her, manage somehow to smooth over this entire situation without ever letting her know I'm aware of its existence. I'll talk to her, tell her I can see she's still brooding about you. If I can make her realize you're best forgotten . . ."

Lyle said softly, "Good Lord, she actually wants to kill me. . . ." He stretched out on the bed again. "Good Lord," he said wonderingly. There was a faint, flattered smile about his lips. It lingered for a moment, then dissolved, his eyes growing thoughtful. He glanced at Melton's back.

"What if you can't?" he said. He was speaking more slowly now. "What if you can't make her see the light? Suppose she takes her gun and comes after me. Don't you think it would be a good idea if I moved to a different hotel?"

"Yes," Melton said, "I suppose it would."

"The only trouble is," Lyle said, "I can't afford to move to a different hotel."

Melton turned from the window.

"I would even leave New York," Lyle said, "if I could afford to. Then you wouldn't have *any* worries about Sylvia getting herself into trouble."

Melton looked at him.

"Where would you go?" he said.

Lyle pondered.

"Dallas," he said. "Dallas, Texas." He thought for a moment. "Or is Houston the big city there? Oh well, Dallas or Houston."

Impassively Melton took out his wallet. Behind the bills he always kept a blank check.

Locked in the crawling traffic of the West Side Highway, Melton considered how best to temper Sylvia from her intended violence without revealing his own knowledge of it. He turned off onto the Merritt Parkway and as he did so he remembered that he had not eaten since breakfast. He stopped at a restaurant, ordered mechanically and ate without interest.

It was past seven o'clock when he guided the Lincoln between the stone posts and up the circular drive toward the front of the house. The Reddens's Plymouth was parked there, with Mrs. Redden in the act of pushing down the lid of the luggage compartment. Melton pulled up behind her and got out of the car.

"Good evening, sir," Mrs. Redden said a bit uncomfortably. "There's some dinner keeping warm on the stove."

"I ate on the road," Melton said.

Mrs. Redden brightened. "We offered to stay on till tomorrow, but Miss Sylvia insisted we shouldn't."

"Where is she?"

"Playing the piano."

Melton went up the steps and to the front door, stopping short as Redden came out with two umbrellas on his arm. "Oh, good evening," Redden said cheerfully. "I finished your packing and brought the suitcases down. There are two telegrams in your room."

"I . . . thanks." Melton caught the door, interrupting its slow swing closed.

"Bon voyage," Redden said.

"Yes, *bon voyage!"* Mrs. Redden called from the car.

"Thanks. Have a good trip." Melton stepped into the house and pulled the door shut after him. He heard Mrs. Redden call out something about Italian food.

His three aluminum suitcases, tagged and labeled, were lined up in a corner of the hall. He looked at them blankly. From the rear of the house came the skipping notes of *The Spinning Song.* Sylvia had been given lessons as a child, but *The Spinning Song* was the only piece she remembered now. She played it rarely and not well. Melton went to the stairs. He listened as he climbed, thinking of all the lessons and practicing that had gone to produce this one awkwardly played selection, and thinking, beneath that, of what he would say to Sylvia.

He went into his room and found the two telegrams. They were from friends, wishing him a safe flight and a pleasant stay on the Riviera. He tossed them on the bed and went into the bathroom.

When he had washed up he came down the stairs again. The piano was silent now. "Sylvia?" he called.

There was no answer. He went into the living room and

11

through it to the music room. She was not there. He returned to the hallway and called her name up the stairs, thinking that perhaps she had gone into her bedroom while he was in the bathroom, but the only answer was silence.

She was in her garden, of course. Melton went down the hall, through the pantry, and into the kitchen. He opened the back door. The sun had gone from the sky and the first blue of dusk was falling. Melton peered across the expanse of lawn, searching for movement behind the high shrubbery that fronted the garden. He moved forward. How like Sylvia, he thought—a walled garden. . . . Birds were calling from the woods beyond. Melton was halfway across the lawn when there was a flutter of movement in the shrubbery and Sylvia came out. She was wearing her gardening smock.

"Sylvia," Melton called.

She gave a little jump. "Oh, hello," she said, smiling. Her glasses were askew and as Melton drew nearer he saw drops of perspiration on her white forehead.

"Working hard?" he said.

"I was beginning to worry. You're late, aren't you? The Reddens have left already."

"I know."

She looked at his jacket. "You're going to change, aren't you?"

"No rush," Melton said. He went over to a wooden bench built around the trunk of an old oak and sat down.

Sylvia followed and stood before him, looking at her watch. "It's twenty of eight," she said.

"I'm afraid the trip is postponed," Melton said.

"What?" She was staring at him.

"There's been some trouble with my passport."

"How could there be trouble with your passport? They renewed it. You showed it to me. How could there be trouble?"

He took her hands and drew her gently to the seat beside him. "Well, as a matter of fact, there *hasn't* been trouble. It's because of you that I'm going to put it off."

"But you told everyone you're leaving!"

12

"So I'll call them tomorrow and tell them I'm not leaving."

"But why?" she said. "Why?"

"Because you're still brooding about Lyle," he said. "I can't leave you this way, Sylvia."

She managed a nervous laugh. "No," she said. "No, I'm not. Honestly I'm not."

"You are, Sylvia," he said. "You know you can't fool *me*."

Her gaze dropped to her lap.

"He's not worth it, Sylvia," Melton said. "Believe me, he's not worth brooding over, not worth hating, not even worth thinking about."

She looked up, suddenly smiling. She took his hand. "Come look at the flowers," she said childishly.

"All right, Sylvia."

They rose and went to the shrubbery and the narrow path that penetrated it. Sylvia parted the branches with her free hand, holding them as she went through so they wouldn't spring back at Melton.

Once on the other side she released his hand and moved forward quickly to a hill of earth at the far side of the garden. She pointed to the ground beside it. "Look!" she said proudly.

Melton came forward and looked. There was a large rectangular hole, very long and quite deep. In the bottom of it, inexplicably, lay Melton's three aluminum suitcases.

He looked at Sylvia wonderingly.

The gun was in her hand. She pushed a wisp of hair up off her forehead. "You ruined my life," she said softly.

Melton stared at her.

"You did," she said. "Ruined it. Thirty-three years. Snooping, spying, arranging things behind my back. Do you think I'm some kind of idiot who can't comb her own hair?" Tears welled up behind her glasses. "That's all there is, a person's life. And you ruined mine!"

"Sylvia . . ."

"Thirty-three years!" It was a scream, cords stretching in

13

her throat. "But no more! Not the rest of it! He's coming back!" Tears were rolling down her flushed cheeks. "Lyle's coming back! Tonight! And he still loves me and this time you're not going to send him away!"

The gun in her hand shot a bolt of heat into Melton's chest. "Sylvia!" he cried.

Melton swayed, trying to speak, trying to tell her that Lyle was no good, that Lyle had been bought off, that Lyle wasn't . . . He stood swaying, staring at her, his hands to his wet chest, and for the first time in his life he saw that her eyes, which had always seemed a dull and empty blue, could burst on occasion to a vivid, gemlike intensity.

"Oh my God," he said, tumbling forward to the ground.

Murder, 1986

·

P.D. James

A two-time winner of the Silver Dagger Award from the British Crime Writers Association, P.D. James has achieved best-seller status with her novels about Chief Superintendent Adam Dalgleish (The Black Tower, Shroud for a Nightingale, Death of an Expert Witness). *She has also published two mysteries featuring private investigator Cordelia Gray* (An Unsuitable Job for a Woman *and* The Skull Beneath the Skin), *nonfiction about crime, and a variety of series and nonseries short stories. "Murder, 1986" is uncharacteristic James in that it has a futuristic setting and plot (it was first published in 1970), but its characterization and deductive elements are the equal of those in any of her contemporary detective stories.*

The girl lay naked on the bed with a knife through her heart. That was the one simple and inescapable fact. No, not simple. It was a fact horrible in its complications. Sergeant Dolby, fighting nausea, steadied his shaking thighs against the foot of the bed and forced his mind into coherence— arranging his thoughts in order, like a child piling brick on colored brick and holding its breath against the inevitable tumble into chaos. He mustn't panic. He must take things slowly. There was a proper procedure laid down for this kind of crisis. There was a procedure laid down for everything.

Dead. That, at least, was certain. Despite the heat of the June morning the slim, girlish body was quite cold, the rigor mortis already well advanced in face and arms. What had they taught him in Detective School about the onset of rigor mortis, that inexorable if erratic stiffening of the muscles, the body's last protest against disintegration and decay? He couldn't remember. He had never been any good at the more academic studies. He had been lucky to be accepted for the Criminal Investigation Department; they had made that clear enough to him at the time. They had never ceased to make it clear. A lost car; a small breaking and entering; a purse snatch. Send Dolby. He had never rated anything more interesting or important than the petty crimes of inadequate men. If it was something no one else wanted to be bothered with, send Dolby. If it was something the C.I.D. would rather not be told about, send Dolby.

And that was exactly how this death would rate. He would have to report it, of course. But it wouldn't be popular news at Headquarters. They were overworked already, depleted in strength, inadequately equipped, forced even to employ him six years after his normal retirement age. No, they wouldn't exactly welcome this spot of trouble. And the reason, as if he didn't know it, was fixed there on the wall for him to read. The statutory notice was pasted precisely over the head of her bed.

He wondered why she had chosen that spot. There was no rule about where it had to be displayed. Why, he wondered, had she chosen to sleep under it as people once slept under a crucifix. An affirmation? But the wording was the same as he would find on the notice in the downstairs hall, in the elevator, on every corridor wall, in every room in the Colony. The Act to which it referred was already two years old:

PRESERVATION OF THE RACE ACT—1984
Control of Interplanetary Disease
Infection Carriers
All registered carriers of the Disease, whether or not they are yet manifesting symptoms, are required under Section 2 of the above Act to conform to the following regulations. . . .

He didn't need to read further. He knew the regulations by heart—the rules by which the Ipdics lived, if you could call it living. The desperate defense of the few healthy against the menace of the many condemned. The small injustices which might prevent the greatest injustice of all, the extinction of man. The stigmata of the Diseased: the registered number tattooed on the left forearm; the regulation Ipdic suit of yellow cotton in summer, blue serge in winter; the compulsory sterilization, since an Ipdic bred only monsters; the rule prohibiting marriage or any close contact with a Normal; the few manual jobs they were permitted to do; the registered Colonies where they were allowed to live.

He knew what they would say at Headquarters. If Dolby had to discover a murder, it would have to be of an Ipdic. And trust him to be fool enough to report it.

But there was no hurry. He could wait until he was calmer, until he could face with confidence whomever they chose to send. And there were things they would expect him to have noticed. He had better make an examination of the scene before he reported. Then, even if they came at once, he would have something sensible to say.

He forced himself to look again at the body. She was lying on her back, eyes closed as if asleep, light brown hair streaming over the pillow. Her arms were crossed over her chest as if in a last innocent gesture of modesty. Below the left breast the handle of a knife stuck out like an obscene horn.

He bent low to examine it. An ordinary handle, probably an ordinary knife. A short-bladed kitchen knife of the kind used to peel vegetables. Her right palm was curved around it, but not touching it, as if about to pluck it out. On her left forearm the registered Ipdic number glowed almost luminous against the delicate skin.

She was neatly covered by a single sheet pulled smooth and taut so that it looked as if the body had been ritually prepared for examination—an intensification of the horror. He did not believe that this childish hand could have driven in the blade with such precision or that, in her last spasms, she had drawn the sheet so tidily over her nakedness. The linen was only a shade whiter than her skin. There had been two months now of almost continuous sunshine. But this body had been muffled in the high-necked tunic and baggy

17

trousers of an Ipdic suit. Only her face had been open to the sun. It was a delicate nut-brown and there was a faint spatter of freckles across the forehead.

He walked slowly around the room. It was sparsely furnished but pleasant enough. The world had no shortage of living space, even for Ipdics. They could live in comfort, even in some opulence, until the electricity, the television, the domestic computer, the micro-oven broke down. Then these things remained broken. The precious skills of electricians and engineers were not wasted on Ipdics. And it was extraordinary how quickly squalor could replace luxury.

A breakdown of electricity in a building like this could mean no hot food, no light, no heating. He had known Ipdics who had frozen or starved to death in apartments which, back in 1980, only six years ago, must have cost a fortune to rent. Somehow the will to survive died quickly in them. It was easier to wrap themselves in blankets and reach for that small white capsule so thoughtfully provided by the Government, the simple painless way out which the whole healthy community was willing for them to take.

But this girl, this female Ipdic PXN 07926431, wasn't living in squalor. The apartment was clean and almost obsessively neat. The micro-oven was out of order, but there was an old-fashioned electric cooker in the kitchen, and when he turned it on the hot plate glowed red. There were even a few personal possessions—a little clutch of seashells carefully arranged on the window ledge, a Staffordshire porcelain figurine of a shepherdess, a child's tea service on a papier-mâché tray.

Her yellow Ipdic suit was neatly folded over the back of a chair. He took it up and saw that she had altered it to fit her. The darts under the breasts had been taken in, the side seams carefully shaped. The hand stitching was neat and regular, an affirmation of individuality, or self-respect. A proud girl. A girl undemoralized by hopelessness. He turned the harsh cotton over and over in his hands and felt the tears stinging the back of his eyes.

He knew that this strange and half-remembered sweetness was pity. He let himself feel it, willing himself not to shrink

18

from the pain. Just so, in his boyhood, he had tentatively placed his full weight on an injured leg after football, relishing the pain in the knowledge that he could bear it, that he was still essentially whole.

But he must waste no more time. Turning on his pocket radio he made his report.

"Sergeant Dolby here. I'm speaking from Ipdic Colony 865. Female Ipdic PXN 07926431 found dead. Room 18. Looks like murder."

It was received as he had expected.

"Oh, God! Are you sure? All right. Hang around. Someone will be over."

While he waited he gave his attention to the flowers. They had struck his senses as soon as he opened the door of the room, but the first sight of the dead girl had driven them from his mind. Now he let their gentle presence drift back into his consciousness. She had died amid such beauty.

The apartment was a bower of wild flowers, their delicate sweetness permeating the warm air so that every breath was an intimation of childhood summers, an evocation of the old innocent days. Wild flowers were his hobby. The slow brain corrected itself, patiently, mechanically: wild flowers had been his hobby. But that was before the Sickness, when the words flower and beauty seemed to have meaning. He hadn't looked at a flower with any joy since 1980.

1980. The year of the Disease. The year with the hottest summer for twenty-one years. That summer when the sheer weight of people had pressed against the concrete bastions of the city like an intolerable force, had thronged its burning pavements, had almost brought its transport system to a stop, had sprawled in checkered ranks across its parks until the sweet grass was pressed into pale straw.

1980. The year when there were too many people. Too many happy, busy, healthy human beings. The year when his wife had been alive; when his daughter Tessa had been alive. The year when brave men, traveling far beyond the moon, had brought back to earth the Sickness—the Sickness which had decimated mankind on every continent of the globe. The

Sickness which had robbed him, Arthur Dolby, of his wife and daughter.

Tessa. She had been only fourteen that spring. It was a wonderful age for a daughter, the sweetest daughter in the world. And Tessa had been intelligent as well as sweet. Both women in his life, his wife and daughter, had been cleverer than Dolby. He had known it, but it hadn't worried him or made him feel inadequate. They had loved him so unreservedly, and relied so much on his manhood, been so satisfied with what little he could provide. They had seen in him qualities he could never discern in himself, virtues which he knew he no longer possessed. His flame of life was meagre; it had needed their warm breaths to keep it burning bright. He wondered what they would think of him now. Arthur Dolby in 1986, looking once more at wild flowers.

He moved among them as if in a dream, like a man recognizing with wonder a treasure given up for lost. There had been no attempt at formal arrangement. She had obviously made use of any suitable container in the apartment and had bunched the plants together naturally and simply, each with its own kind. He could still identify them. There were brown earthenware jars of Herb Robert, the rose-pink flowers set delicately on their reddish stems. There were cracked teacups holding bunches of red clover meadow buttercups, and long-stemmed daisies; jam jars of white campion and cuckoo flowers; egg cups of birdsfoot trefoil—"eggs and bacon," Tessa used to call it—and even smaller jars of rueleaved saxifrage and the soft pink spurs of haresfoot. But, above all, there were the tall vases of cow-parsley, huge bunches of strong hollow-grooved stems supporting their umbels of white flowers, delicate as bridal lace, yet pungent and strong, shedding a white dust on the table, bed, and floor.

And then, in the last jar of all, the only one which held a posy of mixed flowers, he saw the Lady Orchid. It took his breath away. There it stood, alien and exotic, lifting its sumptuous head proudly among the common flowers of the roadside, the white clover, campion, and sweet wild roses. The Lady Orchid. *Orchis Purpurea*.

He stood very still and gazed at it. The decorative spike rose from its shining foliage, elegant and distinctive, seeming to know its rarity. The divisions of the helmet were wine-red, delicately veined and spotted with purple, their somber tint setting off the clear white beauty of the lip. The Lady Orchid. Dolby knew of only one spot, the fringe of a wood in the old Kent County in the Southeast Province, where this flower grew wild. The Sickness had changed the whole of human life. But he doubted if it had changed that.

It was then that he heard the roar of the helicopter. He went to the window. The red machine, like a huge angry insect, was just bouncing down onto the roof landing pad. He watched, puzzled. Why should they send a chopper? Then he understood. The tall figure in the all-white uniform with its gleaming braid swung himself down from the cockpit and was lost to view behind the parapet of the roof. But Dolby recognized at once that helmet of black hair, the confident poise of the head. C. J. Kalvert. The Commissioner of the Home Security Force in person.

He told himself that it couldn't be true—that Kalvert wouldn't concern himself with the death of an Ipdic, that he must have some other business in the Colony. But what business? Dolby waited in fear, his hands clenched so that the nails pierced his palms, waited in an agony of hope that it might not be true. But it was true. A minute later he heard the strong footsteps advancing along the corridor. The door opened. The Commissioner had arrived.

He nodded an acknowledgement to Dolby and, without speaking, went over to the bed. For a moment he stood in silence, looking down at the girl. Then he said, "How did you get in, Sergeant?"

The accent was on the third word.

"The door was unlocked, sir."

"Naturally. Ipdics are forbidden to lock their doors. I was asking what you were doing here."

"I was making a search, sir."

That at least was true. He had been making a private search.

"And you discovered that one more female Ipdic had taken the sensible way out of her troubles. Why didn't you call the Sanitary Squad? It's unwise to leave a body longer than necessary in this weather. Haven't we all had enough of the stench of decay?"

"I think she was murdered, sir."

"Do you indeed, Sergeant. And why?"

Dolby moistened his dry lips and made his cramped fingers relax. He mustn't let himself be intimidated, mustn't permit himself to get flustered. The important thing was to stick to the facts and present them cogently.

"It's the knife, sir. If she were going to stab herself, I think she would have fallen on the blade, letting her weight drive it in. Then the body would have been found face downward. That way, the blade would have done all the work. I don't think she would have had the strength or the skill to pierce her heart lying in that position. It looks almost surgical. It's too neat. The man who drove that knife in knew what he was doing. And then there's the sheet. She couldn't have placed it over herself so neatly."

"A valid point, Sergeant. But the fact that someone considerately tidied her up after death doesn't necessarily mean that he killed her. Anything else?"

He was walking restlessly about the room as he talked, touching nothing, his hands clasped behind his back. Dolby wished that he would stand still. He said, "But why use a knife at all, sir? She must have been issued her euthanasia capsule."

"Not a very dramatic way to go, Dolby. The commonest door for an Ipdic to let life out. She may have exercised a feminine preference for a more individualistic death. Look around this room, Sergeant. Does she strike you as having been an ordinary girl?"

No, she hadn't struck Dolby as ordinary. But this was ground he dare not tread. He said doggedly, "And why should she be naked, sir? Why take all her clothes off to kill herself?"

"Why, indeed. That shocks you, does it, Dolby? It implies

an unpleasant touch of exhibitionism. It offends your modesty. But perhaps she was an exhibitionist. The flowers would suggest it. She made her room into a bower of fragrance and beauty. Then, naked, as unencumbered as the flowers, she stretched herself out like a sacrifice, and drove a knife through her heart. Can you, Sergeant, with your limited imagination, understand that a woman might wish to die like that?''

Kalvert swung round and strode over to him. The fierce black eyes burned into Dolby's. The Sergeant felt frightened, at a loss. The conversation was bizarre. He felt they were playing some private game, but that only one of them knew the rules.

What did Kalvert want of him? In a normal world, in the world before the Sickness when the old police force was at full strength, the Commissioner wouldn't even have known that Dolby existed. Yet here they both were, engaged, it seemed, in some private animus, sparring over the body of an unimportant dead Ipdic.

It was very hot in the room now and the scent of the flowers had been growing stronger. Dolby could feel the beads of sweat on his brow. Whatever happened he must hold on to the facts. He said, ''The flowers needn't be funeral flowers. Perhaps they were for a celebration.''

''That would suggest the presence of more than one person. Even Ipdics don't celebrate alone. Have you found any evidence that someone was with her when she died?''

He wanted to reply, ''Only the knife in her breast.'' But he was silent. Kalvert was pacing the room again. Suddenly he stopped and glanced at his watch. Then, without speaking, he turned on the television. Dolby remembered. Of course. The Leader was due to speak after the midday news. It was already twelve-thirty-two. He would be almost finished.

The screen flickered and the too familiar face appeared. The Leader looked very tired. Even the makeup artist hadn't been able to disguise the heavy shadows under the eyes or the hollows beneath the cheekbones. With that beard and the melancholy, pain-filled face, he looked like an ascetic prophet. But he always had. His face hadn't changed much since the days of his student protest. People said that, even then, he had only really been interested in personal power. Well, he was still under thirty, but he had it now. All the power he could possibly want. The speech was nearly over.

"And so we must find our own solution. We have a tradition in this country of humanity and justice. But how far can we let tradition hamper us in the great task of preserving our race? We know what is happening in other countries, the organized and ceremonial mass suicides of thousands of Ipdics at a time, the humane Disposal squads, the compulsory matings between computer-selected Normals. Some compulsory measures against the Ipdics we must now take. As far as possible we have relied on gentle and voluntary methods. But can we afford to fall behind while other less scrupulous nations are breeding faster and more selectively, disposing of their Ipdics, reestablishing their technology, looking with covetous eyes at the great denuded spaces of the world. One day they will be repopulated. It is our duty to take part in this great process. The world needs our race. The time has come for every one of us, particularly our Ipdics, to ask ourselves with every breath we draw: have I the right to be alive?"

Kalvert turned off the set.

"I think we can forego the pleasure of seeing once again Mrs. Sartori nursing her filthy healthy daughter. Odd to think that the most valuable human being in the world is a healthy fecund female. But you got the message I hope, Sergeant. This Ipdic had the wisdom to take her own way out while she still had a choice. And if somebody helped her, who are we to quibble?"

"It was still murder, sir. I know that killing an Ipdic isn't a capital crime. But the Law hasn't been altered yet. It's still a felony to kill any human being."

"Ah, yes. A felony. And you, of course, are dedicated to the detection and punishment of felonies. The first duty of a policeman is to prevent crime; the second is to detect and punish the criminal. You learned all that when you were in Detective School, didn't you? Learned it all by heart. I remember reading the first report on you, Dolby. It was almost identical with the last. 'Lacking in initiative. Deficient in imagination. Tends to make errors of judgment. Should make a reliable subordinate. Lacks self-confidence.' But it did admit that, when you manage to get an idea into your head, it sticks there. And you have an idea in your head. Murder. And murder is a felony. Well, what do you propose to do about it?''

"In cases of murder the body is first examined by the forensic pathologist.''

"Not this body, Dolby. Do you know how many pathologists this country now has? We have other uses for them than to cut up dead Ipdics. She was a young female. She was not pregnant. She was stabbed through the heart. What more do we need to know?''

"Whether or not a man was with her before she died.''

"I think you can take it there was. Male Ipdics are not yet being sterilized. So we add another fact. She probably had a lover. What else do you want to know?''

"Whether or not there are prints on the knife, sir, and, if so, whose they are.''

Kalvert laughed aloud. "We were short of forensic scientists before the Sickness. How many do you suppose we have now? There was another case of capital murder reported this morning. An Ipdic has killed his former wife because she obeyed the Law and kept away from him. We can't afford to lose a single healthy woman, can we, Dolby? There's the rumor of armed bands of Ipdics roaming the Southeast Province. There's the case of the atomic scientist with the back of his skull smashed in. A scientist, Dolby! Now, do you really want to bother the lab with this petty trouble?''

Dolby said obstinately, "I know that someone was with her when she picked the flowers. That must have been yesterday—they're still fresh even in this heat, and wild flowers fade quickly. I think he probably came back here with her and was with her when she died.''

"Then find him, Sergeant, if you must. But don't ask for help I can't give.''

He walked over to the door without another glance at the

room or at the dead girl, as if neither of them held any further interest for him. Then he turned: "You aren't on the official list of men encouraged to breed daughters in the interest of the race, are you, Sergeant?"

Dolby wanted to reply that he once had a daughter. She was dead and he wanted no other.

"No, sir. They thought I was too old. And then there was the adverse psychologist's report."

"A pity. One would have thought that the brave new world could have made room for just one or two people who were unintelligent, lacking in imagination, unambitious, inclined to errors of judgment. People will persist in going their own obstinate way. Good-bye, Dolby. Report to me personally on this case, will you? I shall be interested to hear how you progress. Who knows, you may reveal unsuspected talents."

He was gone. Dolby waited for a minute as if to cleanse his mind of that disturbing presence. As the confident footsteps died away, even the room seemed to settle itself into peace. Then Dolby began the few tasks which still remained.

There weren't many. First, he took the dead girl's fingerprints. He worked with infinite care, murmuring to her as he gently pressed the pad against each fingertip, like a doctor reassuring a child. It would be pointless, he thought, to compare them with the prints on any of the ordinary objects in the room. That would prove nothing except that another person had been there. The only prints of importance would be those on the knife. But there were no prints on the knife— only an amorphous smudge of whorls and composites as if someone had attempted to fold her hand around the shaft but had lacked the courage to press the fingers firm.

But the best clue was still there—the Lady Orchid, splendid in its purity and beauty, the flower which told him where she had spent the previous day, the flower which might lead him to the man who had been with her. And there was another clue, something he had noticed when he had first examined the body closely. He had said nothing to Kalvert. Perhaps Kalvert hadn't noticed it or hadn't recognized its significance. Perhaps he had been cleverer than Kalvert. He told himself that he wasn't really as stupid as people sometimes thought. It was just that his mind was so easily flustered into incoherence when stronger men bullied or taunted him. Only his wife and daughter had really understood that, had given him the confidence to fight it.

It was time to get started. They might deny him the services of the pathologist and the laboratory, but they still permitted him the use of his car. It would be little more than an hour's drive.

But, before leaving, he bent once more over the body. The Disposal Squad would soon be here for it. He would never see it again. So he studied the clue for the last time—the faint, almost imperceptible circle of paler skin round the third finger of her left hand. The finger that could have worn a ring through the whole of a hot summer day. . . .

He drove through the wide streets and sun-filled squares, through the deserted suburbs, until the tentacles of the city fell away and he was in open country. The roads were pitted and unmended, the hedges high and unkempt, the fields a turbulent sea of vegetation threatening to engulf the unpeopled farmlands. But the sun was pleasant on his face. He could almost persuade himself that this was one of the old happy jaunts into the familiar and well-loved countryside of Old Kent.

He had crossed the boundary into the Southeast Province and was already looking for the remembered landmarks of hillside and church spire when it happened. There was an explosion, a crack like a pistol shot, and the windshield shattered in his face. He felt splinters of glass stinging his cheeks. Instinctively he guarded his face with his arms. The car swerved out of control and lurched onto the grass verge. He felt for the ignition key and turned off the engine. Then he tentatively opened his eyes. They were uninjured. And it was then he saw the Ipdics.

They came out of the opposite ditch and moved toward him, with stones still in their hands. There were half a dozen of them. One, the tallest, seemed to be their leader. The others shuffled at his heels, lumpy figures in their illfitting yellow suits, their feet brown and bare, their hair matted like animals', their greedy eyes fixed on the car. They stood still, looking at him. And then the leader drew his right hand from behind his back, and Dolby saw that it held a gun.

His heart missed a beat. So it was true! Somehow the Ipdics were getting hold of weapons. He got out of the car, trying to recall the exact instructions of such an emergency. Never show fear. Keep calm. Exert authority. Remember that they are inferior, unorganized, easily cowed. Never drop your eyes. But his voice, even to him, sounded feeble, pitched unnaturally high.

"The possession of a weapon by an Ipdic is a capital crime. The punishment is death. Give me that gun."

The voice that replied was quiet, authoritative, the kind of voice one used to call educated.

"No. First you give me the keys to the car. Then I give you something in return. A cartridge in your belly!"

His followers cackled their appreciation. It was one of the most horrible sounds in the world—the laughter of an Ipdic.

The Ipdic pointed the gun at Dolby, moving it slowly from side to side as if selecting his precise target. He was enjoying his power, drunk with elation and triumph. But he waited a second too long. Suddenly his arm jerked upward, the gun leaped from his grasp, and he gave one high desolate scream, falling into the dust of the road. He was in the first spasm of an Ipdic fit. His body writhed and twisted, arched and contracted, until the bones could be heard snapping.

Dolby looked on impassively. There was nothing he could do. He had seen it thousands of times before. It had happened to his wife, to Tessa, to all those who had died of the disease. It happened in the end to every Ipdic. It would have happened to that girl on the bed, at peace now with a knife in her heart.

The attack would leave this Ipdic broken and exhausted. If he survived, he would be a mindless idiot, probably for months. And then the fits would come more frequently. It was this feature of the Disease which made the Ipdics so impossible to train or employ, even for the simplest of jobs.

Dolby walked up to the writhing figure and kicked away the gun, then picked it up. It was a revolver, a Smith and

Wesson .38, old but in good condition. He saw that it was loaded. After a second's thought he slipped it into the pocket of his jacket.

The remaining Ipdics had disappeared, scrambling back into the hedges with cries of anguish and fear. The whole incident was over so quickly that it already seemed like a dream. Only the tortured figure in the dust and the cold metal in his pocket were witnesses to its reality. He should report it at once, of course. The suppression of armed Ipdics was the first duty of the Home Security Force.

He backed the car onto the road. Then, on an impulse, he got out again and went over to the Ipdic. He bent to drag the writhing figure off the road and into the shade of the hedge. But it was no good. Revolted, he drew back. He couldn't bear to touch him. Perhaps the Ipdic's friends would creep back later to carry him away and tend to him. Perhaps. But he, Dolby, had his own problems. He had a murder to solve.

Fifteen minutes later he drove slowly through the village. The main street was deserted but he could glimpse, through the open cottage doors, the garish yellow of an Ipdic suit moving in the dim interior and he could see other yellow-clad figures bending at work in the gardens and fields. None of them looked up as he passed. He guessed that this was one of the settlements which had grown up in the country, where groups of Ipdics attempted to support themselves and each other, growing their own food, nursing their sick, burying their dead. Since they made no demands on the Normals they were usually left in peace. But it couldn't last long. There was no real hope for them.

As more and more of them were overtaken by the last inevitable symptoms, the burden on those left grew intolerable. Soon they too would be helpless and mad. Then the Security Force, the Health Authorities, and the Sanitary Squads would move in, and another colony of the dispossessed would be cleaned up. And it was a question of cleaning up. Dolby had taken part in one such operation. He knew what the final horror would be. But now in the heat of this sun-scented afternoon, he might be driving through the village as he had known it in the days before the Sickness, prosperious, peaceful, sleepy, with the men still busy on the farms.

He left the car at the churchyard gate and slipping the strap of his murder bag over his shoulder, walked up the dappled avenue of elms to the south entrance. The heavy oak door with its carved panels, its massive hinges of hammered iron creaked open at his touch. He stepped into the cool dimness and smelled again the familiar scent of flowers, musty hymn books, and wood polish, saw once again the medieval pillars soaring high to the hammer beams of the room, and, straining his eyes through the dimness he glimpsed the carving on the rood screen and the far gleam of the sanctuary lamp.

The church was full of wild flowers. They were the same flowers as those in the dead girl's apartment but here their frail delicacy was almost lost against the massive pillars and the richly carved oak. But the huge vases of cow-parsley set on each side of the chapel steps made a brave show, floating like twin clouds of whiteness in the dim air. It was a church decked for a bride.

He saw a female Ipdic polishing the brass lectern. He made his way up the aisle toward her and she beamed a gentle welcome as if his appearance were the most ordinary event in the world. Her baggy Ipdic suit was stained with polish and she wore a pair of old sandals, the soles peeling away from the uppers. Her graying hair was drawn back into a loose bun from which wisps of hair had escaped to frame the anxious, sun-stained face.

She reminded him of someone. He let his mind probe once again, painfully, into the past. Then he remembered. Of course. Miss Caroline Martin, his Sunday School superintendent. It wasn't she, of course. Miss Martin would have been over seventy at the time of the Sickness. No one as old as that had survived, except those few Tasmanian aborigines who so interested the scientists. Miss Martin, standing beside the old piano as her younger sister thumped out the opening hymn and beating time with her gloved hand as if hearing some private and quite different music. Afterward, the students had gone to their different classes and had sat in a circle around their teachers. Miss Martin had taught the older children, himself among them. Some of the boys had been unruly, but never Arthur Dolby. Even in those days he had been obedient, law-abiding. The good boy. Not particularly bright, but well-behaved. Good, dull, ineffectual. Teacher's pet.

And when she spoke it was with a voice like Miss Martin's.

"Can I help you? If you've come for Evensong services, I'm afraid it isn't until five-thirty today. If you're looking for Father Reeves, he's at the Rectory. But perhaps you're just a visitor. It's a lovely church, isn't it? Have you seen our sixteenth-century reredos?"

"I hoped I would be in time for the wedding."

She gave a little girlish cry of laughter.

"Dear me, you are late! I'm afraid that was yesterday! But I thought no one was supposed to know about it. Father Reeves said that it was to be quite secret really. But I'm afraid I was very naughty. I did so want to see the bride. After all, we haven't had a wedding here since—"

"Since the Act?"

She corrected him gently, like Miss Martin rebuking the good boy of the class.

"Since 1980. So yesterday was quite an occasion for us. And I did want to see what the bride looked like in Emma's veil."

"In what?"

"A bride has to have a veil, you know." She spoke with gentle reproof, taking pity on his masculine ignorance. "Emma was my niece. I lost her and her parents in 1981. Emma was the last bride to be married here. That was on April 28, 1980. I've always kept her veil and headdress. She was such a lovely bride."

Dolby asked with sudden harshness the irrelevant but necessary question.

"What happened to her bridegroom?"

"Oh, John was one of the lucky ones. I believe he has married again and has three daughters. Just one daughter more and they'll be allowed to have a son. We don't see him, of course. It wasn't to be expected. After all, it is the Law.''

How despicable it was, this need to be reassured that there were other traitors.

"Yes," he said. "It is the Law."

She began polishing the already burnished lectern, chatting to him as she worked.

"But I've kept Emma's veil and headdress. So I thought I'd just place them on a chair beside the font so that this new bride would see them when she came into church. Just in case she wanted to borrow them, you know. And she did. I was so glad. The bridegroom placed the veil over her head and fixed the headdress for her himself, and she walked down the aisle looking so beautiful.''

"Yes," said Dolby. "She would have looked very beautiful.''

"I watched them from behind this pillar. Neither of them noticed me. But it was right for me to be here. There ought to be someone in the church. It says in the prayer book, 'In the sight of God and of this congregation.' She had a small bouquet of wild flowers, just a simple mixed bunch but very charming. I think they must have picked it together.''

"She carried a Lady Orchid," said Dolby. "A Lady Orchid picked by her bridegroom and surrounded by daisies, clover, white campion, and wild roses.''

"How clever of you to guess! Are you a friend, perhaps?''

"No," said Dolby. "Not a friend. Can you describe the bridegroom?''

"I thought that you must know him. Very tall, very dark. He wore a plain white suit. Oh, they were such a handsome couple! I wished Father Reeves could have seen them.''

"I thought he married them."

"So he did. But Father Reeves, poor man, is blind.''

So that was why he risked it, thought Dolby. But what a risk!

"Which prayer book did he use?''

She gazed at him, the milky eyes perplexed. "Father Reeves?''

"No, the bridegroom. He did handle a prayer book, I suppose?"

"Oh, yes. I put one out for each of them. Father Reeves asked me to get things ready. It was I who decorated the church. Poor dears, it wasn't as if they could have the usual printed service sheets. Emma's were so pretty, her initials intertwined with the bridegroom's. But yesterday they had to use ordinary prayer books. I chose them specially from the pews and put them on the two prayer stools. I found a very pretty white one for the bride and this splendid old book with the brass clasp for the bridegroom. It looked masculine, I thought."

It lay on the book ledge of the front pew. She made a move to pick it up, but he shot out his hand. Then he dropped his handkerchief over the book and lifted it by the sharp edges of the binding. Brass and leather. Good for a print. And this man's palm would be moist, clammy, perhaps, with perspiration and fear. A hot day; an illegal ceremony; his mind on murder. To love and to cherish until death us do part. Yes, this bridegroom would have been nervous. But Dolby had one more question.

"How did they get here? Do you know?"

"They came by foot. At least, they walked up to the church together. I think they had walked quite a long way. They were quite hot and dusty when they arrived. But I know how they really came."

She nodded her unkempt head and gave a little conspiratorial nod.

"I've got very good ears, you know. They came by helicopter. I heard it."

A helicopter. He knew almost without thinking exactly who was permitted the use of a helicopter. Members of the Central Committee of Government; high ranking scientists and technicians; doctors; the Commissioner of the Home Security Force, and his Deputy. That was all.

He took the prayer book out into the sun and sat on one of the flat-topped gravestones. He set up the prayer book on its end, then unzipped his murder bag. His hands shook so that he could hardly manage the brush and some of the gray powder was spilt and blew away in the breeze. He willed himself to keep calm, to take his time. Carefully, like a child with a new toy, he dusted the book and clasp with powder gently blowing off the surplus with a small rubber nozzle. It was an old procedure, first practiced when he was a young Detective Constable. But it still worked. It always would. The arches, whorls, and composites came clearly into view.

He was right. It was a beautiful print. The man had made no effort to wipe it clean. Why should he? How could he imagine that this particular book would ever be identified among the many scattered around the church? How could he suspect that he would ever be traced to this despised and unregarded place? Dolby took out his camera and photographed the print. There must be continuity of evidence. He must leave no room for doubt. Then he classified its characteristics, ready for checking.

There was a little delay at the National Identification Computer Center when he phoned, and he had to wait his turn. When it came he gave his name, rank, secret code, and the classification of the print. There was a moment's silence. Then a surprised voice asked, "Is that you, Dolby? Will you confirm your code."

He did so. Another silence.

"Okay. But what on earth are you up to? Are you sure of your print classification?"

"Yes. I want the identification for elimination purposes."

"Then you can eliminate, all right. That's the Commissioner. Kalvert, C. J. Hard luck, Dolby! Better start again."

He switched off the receiver and sat in silence. He had known it, of course. But for how long? Perhaps from the beginning. Kalvert. Kalvert, who had an excuse for visiting an Ipdic Colony. Kalvert, who had the use of a helicopter. Kalvert, who had known without asking that the television set in her room was in working order. Kalvert, who had been too sure of himself to take the most elementary precautions against discovery, because he knew that it didn't matter, because he knew no one would dare touch him. Kalvert, one of the four most powerful men in the country. And it was he, the despised Sergeant Dolby, who had solved the case.

He heard the angry purr of the approaching helicopter without surprise. He had reported the armed attack by the Ipdics. It was certain that Headquarters would have immediately summoned a Squad from the nearest station to hunt them down. But Kalvert would know about the message. He had no doubt that the Commissioner was keeping a watch on him. He would know which way Dolby was heading, would realize that he was dangerously close to the truth. The armed Squad would be here in time. But Kalvert would arrive first.

He waited for five minutes, still sitting quietly on the grave-stone. The air was sweet with the smell of grasses and vibrating with the high-treble midsummer chant of blackbird and thrush. He shut his eyes for a moment, breathing in the beauty, taking courage from its peace. Then he got to his feet and stood at the head of the avenue of elms to wait for Kalvert.

The gold braid on the all-white uniform gleamed in the sun. The tall figure, arrogant with confidence and power, walked unhesitatingly toward him, unsmiling, making no sign. When they were three feet apart, Kalvert stopped. They stood confronting each other. It was Dolby who spoke first. His voice was little more than a whisper.

"You killed her."

He could not meet Kalvert's eyes. But he heard his reply.

"Yes, I killed her. Shall I tell you about it, Sergeant? You seem to have shown some initiative. You deserve to know part of the truth. I was her friend. That is prohibited by Regulation. She became my mistress. That is against the Law. We decided to get married. That is a serious crime. I killed her. That, as you earlier explained, is a felony. And what are you going to do about it, Sergeant?"

Dolby couldn't speak. Suddenly he took out the revolver. It seemed ridiculous to point it at Kalvert. He wasn't even sure that he would be able to fire it. But he held it close to his side and the curved stock fitted comfortably to his palm, giving him courage. He made himself meet Kalvert's eyes, and heard the Commissioner laugh.

"To kill a Normal is also against the Law. But it's something more. Capital murder, Dolby. Is that what you have in mind?"

Dolby spoke out of cracked lips, "But why? *Why?*"

"I don't have to explain to you. But I'll try. Have you the imagination to understand that we might have loved each other, that I might have married her because it seemed a small risk for me and would give her pleasure, that I might have promised to kill her when her last symptoms began? Can you, Sergeant Dolby, enter into the mind of a girl like that? She was an Ipdic. And she was more alive in her condemned cell than you have ever been in your life. Female Ipdic PXN 07926431 found dead. Looks like murder. Remember you reported it, Dolby? A felony. Something to be investigated. Against the Law. That's all it meant to you, isn't it?"

He had taken out his own revolver now. He held it easily, like a man casually dangling a familiar toy. He stood there, magnificent in the sunshine, the breeze lifting his black hair. He said quietly, "Do you think I'd let any Law on earth keep me from the woman I loved?"

Dolby wanted to cry out that it hadn't been like that at all. That Kalvert didn't understand. That he, Dolby, had cared about the girl. But the contempt in those cold black eyes kept him silent. There was nothing they could say to each other. Nothing. And Kalvert would kill him.

The Squad would be here soon. Kalvert couldn't let him live to tell his story. He gazed with fascinated horror at the revolver held so easily, so confidently, in the Commissioner's hand. And he tightened the grip on his own, feeling with a shaking finger for the trigger.

The armored car roared up to the churchyard gate. The Squad were here. Kalvert lifted his revolver to replace it in the holster. Dolby, misunderstanding the gesture, whipped up his own gun and, closing his eyes, fired until the last cartridge was spent. Numbed by misery and panic, he didn't hear the shots or the thud of Kalvert's fall. The first sound to pierce his consciousness was a wild screaming and beating of wings as the terrified birds flew high. Then he was aware of an unnatural silence, and of an acrid smell tainting the summer air.

His right hand ached. It felt empty, slippery with sweat. He saw that he had dropped the gun. There was a long mournful cry of distress. It came from behind him. He turned and glimpsed the yellow-clad figure of the female Ipdic, hand to her mouth, watching him from the shadow of the church. Then she faded back into the dimness.

He dropped on his knees beside Kalvert. The torn arteries were pumping their blood onto the white tunic. The crimson stain burst open like a flower. Dolby took off his jacket with shaking hands and thrust it under Kalvert's head. He wanted to say that he was sorry, to cry out like a child that he hadn't really meant it, that it was all a mistake.

Kalvert looked at him. Was there really pity in those dulling eyes? He was trying to speak. "Poor Dolby! Your final error of judgment."

The last word was hiccupped in a gush of blood. Kalvert turned his head away from Dolby and drew up his knees as if easing himself into sleep. And Dolby knew that it was too late to explain now, that there was no one there to hear him.

He stood up. The Squad were very close now, three of them, walking abreast, guns at hip, moving inexorably forward in the pool of their own shadows. And so he waited, all fear past, with Kalvert's body at his feet. And he thought for the first time of his daughter. Tessa, whom he had allowed to hide from him because that was the Law. Tessa, whom he had deserted and betrayed. Tessa, whom he had sought at last, but had found too late. Tessa, who had led him unwittingly to her lover and murderer. Tessa who would never have picked that Lady Orchid. Hadn't he taught her when she was a child that if you picked a wild orchid it can never bloom again?

It Wouldn't Be Fair

·

Jack Finney

*No matter which of several literary hats he wears, Jack Fin-
ney is a consummate storyteller. He has written with equal
success chilling science fiction* (The Body Snatchers), *nos-
talgic fantasies about time-travel* (The Woodrow Wilson
Dime, Time and Again), *hilarious farce* (Good Neighbor
Sam), *edge-of-the-chair suspense novels* (House of Numbers, Five Against the House, Assault on a Queen), *and a
variety of evocative short stories* (The Third Level, I Love
Galesburg in the Springtime). *"It Wouldn't Be Fair" is Finney under his farcical cap—an amusing send-up of the old-
fashioned fair-play detective story.*

"**S**uppose you found this guy dead," said Charley. He
stood beside the lieutenant's desk, hands in pockets, rocking
gently on his feet, a lean young man with an intelligent face.
"Murdered. Shot and poisoned in his library."

"The library?"

"*His* library; big estate in England."

The lieutenant swung his swivel chair toward the window
behind him. The morning light cut across one shoulder onto
a face made thin by years of insufficient sleep and grooved
from decades of worry. "Out of our jurisdiction," he said.

"You investigate anyway," Charley said cheerfully, "and
find that the dead guy's wife is a homicidal maniac, that her
husband kicked her out into a blizzard on Christmas Eve,
after squandering her fortune on another woman, and that
she happens to own the Webley-Vebley .12-12 pistol which
fired the bullet found in his brain."

38

"Someday," said the lieutenant, "you'll be too smart for your own good. Whatever you're up to or after, I have a feeling, amounting to a conviction, that the answer is going to be no. I never heard of a Webley-Vebley."

"Annie would not be surprised." Charley took a paper clip from the desk and, lowering his head, began carefully bending it straight. "Furthermore, the dead man's wife had run a full page ad in the local newspaper threatening to kill him, she was alone with him during the last ten minutes of his life, and in her handbag are three African darts, each tipped with a poison which kills instantly by turning the blood into putty. You suspect anybody?"

The lieutenant shrugged. "Looks like maybe the wife did it."

"Typical police stupidity." Charley tossed the paper clip at the polished spittoon on the floor and it hit with a ping, then rattled inside. "Annie has often pointed out to me that we constantly leap to conclusions on just such flimsy evidence."

The lieutenant leaned forward, hands clasped, forearms on the desk. "Okay," he said coldly, "just who is this Annie?"

"Annie is a brain. Of a frightening power. A marvel at murder. But a brain bounded on the north by gorgeous brown hair, on the south by a magnificent coastline, and—"

"Spare me," said the lieutenant. "I am an old, old man. Just how does this mighty brain work?"

"While we absurd police, satisfied with our ridiculous evidence, are lounging around the station house or stealing fruit from innocent peddlers, Annie is finding the more subtle clues which blundering police methods invariably miss. And she discovers presently what she suspected all along." Charley hitched his chair closer to the lieutenant's desk. "The wife is innocent. The murdered man's aunt, who raised him from childhood, sacrificed everything to put him through college, and who has been completely paralyzed for thirty-five years except for her ears which she can still wiggle slightly—"

"She did it?"

"Exactly. The rare Webley-Vebley is the only known pistol with a trigger so sensitive it can be fired by a flick of the ear."

The lieutenant leaned back in his chair, and gazed at the ceiling for a considerable time. "Colhaus," he said finally. "You know Colhaus in the Thirteenth Precinct? He has a daughter—"

"No," said Charley. "Annie. I am not interested in anyone's daughter but Annie. You may not understand—"

"I might," said the lieutenant. "Unlikely as it may seem, I was young once. The remedy in a case like yours—I should say the cure—is to marry the girl."

"I can't." Charley's smile disappeared, and his face looked thinner. "In spite of some success during my six years as a member of Homicide, Annie regards me as only a reasonably well-qualified moron in the field of murder investigation. From her experience," he said bitterly, "covering hundreds of cases, she has formed a very low opinion of police and their methods."

The lieutenant gestured with his thumb toward a huge, oak-framed display cabinet which hung on the wall opposite. Its green felt surface under the glass, was paved with dozens of overlapping photographs and deadly mementos: cruelly sharp photos of bodies in every state of violent death; sullen-faced men and women, struggling or passive, in the arms of the police; actual pistols and blackjacks wired in place.

"You were with me on those," said the lieutenant. "Some of them. You did good work, sometimes. *Tell* her about them."

"I did."

"And?"

"Crude and slipshod work. We often arrested and convicted the first guy we suspected. Sometimes, in fact, the only suspect. And often very obviously the obvious suspect. Do you realize what that means?"

"Tell me."

"They were innocent."

The lieutenant smiled bleakly. "Yes? What about the Crowley case? Clear-cut."

"It was," said Charley gravely, "but it took two weeks to break. Perhaps you thought that was fast? Tell me. You sometimes stop to eat, on a case? Even sleep?"

"Yes."

"Fool. There is no time for anything but drinking. Naturally you are pitifully slow."

"This Annie is faster?"

"She often solves cases a full forty-eight pages before Perry Mason."

The lieutenant sighed. "Just what did you have in mind?" he said.

"Well, sir." Charley selected another paper clip. "Singlehanded I have been unable to convince Annie that the murders of fiction, filled with brilliant deductions and subtle clues, have nothing to do with the facts of life. I have told her about our cases. They are dull. No African darts. No guns concealed in the wall which fire when the first frost contracts the woodwork. No hypodermic needles which inject a chemical freezing the blood to dry ice and causing veins to explode. We don't even seem to find any footprints. So what does that mean? The answer is obvious to Annie. We are missing something. We are trampling countless delicate clues under our big flat feet. Convicting innocent men on obvious, ridiculous clues, while *fiends*, ingenious beyond our poor capacity to imagine, are lounging around the city laughing at us. Lieutenant, a man has to have respect from his wife."

"So?"

"So I thought, sir, we'd take Annie along on the next case. Show her a real murder—"

"No." The lieutenant stood up, walked out from behind his desk, and gestured at the walls of his office. "This is not a book from the rental library," he said, "with every killing an excursion trip." With his other hand he gestured at the window toward the police garage three stories below, where a motorcycle idled, its vibrations gently rattling the window

41

pane. "This is Centre Street, Police Headquarters; *real* police with work to do, not a picnic for amateur mystery story—Charley, you know better."

Charley stood up and took his hat from the lieutenant's desk. "I guess so. It's too bad though; Della Street goes everywhere with Perry Mason."

"Colhaus—"

"No," said Charley, "Annie." He put on his hat and stood for a moment, looking at the floor. "I rather expected this. Which brings me to my final hope." He reached inside his suit coat and brought out a bright green-jacketed book which he had held concealed under his arm. "I would like you to read this. The thrilling adventures of Hercule Poirot."

"Why?" the lieutenant demanded.

"It's a very fascinating story. And I would like you to finish it—" he hesitated— "and before you come with me to Annie's tomorrow night."

The lieutenant stared at Charley, his eyes narrowed. "Someday," he said, "you will be too smart for—"

"It's my only hope." Charley opened the door and began backing out. "My only chance is that your gray hairs and ancient wisdom will succeed where I have failed—" the door was closing— "in persuading Annie that the police are as competent, in a much duller way, as Agatha Christie."

Annie's living room, Charley had often noticed, was feminine and suited her perfectly. But he was not prepared, the following evening, for what it did to the lieutenant. The lieutenant—surrounded by dainty, soft-glowing lamps, pastel-tinted slip covers, bright modern paintings—looked as out of place as a bishop in a pool hall.

But Annie was superb. She sat gracefully curled in a corner of the davenport, her hair, as always, even more gloriously brunette than Charley remembered. Her softly tanned face was eager, smiling, and alive. Her large, blue, and beautiful eyes were animated. She seemed confident.

"The lieutenant read Hercule Poirot," Charley announced. "Loved it."

"Oh?" Annie looked interested; she smiled. "Did you figure it out?"

"No," said the lieutenant.

"You mean, not till the end."

"I mean," said the lieutenant—he took a swallow of his drink—"that I never *did* get it. I read the book. I finished it. Read the last chapter twice. And I still don't know who killed Aaron DeCourcey."

"But, Lieutenant. It *said*. It said *Robert* did it; Robert, the adopted son. He confessed."

"I know. We get those confessions all the time; they don't mean a thing." The lieutenant paused, took a thoughtful sip of his drink, then spoke decisively. "I think maybe this Lacy guy did it: Lacy Spreckles."

"But—"

"It figures," said the lieutenant. "He hated the guy, he bought the gun, he had a fake alibi, he needed the money, he was about to be written out of the will, he said he'd do it, nobody else was—"

Annie recovered her voice. "But, Lieutenant! He *couldn't* have done it! Don't you remember? About the sundial?"

"Look, young lady; we had a case two months ago—"

"Oh, those. Lieutenant, don't you remember?" said Annie pleadingly. "He and Lady Gwen were in the garden—"

"Sure I remember! But I didn't get it."

"But it's so *simple*." She forgave him with a smile. "He and Lady Gwen noticed on the sundial in the garden that it was exactly three-thirty. She remarked on it, remember? *Then* they figured out that that was *sun* time, two minutes slower than *real* time, so it was *actually* three-thirty-two, don't you see? But then *Hercule* figured out that the sundial was over three hundred years old and during that time the revolution of the earth changed or something—"

"That's the part I didn't get."

"Well, neither did I, exactly. But anyway the revolution changed the earth's relation to the sun, so the sundial was really *correct*, don't you see? It really *was* three-thirty, so Lacy couldn't *possibly* have done it."

"I thought," said Charley tactfully, "that it could have been Lady Jane."

"No." Annie reached out to tuck Charley's tie neatly inside his coat. "It couldn't have been her, either. Remember she was in the drawing room talking to Blake? The brother-in-law? And he noticed how the sun glinted on her hair bringing out the delicate tones of red and gold? Remember?"

"I guess so," said Charley.

"Well," said Annie happily, "don't you see then? It was cloudy all day."

"Cloudy?"

"Oh, Charley!" She leaned forward impatiently and began ticking off points on her fingertips. "There was no sun all day except *once*, for a second or so. So if Blake saw the sun on Lady Jane's hair, it *must* have been three-thirty. Because that was the *only* time Lacy and Lady Gwen could have told time by the sundial in the garden!" Annie paused. "Lieutenant," she appealed, "*you* see that, don't you?"

"I guess so," said the lieutenant in a strangled voice, "except—well, maybe the sun was out some other time, too. And nobody noticed it."

Annie slumped back on the davenport. "Of course not," she said hopelessly.

"But why?" said the lieutenant.

"Because! It just *couldn't*, that's all!"

The lieutenant glanced at Charley. "But why?" he said plaintively. "Why? Just tell me *why*, that's all!"

"Lieutenant," said Annie with dangerous calm, "don't be absurd. The sun *couldn't* because—why, it wouldn't be *fair*."

There was a long silence during which the lieutenant worked carefully at squeegeeing the moisture from the side of his glass with a forefinger.

Finally Charley looked up and spoke. "Maybe," he said pleasantly, "they commit murders differently in England."

"Yes," said the lieutenant, "they have rules." He turned to Annie. "Look, young lady. In twenty years on the force I have never had a single sundial in any case I've ever been

44

on or ever heard about. And the earth keeps right on revolving in the same old way. The way murders really happen, a guy gets knocked in the head, stabbed with a knife,
or shot with a gun. Once in a while, poisoned. Whoever did
it beats it and we go out and look for him till we find him.
That's all there is to it, nine times out of ten. Clues, yes.
Hard to find, sometimes? Certainly. But no delicate subtle
clues like sundials, and no split-second alibis. Believe me,
murders are practically never committed and they are never,
never solved the way you read about in detective stories."
The lieutenant paused and took a long drink from his empty
glass.

"Your glass," said Annie tenderly, "is empty." She stood
up, gently disengaged his glass from the lieutenant's nerve-
less fingers, and left the room for the kitchen.

"Colhaus," said the lieutenant. "If—"

"No," said Charley. "Annie. But I think you've made a
very strong impression."

"I would like to make an even stronger one. I would like
to show her right now, with a personal demonstration, exactly what murder is like."

Annie returned with the lieutenant's drink and curled up
on the davenport again. "As I understand you, Lieutenant,
any clue in a murder case less obvious than a bloodstained
monkey wrench, with a full set of fingerprints, is hardly worth
bothering about. Because—"

The lieutenant spoke, frowning and studying his glass.
"This drink tastes funny," he said.

"Try some more," said Annie.

The lieutenant drank again. "Still tastes funny."

"I know," said Annie sweetly. "I put salt in it."

The lieutenant set his glass down, carefully. "Salt?" he
asked with deadly politeness. "Why?"

"To show you that if that salt," said Annie, "had been
tse-tsum, you'd be dead right now! Within two seconds."

"*Look—*"

"I'll get you some more," said Annie hastily.

"I don't want any more! Just what is this, anyway?"

45

"Well." Annie looked defensively from the lieutenant to Charley and back again. "You're both so smart that I just wanted to show you. There you'd be on the floor, dead. With *tse-tsum*, a rare jungle poison, analysis shows nothing but heart failure, so they couldn't prove a thing. Anyway, nobody'd suspect me because, as you just explained, murders are *never* committed *this* way."

"Yes?" said the lieutenant pleasantly. "And just where do you get this see-some? At your neighborhood druggist's?"

"You couldn't get it," said Annie aloofly.

The lieutenant took a deep breath. He continued to inhale through flared nostrils, as though he were planning to inflate a large balloon. His face changed from rosy pink to a very attractive shade of orange, the color of a desert sunset. Then the telephone rang.

Annie walked, hastily, out to the hall and answered it.

"Annie's round," said Charley pleasantly, "on points."

"For you, Lieutenant," Annie called sweetly, and the lieutenant, exhaling as he went, came out and picked up the phone, while Annie tiptoed softly back to the davenport.

"Yeah," they heard him say, then silence. "Right away. Send a car. You got the address? Right," he said, then hung up and returned to the room. "Murder," he said softly, "*real* murder. You have never seen a murder, have you? Committed not with see-some, but by blowing a guy's head off with a gun?"

"No," said Annie.

"Get your hat," said the lieutenant grimly, "and we'll drop in on a fresh, warm, and very real killing." He turned suddenly and looked at Charley, his eyes narrowing. "Say, if I thought you'd planned on something like this—"

"Absurd," said Charley. "Such a plan would be far too subtle for a flatfoot like me."

The room in which the dead man lay was a hotel room, not cheap or small, but drab and sad under the mean light of the chandelier on its ceiling. It had one window, shiny black against the night, and was furnished with a dark rug, a bed, a desk, a chair, a bureau, a floor lamp.

But Charley, Annie, and the lieutenant, standing in the doorway, saw none of these things. They saw only the man on his back on the floor, legs out straight, feet apart. One arm lay over his chest, limply, the other was stretched out on the floor, away from the body, palm upward. There was no hair above his eyes; there was no head. The lieutenant gently pushed Annie into the room and closed the door behind them.

Four men, two kneeling at the dead man's side, the other rifling the drawers of the bureau, looked up, nodded at Charley and the lieutenant, glanced curiously at Annie, and resumed their work.

Charley turned to Annie who was still staring, eyes big, at the man on the floor. She was, Charley thought, remarkably pretty for a girl with a green complexion.

"Look," he said softly, "maybe it wasn't too smart bringing you here. I'll take you downstairs and you can—"

Annie turned haughtily. "I am quite all right," she said, apparently using someone else's voice. She stepped bravely closer to the dead man and, frowning a little, stared at his face.

Charley stooped down, hands on knees, beside the medical examiner, who was squatting at the dead man's side. "Identify him?" he said.

"Yeah. Lou knows him. Small-time racketeer; black market in the war. Marijuana, loft robberies."

Charley stood up and joined Annie who was standing in a far corner of the room. Her face was now a comparatively healthy white. "Look, honey," he said gently, "the difference between a real murder investigation and the kind you read—"

Annie interrupted. She seemed excited. "The killer," she whispered, "is redheaded."

Charley looked at her for a moment. "Yeah?" he said.

Annie opened her bag and brought out a notebook. "Look at his fingernails."

Charley looked. In the harsh light from the overhead chandelier he could see, caught in the nails of the dead man's outflung hand, a little fringe of short, dark red hairs. *Red hair*, Annie printed in her notebook.

Charley walked back to the medical examiner who was talking to the lieutenant. "That hair under his nails," he said, "from the rug, isn't it?"

"Of course."

The lieutenant glanced curiously at Charley. "Annie?"

"Yeah."

The lieutenant stood up. "This is almost too easy."

"Wait." Charley remained motionless for a moment thinking. "Maybe this is the way. I was simply going to explain our procedure, but she wants to be smart, let her have her head. Let's give her all the rope she needs."

The door of the room opened and the policeman on guard outside leaned in, a hand on the door knob. A small worried man stepped past him into the room.

"Who are you?" said the lieutenant.

"Mr. Whiteman. Theodore Whiteman, the manager."

"Okay; wait."

Annie caught Charley's eye and Charley crossed the room, the lieutenant joining him. She whispered, "See the mud on his shoes?"

"Yes," said the lieutenant. "So what?"

Annie looked at him contemptuously and produced her notebook. "There is only one place in the entire New York area where you will find soil of that peculiar red color. South Street—" she began writing in her notebook— "around the dock area at South Street."

"Very interesting," said the lieutenant gravely. "You'd say, then, that he's been in South Street lately? Maybe the murderer hangs out there, too."

"Very likely. And the murder was committed at seven-fourteen."

The lieutenant's mouth opened suddenly, then closed again slowly. "You don't say," he said. "How—"

"His watch, of course. It stopped when he was killed."

The lieutenant nodded at Annie approvingly. "Good girl," he said. "Keep it up; keep your eyes open." He nodded at Charley and they walked toward the desk where one of the detectives was standing.

"What about that mud?" said Charley.

"Offhand," said the lieutenant, "I could name you fifty places around town where you'll find red soil."

The detective at the desk looked up.

"How come the guy's watch stopped, Eddie?" said Charley.

The detective shrugged. "Wasn't wound. I tried it."

The lieutenant smiled happily at Charley. "Hello, Hercule," he said. He turned to the hotel manager. "Anyone come up here before?"

The manager shook his head. "Not that I know of. Or any of the help. I checked."

"Anyone call?"

"A man, about an hour ago."

"What'd he say?"

"He said, 'Eight-oh-nine in?' and I said, 'Just came in.' And he hung up. Didn't even say thanks."

The lieutenant nodded as though this were what he expected. "You know the voice?"

"Never heard it before."

The lieutenant indicated the dead man with his foot. "You know this guy?"

"Yessir."

"How come?"

"He stopped here before."

"Know anything about him?"

"Just that."

"You talk to him today?"

The manager nodded. "On the phone."

"When?"

"Seven-thirty."

"What about?"

"He owed a phone bill from the last time he was here. I asked him to pay."

"What did you say?"

"I said, 'This is the manager. Glad you're with us again. There is a small bill—' Then he interrupted."

"What'd he say?"

"He said, 'Okay, Theo, later.' "

"Theo?"

"It's what people call me. He knew me."

The lieutenant looked at the manager for a moment, then turned away. "Stick around," he said. He beckoned to one of the detectives who crossed the room.

"Lou? Charley?" the lieutenant said. "What do you think?"

Charley shrugged. "Routine," he said. "A small-time down and out, who just got his hands on some cash. All his clothes are new. Right, Lou?"

The other detective nodded.

"So he's in the chips again," Charley continued, "and moves in out of the rain. But there's no money here now. Right, Lou?"

Lou nodded again.

"So—" Charley shrugged once more— "somebody dumped him for the money. Maybe it was his money in the first place."

The lieutenant glanced at Lou inquiringly.

"Something like that," said Lou. "Yeah."

"Well, we'll pick him up here or there, sooner or later," said the lieutenant. "Teletype out?"

"Half an hour ago."

"Okay." The lieutenant nodded, dismissing Lou, and turned to Charley. "We might as well go."

They crossed the room to Annie again. Her eyes were fever-bright. "You noticed, didn't you?" she whispered.

"Noticed?" said Charley.

"Oh, *Charley*—the hotel man! When he phoned, he wasn't talking to—the dead man. He *couldn't* have been. It was seven-*thirty* and the man was killed at seven-*fourteen*! Remember?"

Charley nodded dumbly.

50

"So he *must* have been talking to the *murderer*. The phone rang, and—the murderer answered it!"

"No," said the lieutenant.

"No?" said Annie challengingly. "Why?"

"Well—" The lieutenant hesitated. "He said, 'Theo.' He said, 'Okay, Theo, later.' Not likely he'd know the manager's name or use it if he did."

Annie thought for several moments, rubbing her front teeth nervously with a forefinger. "What a break!" she exclaimed. "Don't you see? The murderer lisped!"

Charley felt suddenly guilty. "Look honey," he said contritely. He put an arm around her shoulder protectively. "Maybe I should tell you—"

"Oh, Charley!" she said. "Don't you *see*? Look. We know it was the murderer who answered the phone. We know he wouldn't have said, 'Theo.' So what *did* he say that sounded like it? He must have said, 'Okay, thee you later'! Which sounds almost exactly like, 'Okay, Theo, later'! The murderer lisped!"

Charley looked at Annie hopelessly, his face a mask of guilt and despair. He opened his mouth to speak, then closed it again. He had waited, he realized, too long. It was impossible now to explain—if he ever hoped even to speak to Annie again.

"What's more," said Annie, "he was six feet four inches tall and left-handed."

"Wonderful," said the lieutenant. "How—"

"Look at the phone," said Annie coldly. She pointed to the desk. The phone lay in its cradle, the mouthpiece at the right. "A right-handed person replaces the phone exactly opposite from that. As for his height—"

The lieutenant took Charley's arm and they crossed the room to the desk. "You use this phone?" said the lieutenant quietly to the man at the desk.

The detective looked up. "Of course."

"You left-handed?"

The man glanced at the lieutenant curiously. "No. Why?"

"How come you put the phone back like that?"

The detective looked at the phone, then back again. "I don't know," he said. "I always do."

They returned to Annie. "Marvelous," said the lieutenant. He put his arm around Annie affectionately. "Amazing," he said. "Great little helpmate you'll be for Charley." He looked at Charley solemnly. "Let's get out of here," he said. "Annie's given us enough to work on. The rest will be strictly routine."

And it was. To Annie's outraged astonishment, during the next week, no manhunt took place; no cordon of police was thrown around the city. Even worse, no circular was issued containing Annie's beautifully worked-out dossier on the criminal. The police seemed completely uninterested in Annie's deductions.

Charley tried to explain. They had returned to Annie's apartment from a movie, *Sweet Murder, My Lovely*, and were sitting—several feet apart—on the davenport.

"In this kind of killing," Charley said patiently, "we *know* the kind of guy who did it. And that's all we need. Because we know he'll be picked up sooner or later, somewhere, for something. In a gambling raid, or for petty larceny, jostling in a subway, whatever his racket is. And every possible suspect is always questioned; about this crime and any others we've got."

Annie found this explanation less than satisfactory. She sniffed: a sniff that was close to a snort. "It's like hunting for a needle in a haystack," she said, "blindfolded! And not even hunting! Just waiting till it jabs you!"

"So what? As long as you find the needle."

"But when you have a *description*," Annie wailed, "practically an exact description, and . . ."

Relations between Charley and Annie, some six days later when the killer was found, resembled in tenseness the high E string of an electric guitar connected by mistake to a power line. And the fact that he was caught precisely as Charley had predicted didn't help. The word came one evening at Annie's; Charley answered the phone. And when he returned smiling for the first time in days, he could be pardoned, perhaps, for gloating a little.

"Grab your hat," he said. "We're going to headquarters! And I'll show you a killer caught by the cops without any help from Sam Spade, Inspector Chafik, or even Hercule Poirot!"

They waited at headquarters, seated on yellow wooden folding chairs, in a small, unadorned, white-plastered room. The lieutenant, more worried and sleepless-appearing than ever, sat staring at his feet. Annie looked coldly ahead, while Charley waited happily, both watching the closed door of the room.

The door opened. A man was urged forward by a policeman at his back. He stepped forward into the room, ducking his head as he passed through the doorway, then stood staring sullenly over their heads at the opposite wall. His clothes were unpressed and he wore a cap. He seemed about forty years old.

Annie brought out her notebook and ticked off an item with her pencil. "Six feet four," she said. "Right?"

The lieutenant did not look at Annie. "Four and a half," he said.

Annie leaned forward and whispered to the lieutenant. "His cap," she said. "Do you suppose—"

The lieutenant spoke wearily. "Take off your cap."

The man raised his hand—his left hand—and Annie's pencil flicked once. He pulled off his cap. His hair was almost beautiful: thick and alive, deeply waved, and red.

"Little darker than I thought," Annie murmured, and her pencil flicked once more. "Where was he found, Lieutenant?"

The lieutenant looked up again, very, very wearily. "Where did they pick you up?" he said to the man.

The man looked at them all for a moment, then returned his gaze to the wall before him. "Thouth Thtreet," he said, and Annie's pencil flicked twice. . . .

During the ten-minute cab ride back to Annie's apartment, neither she nor Charley spoke; Charley because he was unable to, and Annie out of compassion. But when they stood at the street door of Annie's building, the cab still waiting at the curb, a voice, not his, came out of Charley's throat. "Tell me, just tell me it *could* have been somebody else? Say a baldheaded guy, five feet two, who spoke with maybe a stutter? Did it ever enter your head that your clues *could* have been wrong? That it *could* have been somebody else? Did it ever—"

"No," Annie said. "Of course not."

"But why?" Charley wailed. "Why? Will you please tell me *why*?"

Annie looked at him sadly, pityingly, and made the final effort of a person who knows it is doomed to failure. "The clues," she said gently, "couldn't be wrong." She opened the door. "They just *couldn't* because—Charley, don't you see? It wouldn't be *fair*!"

Charley and Annie are married, now. They are very happy and contented—because they are not married to each other. Charley's wife thinks he is wonderful, a bulwark of law and order, but then she always did admire policemen—from her earliest memories of riding pickaback on the broad shoulders of her father, Patrolman Colhaus. And Annie's husband—he thinks she is marvelous. He is a writer, a tweed-jacketed, pipe-smoking author of detective stories. And Annie, he says, gives him most of his best ideas.

The Parker Shotgun

•

Sue Grafton

Sue Grafton's novels and short stories featuring private investigator Kinsey Millhone have won her a large readership and several awards, including a Best Novel Shamus from the Private Eye Writers of America for "B" is for Burglar (1985). Her other "alphabet" novels include "A" is for Alibi (1984), "C" is for Corpse (1986), "D" is for Deadbeat (1987), and "E" is for Evidence (1988). In addition to crime fiction, Grafton is an accomplished screenwriter; among her scripting credits are a pair of TV movies adapted from novels by Agatha Christie and co-authored with her husband, Steve Humphrey. "The Parker Shotgun" is arguably the best of Kinsey Millhone's short cases.

The Christmas holidays had come and gone, and the new year was underway. January, in California, is as good as it gets—cool, clear, and green, with a sky the color of wisteria and a surf that thunders like a volley of gunfire in a distant field. My name is Kinsey Millhone. I'm a private investigator, licensed, bonded, insured; white, female, age thirty-two, unmarried, and physically fit. That Monday morning, I was sitting in my office with my feet up, wondering what life would bring, when a woman walked in and tossed a photograph on my desk. My introduction to the Parker shotgun began with a graphic view of its apparent effect when fired at a formerly nice-looking man at close range. His face was still largely intact, but he had no use now for a pocket comb. With effort, I kept my expression neutral as I glanced up at her.

"Somebody killed my husband."

"I can see that," I said.

She snatched the picture back and stared at it as though she might have missed some telling detail. Her face suffused with pink, and she blinked back tears. "Jesus. Rudd was killed five months ago, and the cops have done shit. I'm so sick of getting the runaround I could scream."

She sat down abruptly and pressed a hand to her mouth, trying to compose herself. She was in her late twenties, with a gaudy prettiness. Her hair was an odd shade of brown, like cherry Coke, worn shoulder length and straight. Her eyes were large, a lush mink brown; her mouth was full. Her complexion was all warm tones, tanned, and clear. She didn't seem to be wearing makeup, but she was still as vivid as a magazine illustration, a good four-color run on slick paper. She was seven months pregnant by the look of her; not voluminous yet, but rotund. When she was calmer, she identified herself as Lisa Osterling.

"That's a crime lab photo. How'd you come by it?" I said when the preliminaries were disposed of.

She fumbled in her handbag for a tissue and blew her nose. "I have my little ways," she said morosely. "Actually I know the photographer and I stole a print. I'm going to have it blown up and hung on the wall just so I won't forget. The police are hoping I'll drop the whole thing, but I got news for *them*." Her mouth was starting to tremble again, and a tear splashed onto her skirt as though my ceiling had a leak.

"What's the story?" I said. "The cops in this town are usually pretty good." I got up and filled a paper cup with water from my Sparklett's dispenser, passing it over to her. She murmured a thank-you and drank it down, staring into the bottom of the cup as she spoke. "Rudd was a cocaine dealer until a month or so before he died. They haven't said as much, but I know they've written him off as some kind of small-time punk. What do they care? They'd like to think he was killed in a drug deal—a double cross or something like that. He wasn't, though. He'd given it all up because of this."

56

She glanced down at the swell of her belly. She was wearing a kelly green T-shirt with an arrow down the front. The word "Oops!" was written across her breasts in machine embroidery.

"What's your theory?" I asked. Already I was leaning toward the official police version of events. Drug dealing isn't synonymous with longevity. There's too much money involved and too many amateurs getting into the act. This was Santa Teresa—ninety-five miles north of the big time in L.A., but there are still standards to maintain. A shotgun blast is the underworld equivalent of a bad annual review.

"I don't have a theory. I just don't like theirs. I want you to look into it so I can clear Rudd's name before the baby comes."

I shrugged. "I'll do what I can, but I can't guarantee the results. How are you going to feel if the cops are right?"

She stood up, giving me a flat look. "I don't know why Rudd died, but it had nothing to do with drugs," she said. She opened her handbag and extracted a roll of bills the size of a wad of socks. "What do you charge?"

"Thirty bucks an hour plus expenses."

She peeled off several hundred-dollar bills and laid them on the desk.

I got out a contract.

My second encounter with the Parker shotgun came in the form of a dealer's appraisal slip that I discovered when I was nosing through Rudd Osterling's private possessions an hour later at the house. The address she'd given me was on the Bluffs, a residential area on the west side of town, overlooking the Pacific. It should have been an elegant neighborhood, but the ocean generated too much fog and too much corrosive salt air. The houses were small and had a temporary feel to them, as though the occupants intended to move on when the month was up. No one seemed to get around to painting the trim, and the yards looked like they were kept by people who spent all day at the beach. I followed her in my car, reviewing the information she'd given me as I urged my ancient VW up Capilla Hill and took a right on Presipio.

The late Rudd Osterling had been in Santa Teresa since the sixties, when he migrated to the West Coast in search of sunshine, good surf, good dope, and casual sex. Lisa told me he'd lived in vans and communes, working variously as a roofer, tree trimmer, bean picker, fry cook, and forklift operator—never with any noticeable ambition or success. He'd started dealing cocaine two years earlier, apparently netting more money than he was accustomed to. Then he'd met and married Lisa, and she'd been determined to see him clean up his act. According to her, he'd retired from the drug trade and was just in the process of setting himself up in a landscape maintenance business when someone blew the top of his head off.

I pulled into the driveway behind her, glancing at the frame and stucco bungalow with its patchy grass and dilapidated fence. It looked like one of those households where there's always something under construction, probably without permits and not up to code. In this case, a foundation had been laid for an addition to the garage, but the weeds were already growing up through cracks in the concrete. A wooden outbuilding had been dismantled, the old lumber tossed in an unsightly pile. Closer to the house, there were stacks of cheap pecan wood paneling, sun-bleached in places and warped along one edge. It was all hapless and depressing, but she scarcely looked at it.

I followed her into the house.

"We were just getting the house fixed up when he died," she remarked.

"When did you buy the place?" I was manufacturing small talk, trying to cover my distaste at the sight of the old linoleum counter, where a line of ants stretched from a crust of toast and jelly all the way out the back door.

"We didn't really. This was my mother's. She and my stepdad moved back to the Midwest last year."

"What about Rudd? Did he have any family out here?"

"They're all in Connecticut, I think, real la-di-dah. His

parents are dead, and his sisters wouldn't even come out to the funeral."

"Did he have a lot of friends?"

"All cocaine dealers have friends."

"Enemies?"

"Not that I ever heard about."

"Who was his supplier?"

"I don't know that."

"No disputes? Suits pending? Quarrels with the neighbors? Family arguments about the inheritance?"

She gave me a "no" on all four counts.

I had told her I wanted to go through his personal belongings, so she showed me into the tiny back bedroom, where he'd set up a card table and some cardboard file boxes. A real entrepreneur. I began to search while she leaned against the doorframe, watching.

I said, "Tell me about what was going on the week he died." I was sorting through canceled checks in a Nike shoe box. Most were written to the neighborhood supermarket, utilities, telephone company.

She moved to the desk chair and sat down. "I can't tell you much because I was at work. I do alterations and repairs at a dry cleaner's up at Presipio Mall. Rudd would stop in now and then when he was out running around. He'd picked up a few jobs already, but he really wasn't doing the gardening full time. He was trying to get all his old business squared away. Some kid owed him money. I remember that."

"He sold cocaine on *credit*?"

She shrugged. "Maybe it was grass or pills. Somehow the kid owed him a bundle. That's all I know."

"I don't suppose he kept any records."

"Nuh-uh. It was all in his head. He was too paranoid to put anything down in black and white."

The file boxes were jammed with old letters, tax returns, receipts. It all looked like junk to me.

"What about the day he was killed? Were you at work then?"

She shook her head. "It was a Saturday. I was off work,

but I'd gone to the market. I was out maybe an hour and a half, and when I got home, police cars were parked in front, and the paramedics were here. Neighbors were standing out on the street.'' She stopped talking, and I was left to imagine the rest.

"Had he been expecting anyone?"

"If he was, he never said anything to me. He was in the garage, doing I don't know what. Chauncy, next door, heard the shotgun go off, but by the time he got here to investigate, whoever did it was gone.''

I got up and moved toward the hallway. "Is this the bedroom down here?"

"Right. I haven't gotten rid of his stuff yet. I guess I'll have to eventually. I'm going to use his office for the nursery.''

I moved into the master bedroom and went through his hanging clothes. "Did the police find anything?"

"They didn't look. Well, one guy came through and poked around some. About five minutes' worth.''

I began to check through the drawers she indicated were his. Nothing remarkable came to light. On top of the chest was one of those brass and walnut caddies, where Rudd apparently kept his watch, keys, loose change. Almost idly, I picked it up. Under it there was a folded slip of paper. It was a partially completed appraisal form from a gun shop out in Colgate, a township to the north of us. "What's a Parker?" I said when I'd glanced at it. She peered over the slip.

"Oh. That's probably the appraisal on the shotgun he got.''

"The one he was killed with?"

"Well, I don't know. They never found the weapon, but the homicide detective said they couldn't run it through ballistics, anyway—or whatever it is they do.''

"Why'd he have it appraised in the first place?"

"He was taking it in trade for a big drug debt, and he needed to know if it was worth it.''

"Was this the kid you mentioned before or someone else?"

"The same one, I think. At first, Rudd intended to turn around and sell the gun, but then he found out it was a collector's item so he decided to keep it. The gun dealer called a couple of times after Rudd died, but it was gone by then.''

"And you told the cops all this stuff?''

"Sure. They couldn't have cared less.''

I doubted that, but I tucked the slip in my pocket anyway. I'd check it out and then talk to Dolan in homicide.

The gun shop was located on a narrow side street in Colgate, just off the main thoroughfare. Colgate looks like it's made up of hardware stores, U-haul rentals, and plant nurseries; places that seem to have half their merchandise outside, surrounded by chain link fence. The gun shop had been set up in someone's front parlor in a dinky white frame house. There were some glass counters filled with gun paraphernalia, but no guns in sight.

The man who came out of the back room was in his fifties, with a narrow face and graying hair, gray eyes made luminous by rimless glasses. He wore a dress shirt with the sleeves rolled up and a long gray apron tied around his waist. He had perfect teeth, but when he talked I could see the rim of pink where his upper plate was fit, and it spoiled the effect. Still, I had to give him credit for a certain level of good looks, maybe a seven on a scale of ten. Not bad for a man his age. "Yes ma'am,'' he said. He had a trace of an accent, Virginia, I thought.

"Are you Avery Lamb?''

"That's right. What can I help you with?''

"I'm not sure. I'm wondering what you can tell me about this appraisal you did.'' I handed him the slip.

He glanced down and then looked up at me. "Where did you get this?''

"Rudd Osterling's widow,'' I said.

"She told me she didn't have the gun.''

"That's right.''

His manner was a combination of confusion and wariness. "What's your connection to the matter?''

I took out a business card and gave it to him. "She hired

me to look into Rudd's death. I thought the shotgun might be relevant since he was killed with one.''

He shook his head. ''I don't know what's going on. This is the second time it's disappeared.''

''Meaning what?''

''Some woman brought it in to have it appraised back in June. I made an offer on it then, but before we could work out a deal, she claimed the gun was stolen.''

''I take it you had some doubts about that.''

''Sure I did. I don't think she ever filed a police report, and I suspect she knew damn well who took it but didn't intend to pursue it. Next thing I knew, this Osterling fellow brought the same gun in. It had a beavertail fore-end and an English grip. There was no mistaking it.''

''Wasn't that a bit of a coincidence? His bringing the gun in to you?''

''Not really. I'm one of the few master gunsmiths in this area. All he had to do was ask around the same way she did.''

''Did you tell her the gun had showed up?''

He shrugged with his mouth and a lift of his brows. ''Before I could talk to her, he was dead and the Parker was gone again.''

I checked the date on the slip. ''That was in August?''

''That's right, and I haven't seen the gun since.''

''Did he tell you how he acquired it?''

''Said he took it in trade. I told him this other woman showed up with it first, but he didn't seem to care about that.''

''How much was the Parker worth?''

He hesitated, weighing his words. ''I offered him six thousand.''

''But what's its value out in the marketplace?''

''Depends on what people are willing to pay.''

I tried to control the little surge of impatience he had sparked. I could tell he'd jumped into his crafty negotiator's mode, unwilling to tip his hand in case the gun showed up and he could nick it off cheap. ''Look,'' I said, ''I'm asking you in confidence. This won't go any further unless it becomes a police matter, and then neither one of us will have a choice. Right now, the gun's missing anyway, so what difference does it make?''

He didn't seem entirely convinced, but he got my point. He cleared his throat with obvious embarrassment. "Ninety-six.''

I stared at him. "Thousand dollars?''

He nodded.

"Jesus. That's a lot for a gun, isn't it?''

His voice dropped. "Ms. Millhone, that gun is priceless. It's an A-1 Special 28-gauge with a two-barrel set. There were only two of them made.''

"But why so much?''

"For one thing, the Parker's a beautifully crafted shotgun. There are different grades, of course, but this one was exceptional. Fine wood. Some of the most incredible scroll-work you'll ever see. Parker had an Italian working for him back then who'd spend sometimes five thousand hours on the engraving alone. The company went out of business around 1942, so there aren't any more to be had.''

"You said there were two. Where's the other one, or would you know?''

"Only what I've heard. A dealer in Ohio bought the one at auction a couple years back for ninety-six. I understand some fella down in Texas has it now, part of a collection of Parkers. The gun Rudd Osterling brought in has been missing for years. I don't think he knew what he had on his hands.''

"And you didn't tell him.''

Lamb shifted his gaze. "I told him enough,'' he said carefully. "I can't help it if the man didn't do his homework.''

"How'd you know it was the missing Parker?''

"The serial number matched, and so did everything else. It wasn't a fake, either. I examined the gun under heavy magnification, checking for fill-in welds and traces of markings that might have been overstamped. After I checked it out, I showed it to a buddy of mine, a big gun buff, and he recognized it, too.''

"Who else knew about it besides you and this friend?"

"Whoever Rudd Osterling got it from, I guess."

"I'll want the woman's name and address if you've still got it. Maybe she knows how the gun fell into Rudd's hands."

Again he hesitated for a moment, and then he shrugged. "I don't see why not." He made a note on a piece of scratch paper and pushed it across the counter to me. "I'd like to know if the gun shows up," he said.

"Sure, as long as Mrs. Osterling doesn't object."

I didn't have any other questions for the moment. I moved toward the door, then glanced back at him. "How could Rudd have sold the gun if it was stolen property? Wouldn't he have needed a bill of sale for it? Some proof of ownership?"

Avery Lamb's face was devoid of expression. "Not necessarily. If an avid collector got hold of that gun, it would sink out of sight, and that's the last you'd ever see of it. He'd keep it in his basement and never show it to a soul. It'd be enough if he knew he had it. You don't need a bill of sale for that."

I sat out in my car and made some notes while the information was fresh. Then I checked the address Lamb had given me, and I could feel the adrenaline stir. It was right back in Rudd's neighborhood.

The woman's name was Jackie Barnett. The address was two streets over from the Osterling house and just about parallel; a big corner lot planted with avocado trees and bracketed with palms. The house itself was yellow stucco with flaking brown shutters and a yard that needed mowing. The mailbox read "Squires," but the house number seemed to match. There was a basketball hoop nailed up above the two-car garage and a dismantled motorcycle in the driveway.

I parked my car and got out. As I approached the house, I saw an old man in a wheelchair planted in the side yard like a lawn ornament. He was parchment pale, with baby-fine white hair and rheumy eyes. The left half of his face had been disconnected by a stroke, and his left arm and hand rested uselessly in his lap. I caught sight of a woman peering through the window, apparently drawn by the sound of my car door slamming shut. I crossed the yard, moving toward the front porch. She opened the door before I had a chance to knock.

"You must be Kinsey Millhone. I just got off the phone with Avery. He said you'd be stopping by."

"That was quick. I didn't realize he'd be calling ahead. Saves me an explanation. I take it you're Jackie Barnett."

"That's right. Come in if you like. I just have to check on him," she said, indicating the man in the yard.

"Your father?"

She shot me a look. "Husband," she said. I watched her cross the grass toward the old man, grateful for a chance to recover from my gaffe. I could see now that she was older than she'd first appeared. She must have been in her fifties—at that stage where women wear too much makeup and dye their hair too bold a shade of blonde. She was buxom, clearly overweight, but lush. In a seventeenth-century painting, she'd have been depicted supine, her plump naked body draped in sheer white. Standing over her, something with a goat's rear end would be poised for assault. Both would look coy but excited at the prospects. The old man was beyond the pleasures of the flesh, yet the noises he made—garbled and indistinguishable because of the stroke—had the same intimate quality as sounds uttered in the throes of passion, a disquieting effect.

I looked away from him, thinking of Avery Lamb instead. He hadn't actually told me the woman was a stranger to him, but he'd certainly implied as much. I wondered now what their relationship consisted of.

Jackie spoke to the old man briefly, adjusting his lap robe. Then she came back and we went inside.

"Is your name Barnett or Squires?" I asked.

"Technically it's Squires, but I still use Barnett for the most part," she said. She seemed angry, and I thought at first the rage was directed at me. She caught my look. "I'm

65

sorry," she said, "but I've about had it with him. Have you ever dealt with a stroke victim?"

"I understand it's difficult."

"It's impossible! I know I sound hard-hearted, but he was always short-tempered and now he's frustrated on top of that. Self-centered, demanding. Nothing suits him. Nothing. I put him out in the yard sometimes just so I won't have to fool with him. Have a seat, hon."

I sat. "How long has he been sick?"

"He had the first stroke in June. He's been in and out of the hospital ever since."

"What's the story on the gun you took out to Avery's shop?"

"Oh, that's right. He said you were looking into some fellow's death. He lived right here on the Bluffs, too, didn't he?"

"Over on Whitmore . . ."

"That was terrible. I read about it in the papers, but I never did hear the end of it. What went on?"

"I wasn't given the details," I said briefly. "Actually, I'm trying to track down a shotgun that belonged to him. Avery Lamb says it was the same gun you brought in."

She had automatically proceeded to get out two cups and saucers, so her answer was delayed until she'd poured coffee for us both. She passed a cup over to me, and then she sat down, stirring milk into hers. She glanced at me self-consciously. "I just took the gun to spite *him*," she said with a nod toward the yard. "I've been married to Bill for six years and miserable for every one of them. It was my own damn fault. I'd been divorced for ages and I was doing fine, but somehow when I hit fifty, I got in a panic. Afraid of growing old alone, I guess. I ran into Bill, and he looked like a catch. He was retired, but he had loads of money, or so he said. He promised me the moon. Said we'd travel. Said he'd buy me clothes and a car and I don't know what all. Turns out he's a penny-pinching miser with a mean mouth and a quick fist. At least he can't do that anymore." She paused to shake her head, staring down at her coffee cup.

''The gun was his?''

''Well, yes, it was. He has a collection of shotguns. I swear he took better care of them than he did of me. I just despise guns. I was always after him to get rid of them. Makes me nervous to have them in the house. Anyway, when he got sick, it turned out he had insurance, but it only paid eighty percent. I was afraid his whole life savings would go up in smoke. I figured he'd go on for years, using up all the money, and then I'd be stuck with his debts when he died. So I just picked up one of the guns and took it out to that gun place to sell. I was going to buy me some clothes.''

''What made you change your mind?''

''Well, I didn't think it'd be worth but eight or nine hundred dollars. Then Avery said he'd give me six thousand for it, so I had to guess it was worth at least twice that. I got nervous and thought I better put it back.''

''How soon after that did the gun disappear?''

''Oh, gee, I don't know. I didn't pay much attention until Bill got out of the hospital the second time. He's the one who noticed it was gone,'' she said. ''Of course, he raised plu-perfect hell. You should have seen him. He had a conniption fit for two days, and then he had another stroke and had to be hospitalized all over again. Served him right if you ask me. At least I had Labor Day weekend to myself. I needed it.''

''Do you have any idea who might have taken the gun?''

She gave me a long, candid look. Her eyes were very blue and couldn't have appeared more guileless. ''Not the faintest.''

I let her practice her wide-eyed stare for a moment, and then I laid out a little bait just to see what she'd do. ''God, that's too bad,'' I said. ''I'm assuming you reported it to the police.''

I could see her debate briefly before she replied. Yes or no. Check one. ''Well, of course,'' she said.

She was one of those liars who blush from lack of practice.

I kept my tone of voice mild. ''What about the insurance? Did you put in a claim?''

67

She looked at me blankly, and I had the feeling I'd taken her by surprise on that one. She said, "You know, it never even occurred to me. But of course he probably would have it insured, wouldn't he?"

"Sure, if the gun's worth that much. What company is he with?"

"I don't remember offhand. I'd have to look it up."

"I'd do that if I were you," I said. "You can file a claim, and then all you have to do is give the agent the case number."

"Case number?"

"The police will give you that from their report."

She stirred restlessly, glancing at her watch. "Oh, lordy, I'm going to have to give him his medicine. Was there anything else you wanted to ask while you were here?" Now that she'd told me a fib or two, she was anxious to get rid of me so she could assess the situation. Avery Lamb had told me she'd never reported it to the cops. I wondered if she'd call him up now to compare notes.

"Could I take a quick look at his collection?" I said, getting up.

"I suppose that'd be all right. It's in here," she said. She moved toward a small paneled den, and I followed, stepping around a suitcase near the door.

A rack of six guns was enclosed in a glass-fronted cabinet. All of them were beautifully engraved, with fine wood stocks, and I wondered how a priceless Parker could really be distinguished. Both the cabinet and the rack were locked, and there were no empty slots. "Did he keep the Parker in here?"

She shook her head. "The Parker had its own case." She hauled out a handsome wood case from behind the couch and opened it for me, demonstrating its emptiness as though she might be setting up a magic trick. Actually, there was a set of barrels in the box, but nothing else.

I glanced around. There was a shotgun propped in one corner, and I picked it up, checking the manufacturer's imprint on the frame. L. C. Smith. Too bad. For a moment I'd thought it might be the missing Parker. I'm always hoping for the obvious. I set the Smith back in the corner with regret.

"Well, I guess that'll do," I said. "Thanks for the coffee."

"No trouble. I wish I could be more help." She started easing me toward the door.

I held out my hand. "Nice meeting you," I said. "Thanks again for your time."

She gave my hand a perfunctory shake. "That's all right. Sorry I'm in such a rush, but you know how it is when you have someone sick."

Next thing I knew, the door was closing at my back and I was heading toward my car, wondering what she was up to.

I'd just reached the driveway when a white Corvette came roaring down the street and rumbled into the drive. The kid at the wheel flipped the ignition key and cantilevered himself up onto the seat top. "Hi. You know if my mom's here?"

"Who, Jackie? Sure," I said, taking a flyer. "You must be Doug."

He looked puzzled. "No, Eric. Do I know you?"

I shook my head. "I'm just a friend passing through."

He hopped out of the Corvette. I moved on toward my car, keeping an eye on him as he headed toward the house. He looked about seventeen, blond, blue-eyed, with good cheekbones, a moody, sensual mouth, lean surfer's body. I pictured him in a few years, hanging out in resort hotels, picking up women three times his age. He'd do well. So would they.

Jackie had apparently heard him pull in, and she came out onto the porch, intercepting him with a quick look at me. She put her arm through his, and the two moved into the house. I looked over at the old man. He was making noises again, plucking aimlessly at his bad hand with his good one. I felt a mental jolt, like an interior tremor shifting the ground under me. I was beginning to get it.

I drove the two blocks to Lisa Osterling's. She was in the backyard, stretched out on a chaise in a sunsuit that made her belly look like a watermelon in a laundry bag. Her face and arms were rosy, and her tanned legs glistened with tanning oil. As I crossed the grass, she raised a hand to her eyes, shading her face from the winter sunlight so she could look at me. "I didn't expect to see you back so soon."

"I have a question," I said, "and then I need to use your phone. Did Rudd know a kid named Eric Barnett?"

"I'm not sure. What's he look like?"

I gave her a quick rundown, including a description of the white Corvette. I could see the recognition in her face as she sat up.

"Oh, him. Sure. He was over here two or three times a week. I just never knew his name. Rudd said he lived around here somewhere and stopped by to borrow tools so he could work on his motorcycle. Is he the one who owed Rudd the money?"

"Well, I don't know how we're going to prove it, but I suspect he was."

"You think he killed him?"

"I can't answer that yet, but I'm working on it. Is the phone in here?" I was moving toward the kitchen. She struggled to her feet and followed me into the house. There was a wall phone near the back door. I tucked the receiver against my shoulder, pulling the appraisal slip out of my pocket. I dialed Avery Lamb's gun shop. The phone rang twice.

Somebody picked up on the other end. "Gun shop."

"Mr. Lamb?"

"This is Orville Lamb. Did you want me or my brother, Avery?"

"Avery, actually. I have a quick question for him."

"Well, he left a short while ago, and I'm not sure when he'll be back. Is it something I can help you with?"

"Maybe so," I said. "If you had a priceless shotgun— say, an Ithaca or a Parker, one of the classics—would you shoot a gun like that?"

"You could," he said dubiously, "but it wouldn't be a good idea, especially if it was in mint condition to begin with. You wouldn't want to take a chance on lowering the value. Now if it'd been in use previously, I don't guess it would matter much, but still I wouldn't advise it—just speaking for myself. Is this a gun of yours?''

But I'd hung up. Lisa was right behind me, her expression was anxious. ''I've got to go in a minute,'' I said, ''but here's what I think went on. Eric Barnett's stepfather has a collection of fine shotguns, one of which turns out to be very, very valuable. The old man was hospitalized, and Eric's mother decided to hock one of the guns in order to do a little something for herself before he'd blown every asset he had on his medical bills. She had no idea the gun she chose was worth so much, but the gun dealer recognized it as the find of a lifetime. I don't know whether he told her that or not, but when she realized it was more valuable than she thought, she lost her nerve and put it back.''

''Was that the same gun Rudd took in trade?''

''Exactly. My guess is that she mentioned it to her son, who saw a chance to square his drug debt. He offered Rudd the shotgun in trade, and Rudd decided he'd better get the gun appraised, so he took it out to the same place. The gun dealer recognized it when he brought it in.''

She stared at me. ''Rudd was killed over the gun itself, wasn't he?'' she said.

''I think so, yes. It might have been an accident. Maybe there was a struggle and the gun went off.''

She closed her eyes and nodded. ''Okay. Oh, wow. That feels better. I can live with that.'' Her eyes came open, and she smiled painfully. ''Now what?''

''I have one more hunch to check out, and then I think we'll know what's what.''

She reached over and squeezed my arm. ''Thanks.''

''Yeah, well, it's not over yet, but we're getting there.''

When I got back to Jackie Barnett's, the white Corvette was still in the driveway, but the old man in the wheelchair had apparently been moved into the house. I knocked, and after an interval, Eric opened the door, his expression altering only slightly when he saw me.

I said, "Hello again. Can I talk to your mom?"

"Well, not really. She's gone right now."

"Did she and Avery go off together?"

"Who?"

I smiled briefly. "You can drop the bullshit, Eric. I saw the suitcase in the hall when I was here the first time. Are they gone for good or just for a quick jaunt?"

"They said they'd be back by the end of the week," he mumbled. It was clear he looked a lot slicker than he really was. I almost felt bad that he was so far outclassed.

"Do you mind if I talk to your stepfather?"

He flushed. "She doesn't want him upset."

"I won't upset him."

He shifted uneasily, trying to decide what to do with me.

I thought I'd help him out. "Could I just make a suggestion here? According to the California penal code, grand theft is committed when the real or personal property taken is of a value exceeding two hundred dollars. Now that includes domestic fowl, avocados, olives, citrus, nuts, and artichokes. Also shotguns, and it's punishable by imprisonment in the county jail or state prison for not more than one year. I don't think you'd care for it."

He stepped away from the door and let me in.

The old man was huddled in his wheelchair in the den. The rheumy eyes came up to meet mine, but there was no recognition in them. Or maybe there was recognition but no interest. I hunkered beside his wheelchair. "Is your hearing okay?"

He began to pluck aimlessly at his pant leg with his good hand, looking away from me. I've seen dogs with the same expression when they've done pottie on the rug and know you've got a roll of newspaper tucked behind your back.

"Want me to tell you what I think happened?" I didn't really need to wait. He couldn't answer in any mode that I could interpret. "I think when you came home from the hospital the first time and found out the gun was gone, the shit hit the fan. You must have figured out that Eric took it. He'd probably taken other things if he'd been doing cocaine for long. You probably hounded him until you found out what he'd done with it, and then you went over to Rudd's to get it. Maybe you took the L. C. Smith with you the first time, or maybe you came back for it when he refused to return the Parker. In either case, you blew his head off and then came back across the yards. And then you had another stroke."

I became aware of Eric in the doorway behind me. I glanced back at him. "You want to talk about this stuff?" I asked.

"Did he kill Rudd?"

"I think so," I said. I stared at the old man.

His face had taken on a canny stubbornness, and what was I going to do? I'd have to talk to Lieutenant Dolan about the situation, but the cops would probably never find any real proof, and even if they did, what could they do to him? He'd be lucky if he lived out the year.

"Rudd was a nice guy," Eric said.

"God, Eric. You *all* must have guessed what happened," I said snappishly.

He had the good grace to color up at that, and then he left the room. I stood up. To save myself, I couldn't work up any righteous anger at the pitiful remainder of a human being hunched in front of me. I crossed to the gun cabinet.

The Parker shotgun was in the rack, three slots down, looking like the other classic shotguns in the case. The old man would die, and Jackie would inherit it from his estate. Then she'd marry Avery and they'd all have what they wanted. I stood there for a moment, and then I started looking through the desk drawers until I found the keys. I unlocked the cabinet and then unlocked the rack. I substituted the L. C. Smith for the Parker and then locked the whole business up again. The old man was whimpering, but he never looked at me, and Eric was nowhere in sight when I left.

The last I saw of the Parker shotgun, Lisa Osterling was holding it somewhat awkwardly across her bulky midriff. I'd talk to Lieutenant Dolan all right, but I wasn't going to tell him everything. Sometimes justice is served in other ways.

Never Marry Murder

·

William Campbell Gault

An award-winning author of crime, sports, and juvenile fiction, William Campbell Gault has been entertaining readers young and old for more than fifty years. He was a prolific contributor to the detective and sports pulps from 1936 until the collapse of the pulp markets in the early fifties. His first mystery novel, Don't Cry for Me, *was the recipient of an MWA Edgar for Best First Novel of 1952; and his first juvenile sports novel,* Thunder Road, *also published in 1952, was in print continuously for more than thirty years. Gault's most popular series character, Brock "The Rock" Callahan, has appeared in a dozen excellent mystery novels, the most recent of which is* Cat and Mouse *(1987). "Never Marry Murder," about a man who killed two wives for money and is driven to murder a third for love, is a solid example of Gault's proficiency with the short crime story.*

This time, he had told himself, he'd marry for love. And he had. This time it would be for keeps, and he would rejoin the society of normal citizens. He would vote and argue politics and play poker and take up golf. This was to be the peace he'd earned; there was no longer any reason why he couldn't be normal. He could afford it now.

He sat in the breakfast nook this morning, reading the sports pages of the morning paper, feeling smug and contented and cheerful.

"The honeymoon is over," Eve said. "Reading at breakfast. This is the first time."

He put the paper away and smiled at her. "I couldn't tell you a word I've read. But it seemed like the thing to do."

"You're the strangest one," Eve said. "What did you mean by that?"

"I meant," he said lightly, "that it seemed like the accepted thing to do. In all the plays and movies and comic strips about domestic bliss, the husband is always reading the paper at breakfast. That's why I ordered it. I don't like that paper at all."

Her warm brown eyes regarded him curiously. "I can never tell when you're joking. You're joking now, aren't you?"

"I am," he admitted. "Darling, the honeymoon will never be over with us, will it?"

"Not for me," she said, and her smile was a promise. "Happy?"

"I've never been happier," he told her honestly. "I never expected to be this happy."

She sighed contentedly. "More coffee?"

"A little." He looked at her and wondered at his luck. But of course, he'd always had a way with women.

But not always luck. Jane, now, and Martha—they'd served their purpose; they'd made it possible for him to marry Eve. But he would always think of them as Plain Jane and Mammoth Martha. He shuddered a little, remembering.

"What's the matter?" Eve said quickly. "You had the bleakest look on your face just then."

"I was thinking," he said, "what a horrible world this would be if I hadn't been in Fort Lauderdale on January seventeenth, in the dining room of the Seminole Hotel." That was where they'd met.

She made a face. "Do you think it was fate?"

"Don't you?"

"It must have been," she agreed, and her voice was teasing. "I was down to my last five thousand dollars. I'd have gone to work in June if it hadn't been for you."

He grinned at her. "And you're working for me. But as

soon as we get another wing on this house, I'll get some help, honey. Then we'll really enjoy life."

"I'm enjoying it now," she said, "and I want us to be alone for a while. Is that selfish, Perry?"

"If it is," he said, "I share it. I want us to be alone, too."

He finished his coffee, kissed her lightly on the forehead and went out to move the sprinkler.

Joe Judson, his neighbor to the north, was trimming his hedge. Joe said, "Those Cards look like the team to beat, don't they?"

"They sure do," Perry said. He'd have to look up the Cards. That was, let's see, the St. Louis team in one of the leagues. Perry said, "This grass needs something besides water, to look at it."

"A little top dressing wouldn't hurt," Joe said thoughtfully. "Peat moss and a good fertilizer, about half and half, I'd say. Lot of clay in the soil around here."

"You've got the lawn, in this neighborhood," Perry said. "You must have put a lot of time into it, Joe."

Joe tried not to look pleased, and failed. "For that I'll get you a can of beer."

They sat on Joe's front porch, drinking the beer and soaking up the sun. Perry felt relaxed, and for the moment he forgot Plain Jane and Mammoth Martha. For the first time in months. A murderer shouldn't have a conscience, and Perry had almost succeeded in killing his. But there were times. . . .

They played bridge with the Judsons that evening. And poker, penny poker, with the Judsons and the Velters on Saturday evening.

Stan Velter said, "Joe, we'll have to get Perry in our Monday night games." He winked at Joe. "If he can leave Eve that long."

Joe looked at Perry. "Well, as soon as he loses that honeymoon bloom. It would be *too* cruel to take him away from home for a while. He looks happy there."

Eve said, "I think you boys are mean. Perry can play

poker any time he wants to, and he knows it. Perry's his own boss.''

"We all are," Joe said. "More or less."

They laughed, and Eve said, "You just don't want Perry. You're afraid he'll win all your money.''

"Those are fighting words," Joe said. "Perry, it's your decision. Remember, you're your own boss."

Perry looked doubtfully at Eve, and they laughed again. Eve was laughing, too. She said, "Perry, don't make a liar out of me.''

"It's a free-wheeling game," Joe warned him. "None of this penny stuff.''

"I'll be there," Perry said. And then, because it seemed like the right thing to say, he added, "With bells on."

Joe Judson, Stan Velter, Pete Cummer, Al Sternig, Woody Griebling—these were the other participants in the "free-wheeling" game on Monday night. Perry hadn't known what the stakes would be, but learned that quarter limit was as free as they cared to wheel.

Of course, these boys earned their money. There had been no Plain Janes and Mammoth Marthas in their lives. These were the solid citizens, and Perry was one of them now.

With a complete lack of skill and an overbundance of luck, Perry won thirty-two dollars that Monday night. Over the beer and sandwiches that followed the game they all agreed he'd held unreasonably powerful hands.

"Lucky in cards and lucky in love," Stan commented. "You're holding all the aces, Perry."

"I think so," Perry agreed. Nobody had ever said that to him about Jane or Martha.

He drove Joe home with him, and Joe stood for a while near the garage, gassing. Perry was bored by now and wanted to go in, but Joe talked and talked and talked.

Perry's head began to ache, and finally he said, "I'm bushed, Joe. I've got to hit the hay."

"Sure," Joe said. "See you tomorrow."

Inside, his headache persisted, and he searched the medicine cabinet in the bathroom for an aspirin. There was none.

Then he remembered that Eve had brought him an aspirin after breakfast this morning and they were still in the kitchen.

There were just two left. He popped them in his mouth, washed them down with a glass of water. Then he stepped on the foot pedal of the garbage can, intending to throw the box away.

He stood there for seconds, looking down at the opened top of the prettily enameled receptacle. There were coffee grounds in there, and potato parings. There were ashes and lipstick-smeared cigarette stubs.

And there was one badly mangled cigar stub.

There was a sickness in him beyond the headache now, an unreasoning rage in him. He dropped the box in and let the lid fall shut.

From the bedroom, Eve called, "Aren't you coming to bed, Perry? Are you raiding the ice box?"

"I've a headache," he said. "I'm taking an aspirin."

He heard her moving around in the bedroom, and then she appeared through the door to the dining room. "Well, I'm hungry," she said. "I couldn't sleep a wink."

"You should have gone next door and visited with Grace," he said. "It wasn't necessary to be alone."

He emphasised the word *alone*.

She was taking a bottle of milk from the refrigerator. "Alone? For over an hour I sat and listened to *that man*. Big fat thing smoking that vile cigar . . ." She was bringing out some cheese, now.

"Man?" Perry said. "What man?"

"I don't know his name," Eve said, "but he was selling lots, *cemetery lots*. He said *now* was the time to think of that, now that we'd begun life's journey together. Oh, it was grisly, and that awful, stinking cigar . . ."

Perry took a deep breath and expelled it.

Eve was plugging in the toaster. She looked at him wonderingly. "You sound relieved. Glad to be home?"

He laughed shakily. "I saw the cigar, honey. When I was throwing the aspirin tin away. I thought . . . I mean . . ."

"Perry Hopkins!" she said. "You didn't think, for one minute, I'd been . . . I was . . ."

He looked at her abjectly and nodded. "It was rotten of me, wasn't it? But you're so beautiful, and I'm so scared."

Then she was in his arms, and it was like that first day when he'd seen her in the dining room, down in Florida. He was lucky.

"I don't want you ever," she said later, "to think that way again. There's only you, Perry. That's all there's ever going to be, just you."

And he believed her.

He didn't think of Jane or Martha much, after that. He'd given Jane two years of his life, and Martha four. He'd given both of them the romance in their lives they never would have had if he hadn't come along. He'd given them both that small grasp at happiness before Martha, with his help, had drowned; before Jane, with charming naivete, had consumed the conine he'd mixed with her after-dinner drink.

They'd been up at Jane's cabin in the woods when she died, and Perry had rowed her body out to the middle of the lake that night and dumped it. It was adequately weighted and there'd be no kickback there. Both of them had thoughtfully put their estates in his name before their deaths. He had a way with women.

Because of them, he could live with Eve the way a man should live, without grubbing for money or worrying or fighting for survival.

It was a beautiful life.

They joined the Bryn Meadows Country Club in the latter part of June. Most of the gang belonged to it, and Perry was determined to be one of the gang.

He went in with Stan Velter on a subdivision venture, and it was successful from the start. Perry had a definite salesman's talent, he discovered, and was proud of the discovery.

If Eve was too popular at the country club dances, it was a small fly in his ointment. Eve was beautiful, and men were men, and there was no sense making a scene about nothing. Though many were the occasions he was inwardly raging.

He was popular enough with the ladies, but Eve didn't seem to mind. She kidded him about it. He would have preferred her anger.

In August, he and Stan had a chance to sell out the still undeveloped section of their subdivision at a handsome price. The deal was closed in town, and Perry left Stan there.

Perry went to the finest jeweler in the city and bought a star sapphire ring Eve had admired one time. The store was on the first floor of one of the city's better hotels, and Perry went through the lobby with his purchase.

He was just heading for the door to the street when he saw Eve. She was at the desk talking to the clerk, and his first impulse was to go over.

But he didn't. He remembered that Monday night in June, and he stood where he was, watching her. He was effectively screened from her casual view, as he stood in the darker part of the lobby.

She finished talking to the clerk and headed over toward one of the chairs in a corner. Perry went over to stand near the magazine counter, where he could watch her, unseen.

He saw the man come from the elevator and head directly for the corner where his wife waited. He saw the man take a chair opposite her, and saw the stricken look on Eve's face as she started to talk to him.

The man wasn't fat and wasn't the kind Eve would call a *thing*. But he was smoking a cigar. He was a virile-looking gent, with broad shoulders and crisp, black hair.

Perry felt his hands clench, and his vision of them was blurred by the red haze of his anger. The sickness came again and he went out into the August sunshine.

He was cold, despite the heat. It wasn't only jealousy; it was the chilling knowledge that this front of respectability he'd labored so hard to build could be destroyed in the lurid publicity of the divorce court. He'd been very careful, always; he'd been painstaking about details, about avoiding even the appearance of scandal.

He had worked long to establish himself in this community; his solid reputation was his best assurance of continued freedom.

He didn't remember driving home, but the car was in the drive, and he still sat there, staring at the garage doors, but not seeing them.

Ever since June she'd been seeing this man. Everything he'd done, he'd done for her. . . . And they'd called him lucky.

He was out on the front porch when she came home. He watched her pay the cabbie, and then she waved at him. He waved back.

She came up the walk, and he saw that her face was wan and tired, her whole attitude dispirited.

"What a day," she said, and slumped in the wicker chair next to him. "Would you fix me a drink, Perry?"

"Of course," he said. "Bad day, honey?"

"Horrible." She sighed. "Trying to find a decent dress. There just aren't any to be had. Everything looks like a sack on me."

He reached into his pocket and brought out the small jeweler's box. He handed it to her without a word.

She stared at it, opened the box and stared again. "Perry—Perry, darling, of all the beautiful . . . Oh, Perry, you shouldn't have. . . ."

She was in his lap and kissing him, her mouth soft on his, her perfume fanning the fire in his brain.

He disentangled himself finally. He rose and said, "What will the neighbors think?"

"I don't care," she said. "Do you?"

"I'll fix your drink," he said, and went into the kitchen.

When he'd finished mixing it, he looked at it for seconds, thinking of Martha and Jane. Something stirred in him, something like pleasure, something that lifted the red mists of anger in his mind.

Out on the porch, Eve was looking at the jeweler's name on the box. "Aren't they in the Revere Hotel?" she asked.

He nodded. His hand trembled as he handed her the drink.

"When did you get it?" She wasn't looking at him. Her voice had missed being casual by just a shade.

"This morning," he lied. "Why, honey?"

"I just wondered," she said, and there was no mistaking the relief in her voice now.

Perry thought back to that Monday night in June and realized she'd known, before he told her, that he'd seen the cigar in the garbage. She'd been awake and heard the slam of the lid. And if he'd accosted her at the hotel this afternoon, she'd have had an answer then, too.

He'd play it differently from now on. He'd give her enough rope to hang herself.

He sat there on the porch after she'd gone in to make dinner, thinking it all out, planning. The prowl car went by, and the cops in it waved at Perry and he waved back. That was ironic; Perry Hopkins, the solid citizen, the good neighbor, the quarter-limit, golf-dub, wife-adoring taxpayer.

They should know, he thought. They should know about Jane and Martha. These smug suburbanites with their kids and year-before-last sedans and Sunday foursomes. Wouldn't they be shocked out of their complacency if they knew?

But they never would. Nobody had ever known about Martha and Jane. Nobody would guess about Eve.

Joe Judson drove into his yard next door and waved at Perry. Perry went over to the hedge.

Joe said, "How's it going? That deal go through today?"

Perry nodded glumly.

"You don't look happy about it. Aren't you feeling well, boy?"

"I'm all right," Perry said. He looked hesitantly at Joe. "It's Eve, Joe. She's been so sort of depressed lately. Kind of gives me the shivers."

"Any reason for it?" Joe asked, "Is she feeling all right?"

"Physically, she's all right." Perry looked away. "Oh, forget I mentioned it, Joe. I . . . just had to talk to somebody. She's—she means so much to me." He turned and walked quickly toward the house. He could almost feel Joe's stare.

That was the beginning of the campaign.

Monday, Stan phoned to remind him of the poker game, and Perry told him, "I won't be able to make it tonight, Stan. I—I wouldn't feel right, leaving Eve." He kept his voice low.

"Is Eve sick?" Stan asked.

"Oh, it's something I'll tell you about when I see you, Stan. I'd rather not talk about it now."

When he came out onto the porch, Eve said, "Who's got the poker game tonight?"

"Stan," he said. "I don't know if I'll go or not."

"You should," she said. "You've been so gloomy the last couple of days. It will do you good to get out."

"I'll run over and see if Pete Cummer's going," he said. He kissed her lightly on the lips and went down the side steps toward the rear of the house.

Pete lived directly behind them and it was logical he'd cut across the backyards, rather than go around the block. But as soon as he reached the end of the house, he cut quietly along to the rear door and into the hall there.

The kitchen door was open, and he could hear her feet walking along the wooden porch and into the tile of the front hall.

He could hear her dial, hear her say, "Mr. Steele's room, please."

A pause, and she said, "It's all right for tonight, I think. If it isn't, I'll try and call back."

When he heard her steps on the porch again, he left the hall and went across the lawn in the rear to Cummer's.

Pete was out in back, looking over his flowers.

Perry said, "Did Eve give you that bottle of nicotine I had, Pete? She says she lent it to someone, but she can't remember who. Those aphids are going to town on my roses."

"Not to me," Pete said. "You going to the game tonight, I suppose?"

"I shouldn't," Perry said. "Eve's been so—so sort of restless and absentminded lately. She practically took my head off when I asked her about the nicotine."

"Maybe it'll do her good to get out of her sight for a few hours," Pete said. "Women are strange creatures."

"I'm beginning to realize that," Perry admitted. "I guess I'll go along with the gang. I told Stan I wouldn't be there. Maybe I'd better call him." He paused for just the right dramatic effect. "And don't say anything about the nicotine, will you, Pete? I don't want Eve to get the idea I'm . . . spying on her."

He was quiet at the poker session. He gave a good interpretation of a man putting up a brave front, and he sensed that Pete and Stan and Joe admired him for it.

He drove home with Joe and Pete, and they were both abnormally quiet. After Pete had gone across to his house, Joe lingered. He asked gently, "How's Eve been?"

"She'll pull out of it," Perry said. "At times, she's fine. Then she gets one of those spells, and I can't seem to get through to her." He shook his head. "She's just got to pull out of it, Joe."

"Maybe," Joe said, "you ought to take a trip up north. This heat's been terrific the last week."

"That might be a good idea," Perry said, and added very distinctly, "I'm glad you thought of it, Joe. That might be just the thing for her."

He put a hand on Joe's arm. "Sorry I've been such a sourpuss. But—"

"I understand," Joe said. "That's what friends are for."

It was dark enough out so that Perry could permit himself the luxury of a smile.

Eve was in the living room when he came in. There was only a dim light on in one of the table lamps. Her eyes were glazed, and she looked at Perry without recognition.

The smell of liquor was heavy in the room.

"I'm drunk, Perry," she said. "I'm drunk and sick. I missed you, Perry." She was looking at him woodenly.

He stared at her for a few seconds, before saying, "I'll make you some coffee."

He went into the kitchen and saw the empty fifth of bourbon there. It had been about half full. There was some rye gone, too. And Eve *never* drank rye; she couldn't stomach it.

Steele must have been here. What a fool she was to have visitors in a neighborhood like this, where everybody knew everybody else. She was playing with fire; how stupid did she think they all were?

He made the coffee. He made it strong and gave it to her black, and she began to get control of herself.

As she finished the second cup he said, "This heat is getting me, too, Eve. Why don't we go up north, get a cabin? Near some lake, where we can be alone?"

She looked at him and smiled. "I'd love it, Perry. Anything to get away from here. I've got to get away from here for a while."

He tried to keep his voice casual. "Nothing's happened, Eve? You sound so—so frightened, sort of."

She shook her head, not looking at him. "I just have to get away, that's all. The—the heat . . ."

"You shouldn't have drunk that rye."

"Rye?" she said. "Did I drink some rye?"

His voice was cold. "You must have. There's some gone."

She stared at him, as though trying to read his mind. Then she said, "I must have."

Joe came over before breakfast in the morning, and Perry cautioned him to be quiet. "Eve's sleeping, finally," he said. "She's been up all night."

Joe said, "I want to tell you about this place Stan has, up near Lancaster. Small lake but deep, and damned good fishing. And Stan's cottage is the only one on the lake." Joe looked flustered. "I thought, maybe, you know—a second honeymoon, sort of."

Perry smiled sadly. "Thanks, Joe. I'll call Stan this morning."

Eve got up around noon, and Perry had arranged it all by then. He told her about it at lunch.

"Can't we leave today?" Eve asked. "It sounds heavenly, Perry."

"We'll leave in an hour," he said.

At one-thirty he took the house key over to Grace Judson. "I don't know how long we'll be gone," he said, "but I'd appreciate it if you'd look around from time to time. Eve apologizes for not coming over, but she had a bad night, and she's a little vain, you know, about her beauty."

Grace's smile was understanding. "Of course. Everything's going to be fine, Perry. Everything's going to be all right."

Perry could guess that Grace would be watching when Eve came out, and Eve did look worn out. That binge of hers last night had been a stroke of luck.

They got to the cabin about seven o'clock. The last two miles had been rugged, little more than a cow-path through the cut-over timber.

But the cabin was worth the trip. The cabin was low and wide, fronting almost on the edge of the water, and the lake was like a mirror in the evening calm.

"We ought to take a dip before supper," Perry said.

"There's just the pier," Eve said doubtfully. "And I can't swim, Perry. There's no beach."

"There's a boat, though," Perry said. "We'll take a row around the lake when the stars come out."

He opened the luggage compartment while Eve went up on the cabin porch. The chains were still there, tire chains heavy with rust. He'd have to get them to the boat when Eve was otherwise occupied.

The cabin was fairly clean; the Velters had spent the previous weekend there. Perry brought the groceries and the whiskey.

"Drink before dinner?" he asked her.

She shook her head and smiled. "Not after last night. Not for a few days yet."

"I'll have to drink alone then," he said.

"After that ride we're going to take, the boat ride," she said. "I don't want any liquor in you while I'm in the boat. My life is in your hands there, honey."

It was a half-hour before he had a chance to take the chains and a hammer down to the boat. He stored them under the front seat and stood on the pier a moment, looking out at the quiet, deserted water, thinking of the past four months.

He'd had no compunctions about Jane or Martha; he'd felt relieved when they were gone. But Eve . . . Eve had given him four unforgettable months. Maybe . . . No, no, the fever was strong in him, and he kept seeing that cigar. It was a symbol to him now, tied up in some way with the solid-citizen role he'd been portraying so successfully these past months.

They'd finished dinner; and Eve had changed to slacks and a sweater. The sun had gone down and the breeze coming from across the lake was cool and fresh.

He helped Eve into the boat, and she sat facing the prow, where she'd be facing him when he sat by the oars. He unhooked the chain from the pier and shoved the boat clear. His hands were trembling violently.

"Isn't it beautiful?" she said. "Oh, I'm glad we came, Perry."

"So am I," he said. "I'm glad we're alone finally."

He couldn't see her clearly in the dimness, but he thought she looked at him sharply. He was wondering about the chains. He was thinking that if somebody should get suspicious and they dragged the lake the chains would be a giveaway.

Unless he went back to town tonight. Unless his story was that Eve had left him, that there was another man and they'd left town. There'd be no reason to drag the lake then.

"You've been so sort of tense lately," Eve said. "As though you've some secret, Perry. You haven't any troubles you're not telling me about, have you?"

"None," he said. That was a rich one, he thought. *Her* talking about a secret.

Now his trembling was worse, and he had difficulty with the oars, and the redness in his brain was like a flame. They were near the middle of the lake, and he bent over the side to look down into the water. He couldn't wait. If he waited . . .

"Look at those fish," he said. "Phosphorescent fish. They're like fireflies under water."

He saw her sleek head outlined in the dimness, and he saw the soft curve at the back of her neck. The hammer was in his hand, and he struck at the back of her neck. She didn't utter a sound.

An hour later he'd disposed of her clothes and decided on the running-off-with-another-man story. It would bring Steele into it, if he let it be known about Steele. A woman caught in one infidelity can be doubted about others.

He was going over to get a drink when he saw the headlights, far below, on the road. Who could it be? Whoever it was, it was a bad time for a visitor. But the sense of power was still strong in Perry, and he wasn't as worried as he might have been.

He poured himself a good, stiff jolt of rye. He lifted it, in a triumphant salute to himself and poured it down.

It seemed to hit his legs first, a sharp pain that made him cry out. Then the top of his head seemed to explode, and his stomach twisted as though tied into one gigantic knot. He fell to the floor, twisting and crying, and then it got to his heart. His last thought was the remembrance that Eve didn't drink rye.

Steele twisted the cigar in his mouth and displayed his credentials to the sheriff. The sheriff looked at them.

"Gilbralter, huh?" he said. "Investigator. I carry Gilbralter insurance myself, Mr. Steele."

"Hopkins didn't," Steele said, "so I suppose this one won't be my baby. But I've been on her trail a long time."

"Married before, was she?"

"Twice," Steele said, "and both husbands died. I couldn't get anything conclusive, you understand, but I was in town in June, so I looked her up. I pretended I was an adjuster for the company, and wanted to know if everything had been settled to her satisfaction. She acted strange and didn't want me to meet her husband. She told me he didn't know about her previous marriages, and she didn't want him to know about them. It smelled like fish to me, so I went back to Tacoma for some further checking.''

"That's where her last husband died?"

Steele nodded. "I got new evidence, all right, almost enough to nail her, so I came back to town. I talked to her twice, and she was going to crack, I think. Then I heard about this trip when I went over to see her this afternoon. It took me a long time to find out where they'd gone; the neighbors were kind of bent on keeping it a secret." He shook his head. "If I'd have got there ten minutes sooner, Hopkins would still be alive."

"Well," the sheriff consoled him, "it's not your fault. You did all you could. This Hopkins was pretty well thought of, huh?"

"A solid citizen," Steele said sadly. "A real solid citizen."

"And where do you think she is now?"

Steele shrugged. "She could wind up in Brooklyn or Singapore. She might be hiding right around here, and we'd never find her. I've no idea where she is. God alone knows where she is."

The Case of the Emerald Sky

·

Eric Ambler

For several decades Eric Ambler has had the distinction of being one of the world's leading writers of espionage fiction. A Coffin for Dimitrios *(1939) is surely among the half dozen finest spy novels published during this century; and such others as* Cause for Alarm *(1938),* Journey into Fear *(1940), and* Dirty Story *(1967) are widely respected. Much less well known—regrettably so—are Ambler's six detective stories featuring Czechoslovakian refugee Dr. Jan Czissar, "late Prague police," which appeared in* The Sketch *(London) in 1940. These are much lighter in tone, as the good doctor indulges his "hobby" of exasperating Scotland Yard by solving such crimes as "The Case of the Emerald Sky" before they can.*

Assistant Commissioner Mercer of Scotland Yard stared, without speaking, at the card which Sergeant Flecker had placed before him.

There was no address, simply:

DR. JAN CZISSAR
Late Prague Police

It was an inoffensive-looking card. An onlooker, who knew only that Dr. Czissar was a refugee Czech with a brilliant record of service in the criminal investigation department of the Prague police, would have been surprised at the expression of dislike that spread slowly over the assistant commissioner's healthy face.

90

Yet, had the same onlooker known the circumstances of Mercer's first encounter with Dr. Czissar, he would not have been surprised. Just one week had elapsed since Dr. Czissar had appeared out of the blue with a letter of introduction from the mighty Sir Herbert at the home office, and Mercer was still smarting as a result of the meeting.

Sergeant Flecker had seen and interpreted the expression. Now he spoke.

"Out, sir?"

Mercer looked up sharply. "No, sergeant. In, but too busy," he snapped.

Half an hour later Mercer's telephone rang.

"Sir Herbert to speak to you from the Home Office, sir," said the operator.

Sir Herbert said, "Hello, Mercer, is that you?" And then, without waiting for a reply: "What's this I hear about your refusing to see Dr. Czissar?"

Mercer jumped but managed to pull himself together. "I did not refuse to see him, Sir Herbert," he said with iron calm. "I sent down a message that I was too busy to see him."

Sir Herbert snorted. "Now look here, Mercer; I happen to know that it was Dr. Czissar who spotted those Seabourne murderers for you. Not blaming you, personally, of course, and I don't propose to mention the matter to the commissioner. You can't be right every time. We all know that as an organization there's nothing to touch Scotland Yard. My point is, Mercer, that you fellows ought not to be above learning a thing or two from a foreign expert. Clever fellows, these Czechs, you know. No question of poaching on your preserves. Dr. Czissar wants no publicity. He's grateful to this country and eager to help. Least we can do is to let him. We don't want any professional jealousy standing in the way."

If it were possible to speak coherently through clenched teeth, Mercer would have done so. "There's no question either of poaching on preserves or of professional jealousy, Sir Herbert. I was, as Dr. Czissar was informed, busy when he called. If he will write in for an appointment, I shall be pleased to see him.''

"Good man," said Sir Herbert cheerfully. "But we don't want any of this red tape business about writing in. He's in my office now. I'll send him over. He's particularly anxious to have a word with you about this Brock Park case. He won't keep you more than a few minutes. Good-bye.''

Mercer replaced the telephone carefully. He knew that if he had replaced it as he felt like replacing it, the entire instrument would have been smashed. For a moment or two he sat quite still. Then, suddenly, he snatched the telephone up again.

"Inspector Cleat, please." He waited. "Is that you, Cleat? Is the commissioner in? . . . I see. Well, you might ask him as soon as he comes in if he could spare me a minute or two. It's urgent. Right.''

He hung up again, feeling a little better. If Sir Herbert could have words with the commissioner, so could he. The old man wouldn't stand for his subordinates being humiliated and insulted by pettifogging politicians. Professional jealousy!

Meanwhile, however, this precious Dr. Czissar wanted to talk about the Brock Park case. Right! Let him! He wouldn't be able to pull that to pieces. It was absolutely watertight. He picked up the file on the case which lay on his desk.

Yes, absolutely watertight.

Three years previously, Thomas Medley, a widower of sixty with two adult children, had married Helena Merlin, a woman of forty-two. The four had since lived together in a large house in the London suburb of Brock Park. Medley, who had amassed a comfortable fortune, had retired from business shortly before his second marriage, and had devoted most of his time since to his hobby, gardening. Helena Merlin was an artist, a landscape painter, and in Brock Park it was whispered that her pictures sold for large sums. She dressed fashionably and smartly, and was disliked by her neighbors. Harold Medley, the son, aged twenty-five, was a medical student at a London hospital. His sister, Janet, was three years younger, and as dowdy as her stepmother was smart.

In the early October of that year, and as a result of an extra heavy meal, Thomas Medley had retired to bed with a bilious attack. Such attacks had not been unusual. He had had an enlarged liver, and had been normally dyspeptic. His doctor had prescribed in the usual way. On his third day in bed the patient had been considerably better. On the fourth day, however, at about four in the afternoon, he had been seized with violent abdominal pains, persistent vomiting, and severe cramps in the muscles of his legs.

These symptoms had persisted for three days, on the last of which there had been convulsions. He had died that night. The doctor had certified the death as being due to gastroenteritis. The dead man's estate had amounted to, roughly, £110,000. Half of it went to his wife. The remainder was divided equally between his two children.

A week after the funeral, the police had received an anonymous letter suggesting that Medley had been poisoned. Subsequently, they had received two further letters. Information had then reached them that several residents in Brock Park had received similar letters, and that the matter was the subject of gossip.

Medley's doctor was approached later. He had reasserted that the death had been due to gastroenteritis, but admitted that the possibility of the condition having been brought on by the willful administration of poison had not occurred to him. The body had been exhumed by license of the home secretary, and an autopsy performed. No traces of poison had been found in the stomach; but in the liver, kidneys, and spleen a total of 1.751 grains of arsenic had been found.

Inquiries had established that on the day on which the poisoning symptoms had appeared, the deceased had had a small luncheon consisting of breast of chicken, spinach (canned), and one potato. The cook had partaken of spinach from the same tin without suffering any ill effects. After his luncheon, Medley had taken a dose of the medicine prescribed for him by the doctor. It had been mixed with water for him by his son, Harold.

Evidence had been obtained from a servant that, a fortnight before the death, Harold had asked his father for £100 to settle a racing debt. He had been refused. Inquiries had revealed that Harold had lied. He had been secretly married for some time, and the money had been needed not to pay racing debts but for his wife, who was about to have a child.

The case against Harold had been conclusive. He had needed money desperately. He had quarreled with his father. He had know that he was the heir to a quarter of his father's estate. As a medical student in a hospital, he had been in a position to obtain arsenic. The poisoning that appeared had shown that the arsenic must have been administered at about the time the medicine had been taken. It had been the first occasion on which Harold had prepared his father's medicine.

The coroner's jury had boggled at indicting him in their verdict, but he had later been arrested and was now on remand. Further evidence from the hospital as to his access to supplies of arsenical drugs had been forthcoming. He would certainly be committed for trial.

Mercer sat back in his chair. A watertight case. Sentences began to form in his mind. "This Dr. Czissar, Sir Charles, is merely a time-wasting crank. He's a refugee and his sufferings have probably unhinged him a little. If you could put the matter to Sir Herbert, in that light . . ."

And then, for the second time that afternoon, Dr. Czissar was announced.

Mercer was angry, yet, as Dr. Czissar came into the room, he became conscious of a curious feeling of friendliness toward him. It was not entirely the friendliness that one feels toward an enemy one is about to destroy. In his mind's eye he had been picturing Dr. Czissar as an ogre. Now, Mercer saw that, with his mild eyes behind their thick spectacles, his round, pale face, his drab raincoat and his unfurled umbrella, Dr. Czissar was, after all, merely pathetic. When, just inside the door, Dr. Czissar stopped, clapped his umbrella to his side as if it were a rifle, and said loudly: "Dr. Jan Czissar. Late Prague Police. At your service." Mercer very nearly smiled.

Instead he said: "Sit down, doctor. I am sorry I was too busy to see you earlier."

"It is so good of you . . ." began Dr. Czissar earnestly.

"Not at all, doctor. You want, I hear, to compliment us on our handling of the Brock Park case."

Dr. Czissar blinked. "Oh, no, Assistant Commissioner Mercer," he said anxiously. "I would like to compliment, but it is too early, I think. I do not wish to seem impolite, but . . ."

Mercer smiled complacently. "Oh, we shall convict our man, all right, doctor. I don't think you need to worry."

Dr. Czissar's anxiety became painful to behold. "Oh, but I do worry. You see—" he hesitated diffidently, "—he is not guilty."

Mercer hoped that the smile with which he greeted the statement did not reveal his secret exultation. He said blandly, "Are you aware, doctor, of all the evidence against him?"

"I attended the inquest," said Dr. Czissar mournfully. "But there will be more evidence from the hospital, no doubt. This young Mr. Harold could no doubt have stolen enough arsenic to poison a regiment without the loss being discovered."

The fact that the words had been taken out of his mouth disconcerted Mercer only slightly. He nodded. "Exactly."

A faint, thin smile stretched the doctor's full lips. He settled his glasses on his nose. Then he cleared his throat, swallowed hard and leaned forward. "Attention, please," he said sharply.

For some reason that he could not fathom, Mercer felt his self-confidence ooze suddenly away. He had seen that same series of actions, ending with the peremptory demand for attention, performed once before, and it had been the prelude to humiliation, to . . . He pulled himself up sharply. The Brock Park case was watertight. He was being absurd.

"I'm listening," he said.

"Good." Dr. Czissar wagged one solemn finger. "According to the medical evidence given at the inquest, arsenic was found in the liver, kidneys, and spleen. No?"

Mercer nodded firmly. "One point seven five one grains. That shows that much more than a fatal dose had been administered. Much more."

Dr. Czissar's eyes gleamed. "Ah, yes. Much more. It is odd, is it not, that so much was found in the kidneys?"

"Nothing odd at all about it."

"Let us leave the point for the moment. Is it not true, Assistant Commissioner Mercer, that all post-mortem tests for arsenic are for arsenic itself and not for any particular arsenic salt?"

Mercer frowned. "Yes, but it's unimportant. All arsenic salts are deadly poisons. Besides, when arsenic is absorbed by the human body, it turns to the sulphide. I don't see what you are driving at, doctor."

"My point is this, assistant commissioner, that usually it is impossible to tell from a delayed autopsy which form of arsenic was used to poison the body. You agree? It might be arsenious oxide, or one of the arsenates or arsenites, copper arsenite, for instance; or it might be a chloride, or it might be an organic compound of arsenic."

"Precisely."

"But," continued Dr. Czissar, "what sort of arsenic should we expect to find in a hospital, eh?"

Mercer pursed his lips. "I see no harm in telling you, doctor, that Harold Medley could easily have secured supplies of either salvarsan or neosalvarsan. They are both important drugs."

"Yes, indeed," said Dr. Czissar. "Very useful in one-tenth of a gram doses, but very dangerous in larger quantities." He stared at the ceiling. "Have you seen any of Helena Merlin's paintings, assistant commissioner?"

The sudden change of subject took Mercer unawares. He hesitated. Then: "Oh, you mean Mrs. Medley. No, I haven't seen any of her paintings."

"Such a chic, attractive woman," said Dr. Czissar. "After

I had seen her at the inquest I could not help wishing to see some of her work. I found some in a gallery near Bond Street.'' He sighed. "I had expected something clever, but I was disappointed. She paints what she thinks instead of what is.''

"Really? I'm afraid, doctor, that I must . . .''

"I felt,'' persisted Dr. Czissar, bringing his cowlike eyes once more to Mercer's, "that the thoughts of a woman who thinks of a field as blue and of a sky as emerald green must be a little strange.''

"Modern stuff, eh?'' said Mercer shortly. "I don't much care for it either. And now, doctor, if you've finished, I'll ask you to excuse me. I . . .''

"Oh, but I have not finished yet,'' said Dr. Czissar kindly. "I think, assistant commissioner, that a woman who paints a landscape with a green sky is not only strange, but also interesting, don't you? I asked the gentleman at the gallery about her. She produces only a few pictures—about six a year. He offered to sell me one of them for 15 guineas. She earns £100 a year from her work. It is wonderful how expensively she dresses on that sum.''

"She had a rich husband.''

"Oh, yes. A curious household, don't you think? The daughter Janet is especially curious. I was so sorry that she was so much upset by the evidence at the inquest.''

"A young woman probably would be upset at the idea of her brother being a murderer,'' said Mercer dryly.

"But to accuse herself so violently of the murder. That was odd.''

"Hysteria. You get a lot of it in murder cases.'' Mercer stood up and held out his hand. "Well, doctor, I'm sorry you haven't been able to upset our case this time. If you'll leave your address with the sergeant as you go, I'll see that you get a pass for the trial,'' he added with relish.

But Dr. Czissar did not move. "You are going to try this young man for murder, then?'' he said slowly. "You have not understood what I have been hinting at?''

Mercer grinned. "We've got something better than hints,

doctor—a first-class circumstantial case against young Medley. Motive, time, and method of administration; source of the poison. Concrete evidence, doctor! Juries like it. If you can produce one scrap of evidence to show that we've got the wrong man, I'll be glad to hear it.''

Dr. Czissar's back straightened, and his cowlike eyes flashed. He said, sharply, ''I, too, am busy. I am engaged on a work on medical jurisprudence. I desire only to see justice done. I do not believe that on the evidence you have you can convict this young man under English law; but the fact of his being brought to trial could damage his career as a doctor. Furthermore, there is the real murderer to be considered. Therefore, in a spirit of friendliness, I have come to you instead of going to Harold Medley's legal advisers. I will now give you your evidence.''

Mercer sat down again. He was very angry. ''I am listening,'' he said grimly; ''but if you . . .''

''Attention, please,'' said Dr. Czissar. He raised a finger. ''Arsenic was found in the dead man's kidneys. It is determined that Harold Medley could have poisoned his father with either salvarsan or neosalvarsan. There is a contradiction there. Most inorganic salts of arsenic, white arsenic, for instance, are practically insoluble in water, and if a quantity of such a salt had been administered, we might expect to find traces of it in the kidneys. Salvarsan and neosalvarsan, however, are compounds of arsenic and are very soluble in water. If either of them had been administered through the mouth, we should *not* expect to find arsenic in the kidneys.''

He paused, but Mercer was silent.

''In what form, therefore, was the arsenic administered?'' he went on. ''The tests do not tell us, for they detect only the presence of the element, arsenic. Let us then look among the inorganic salts. There is white arsenic, that is arsenious oxide. It is used for dipping sheep. We would not expect to find it in Brock Park. But Mr. Medley was a gardener. What about sodium arsenite, the weed-killer? But we heard at the inquest that the weed-killer in the garden was of the kind harmful only to weeds. We come to copper arsenite. Mr.

Medley was, in my opinion, poisoned by a large dose of copper arsenite."

"And on what evidence," demanded Mercer, "do you base that opinion?"

"There is, or there has been, copper arsenite in the Medley's house." Dr. Czissar looked at the ceiling. "On the day of the inquest, Mrs. Medley wore a fur coat. I have since found another fur coat like it. The price of the coat was 400 guineas. Inquiries in Brock Park have told me that this lady's husband, besides being a rich man, was also a very mean and unpleasant man. At the inquest, his son told us that he had kept his marriage a secret because he was afraid that his father would stop his allowance or prevent his continuing his studies in medicine. Helena Medley had expensive tastes. She had married this man so that she could indulge them. He had failed her. That coat she wore, assistant commissioner, was unpaid for. You will find, I think, that she had other debts, and that a threat had been made by one of the creditors to approach her husband. She was tired of this man so much older than she was—this man who did not even justify his existence by spending his fortune on her. She poisoned her husband. There is no doubt of it."

"Nonsense!" said Mercer. "Of course we know that she was in debt. We are not fools. But lots of women are in debt. It doesn't make them murderers. Ridiculous!"

"All murderers are ridiculous," agreed Dr. Czissar solemnly; "especially the clever ones."

"But how on earth . . . ?" began Mercer.

Dr. Czissar smiled gently. "It was the spinach that the dead man had for luncheon before the symptoms of poisoning began that interested me," he said. "Why give spinach when it is out of season? Canned vegetables are not usually given to an invalid with gastric trouble. And then, when I saw Mrs. Medley's paintings, I understood. The emerald sky, assistant commissioner. It was a fine, rich emerald green, that sky—*the sort of emerald green that the artist gets when there is aceto-arsenite of copper in the paint*! The firm which supplies Mrs. Medley with her working materials will be able to tell you when she bought it. I suggest, too, that you take the picture—it is in the Summons Gallery—and remove a little of the sky for analysis. You will find that the spinach was prepared at her suggestion and taken to her husband's bedroom by her. Spinach is *green* and *slightly bitter* in taste. *So is copper arsenite.*" He sighed. "If there had not been anonymous letters . . ."

"Ah!" interrupted Mercer. "The anonymous letters! Perhaps you know . . ."

"Oh, yes," said Dr. Czissar simply. "The daughter Janet wrote them. Poor child! She disliked her smart stepmother and wrote them out of spite. Imagine her feelings when she found that she had—how do you say?—put a noose about her brother's throat. It would be natural for her to try to take the blame herself."

The telephone rang and Mercer picked up the receiver.

"The commissioner to speak to you, sir," said the operator.

"All right. Hello . . . Hello, Sir Charles. Yes, I did want to speak to you urgently. It was—" He hesitated. "—it was about the Brock Park case. I think that we will have to release young Medley. I've got hold of some new medical evidence that . . . Yes, yes I realize that, Sir Charles, and I'm very sorry that . . . All right, Sir Charles, I'll come immediately."

He replaced the telephone.

Dr. Czissar looked at his watch. "But it is late and I must get to the museum reading room before it closes." He stood up, clapped his umbrella to his side, clicked his heels and said loudly: "Dr. Jan Czissar. Late Prague Police. At your service!"

Woman Missing

•

Helen Nielsen

Helen Nielsen began her distinguished career in 1951 with
The Kind Man, *and followed that novel with such other crit-*
ical and commercial successes as Detour *(1953),* Sing Me a
Murder *(1960), and* A Killer in the Street *(1967). She was*
also a regular contributor to all the major mystery magazines
in the fifties and sixties, most notably Manhunt *and* Alfred
Hitchcock's Mystery Magazine; *and a scriptwriter for such*
TV shows as Perry Mason *and* Alfred Hitchcock Presents.
After a hiatus of several years, she has begun writing again:
short stories and a new novel. "Woman Missing" is vintage
Nielsen—a twisty, suspenseful tale of a disappearance whose
motive at first seems obvious but turns out to be anything but.

Einar Peterson's body was wearying of life. He slept at the
touch of his silvered head on the pillow; but when his wife,
Amelia, fastened her hands on his shoulders and shook with
all her housewife strength, he awakened, trying to remember
where he was, and why he was no longer the boy he'd been
dreaming of, sailing his small boat on a bright Sunday on
Lake Vattern. Without his glasses, Amelia's face bobbed
above him like a pale balloon.

"Einar—Einar. Something's wrong in back!"

"What? Where?" Einar mumbled.

"In the tenant's house in back. I think it's Mrs. Tracy sick
again."

Einar Peterson pulled himself up in the bed and groped on
the night table until his slightly arthritic fingers located his

eye glasses. With them in place, the pale balloon now had gray hair and troubled eyes.

"Mrs. Tracy?" he repeated. "What is it, Mother? What's wrong?"

"I don't know. I woke up because of the lights in the driveway and the motor running."

"Maybe it's the Mister."

"In the driveway? You know the Mister always comes home up the alley. Anyway, it's only ten-thirty. I looked at the clock when the lights woke me up. Get up, Einar. Go see. That poor little Mrs. Tracy—"

Amelia liked to worry about people, and the night air was damp and chilly outside the blankets. Einar didn't want to get up; but now he could see that the light reflected on his wife's face wasn't from the ceiling fixture—it was from a glaring beam outside the bedroom window, and the noise he heard wasn't from the old refrigerator in the kitchen—it was the sound of an automobile motor. Reluctantly, he parted himself from snug comfort and padded to the window to which Amelia had preceded him.

"Somebody went back to the tenant house," she whispered. "It was a man."

"Did you see him?" Einar asked.

"Hush, not so loud. No, I didn't see; but I heard the footsteps. I think it must be a doctor."

"A doctor! Why would a doctor leave the motor running?"

"I think it's an ambulance. There's a funny light on top."

The window was open two inches. Einar lifted the sash quietly and poked out his head. Amelia was right. The automobile he saw certainly did have a light on top.

"It's a taxi," he said.

"A taxi? Here?"

"Quiet!" Einar drew back inside. Somebody's coming."

Einar Peterson watched the brightness in front of the headlights; but the heavy, manlike footsteps skirted the light and passed by the window in shadows. They stopped at the taxi. A door opened; then silence behind the idling motor, and darkness behind the lights except for the small, round glow of a cigarette.

"Look," Amelia whispered. "She's coming."

Linda Tracy was such a very young woman, it was difficult to realize that she was married to Mr. Tracy and would have been the mother of his child if it had been God's will. She looked more like one of Einar Peterson's teenage granddaughters except for something. . . . Einar Peterson's mind always caught on that odd feeling when he thought of Mrs. Tracy. Something. She walked rapidly into the headlights, head down except for an instant when she turned and stared almost directly at the dark window behind which the two unseen watchers were hidden. She was wearing a light colored coat and very noisy heels, and, this they would remember to tell the police, a very fearful expression on her face. She passed the window and entered the cab. The glow of a burning cigarette spun into space and was lost in the darkness. The door of the taxi slammed shut. In a matter of seconds, the taxi was gone.

"Well," said Amelia. "What was that?"

Einar Peterson removed his glasses and padded back to the bed.

"Einar, I'm worried. Mrs. Tracy never goes out at night. Her lights always go off just after ten o'clock. Einar—"

Einar's answer was a snore. She lowered the window to within two inches of the sill and returned to bed; but she didn't sleep. There was something strange about Linda Tracy. Amelia had never mentioned her feelings to anyone, not even Einar; but there was something. . . .

Chester Tracy was a slight, sandy-haired man with a peering face. That was how he impressed Sergeant Mike Shelly. He had probably started peering when he was a kid, his nose pressed against the store windows full of Christmas toys he would never receive. Children who had done that never lost the look; it grew older with them. There was fear in his face, too; fear muted by shock. Shelly had to pry words out of him.

"When did you get home, Mr. Tracy?" he asked. "At what time—exactly."

Tracy was possibly forty. He wore suntan cotton pants and a brown leather zipper jacket with an I.D. badge from Flight Research pinned to the breast pocket. The photo on the badge would have embarrassed the Passport Bureau.

"The usual time," he said. "I work the five-forty-five P.M. to two-forty-five A.M. shift."

"What time?" Shelly persisted.

"It takes me eighteen minutes to drive home. I've clocked it a hundred times—just to keep awake. It may take eighteen and a half if I miss the green light at Slauson."

"Then you were home at a few minutes past three."

"At three minutes past—exactly. I looked at the kitchen clock when I came in."

"The light was on?" Shelly asked.

"It's always on when I come home. Linda leaves it for me when she goes to bed."

"And so everything seemed normal."

"Until I started down the hall to the bathroom," Tracy said. "I saw that the bedroom door was open. It's usually closed because of that light in the kitchen. I looked in to see if Linda was all right, and that's when I discovered—" Tracy's eyes were less glazed now. Emotion was breaking through the numbness. "Why are you asking all these dumb questions?" he demanded. "My wife's gone—don't you understand? I called you because Linda's gone!"

A missing wife can mean many things—Mike Shelly had carried a police badge in his pocket long enough to know that. He'd talked to the old people up front, but he had to question Tracy alone. Outside, Shelly's partner, Sergeant Keonig, was searching the grounds. Inside, Shelly stood in a living room just large enough for one small divan and two slip-covered chairs, pried away at Chester Tracy, and puzzled over the photographs he'd found in a double frame on the side table. One side of the frame showed Linda Tracy close-up: blond, smiling, lovely; the other held a full-length Linda attired in an abbreviated bathing suit: blond, smiling, lovely. She was nineteen years old. The forty-year-old man with the peering face had told him that.

"I know that your wife's gone," Shelly answered quietly. "I'm looking for her. I've been looking for her ever since I got here. A photograph isn't enough, Mr. Tracy. I need to know what kind of woman your wife is."

Reactions could be startling, particularly in the predawn hours of a torturous night. Color flooded to Chester Tracy's face.

"What kind of woman?" he echoed. "Is that any way to talk to a man in my position?"

"Mr. Tracy—"

"She's my wife. That's the kind of woman she is! She's my wife!"

If someone had bought the finest toy in the shop for that kid with his face pressed against the window, and then taken it away, the emotional response would have matched what was written on Chester Tracy's face.

"I was thinking more of her habits," Shelly explained. "Where she goes. Who she sees . . ."

"But she doesn't see anyone! She doesn't go anywhere—not without me! My wife lost a baby four months ago. Since that time, she hasn't been well. She never goes out unless I take her in the car."

"Where do you go?"

"To the market. Once in awhile to a drive-in movie."

"Never to friends?"

"With me working the hours I work? I went on swing shift for the extra money after Linda got pregnant. Since then, we have no friends. Ask the Petersons up front. Linda walks up to get the mail every morning—the box is on Peterson's house. That's as much as she goes out without me. Every night I call home during the ten o'clock coffee break—"

"Ten o'clock," Shelly echoed. "Did you talk to your wife at ten o'clock tonight?"

"I did."

"Did she seem nervous or upset?"

"No more than usual. Linda's been nervous and upset ever since she lost the baby. That's why I call her every night. I catch her just before she takes her sleeping pills—"

Tracy's voice ceased as the front door opened. It was Keonig. He glanced at Tracy, then turned to Sergeant Shelly.

"I didn't find a single footprint," he said. "This house is built on a cement slab. It extends along the right side for the width of about ten feet, all the way to the alley. There's an old station wagon parked on that extension."

"That's mine," Tracy volunteered.

"In front," Keonig added, "the cement narrows to a walk leading to Peterson's driveway—the way we came. I'd hoped our man might have stepped off the walk and left a print in the soft flower bed under the Peterson's windows, but all I found was this—"

Cupped in the palm of Keonig's hand was a cigarette butt— standard brand, filter tip.

"Peterson said the man who came for Mrs. Tracy tossed a cigarette into the flower bed," Shelly reflected. "Keep it."

"It was all I could find," Keonig repeated.

"Try the bathroom," Shelly said. "Or does your wife keep those sleeping pills in her bedroom, Mr. Tracy?" Shelly set the double-framed photograph back on the table and turned toward the hall. "You take the bathroom," he told Keonig, "and I'll take the bedroom. You come with me, Tracy. I'll need you."

In a square cell with one window, curtained, shade drawn, the bed was turned down and a soft, pink nightgown laid out for its missing occupant. Shelly studied the display while Chester Tracy, at his request, took stock of his wife's closet.

"I think there's a blue dress missing," he reported.

"A blue dress," Shelly repeated.

"Sort of a suit. You know, a dress with a jacket over it."

"What else?" Shelly prodded. "Shoes?"

The shoe rack held, at quick glance, a good dozen pairs of slippers and pumps.

"I think she usually wore black pumps with the blue dress," Chester said. "I don't see them here."

"Black shoes," Shelly echoed. "What coat?"

"The Petersons said a light coat. That would be the one she called a cashmere. It was new. I got it for her with my last big overtime check."

Shelly picked up one of the pumps from the rack and examined it. Size 5A. It was clear plastic with a spike heel. He turned it over in his hands. The soles were badly worn, especially at the toe. The heels weren't.

"Are these new, too?" he asked.

"I got them for her for Christmas," Chester answered.

"Is anything else missing?"

The question kept Chester busy, while Shelly examined the rest of the rack. Most of the shoes were dress pumps or sandals, but there was one conspicuous pair of walking flats. When Keonig came in from the bathroom with the sleeping pills, Shelly still held one of the flats in his hand. A small crust of dried mud loosened at the prod of his fingernail and fell to the floor.

"I had to dig, but I found them in the medicine chest," Keonig said. "Now maybe you'll tell me why."

"Because Mrs. Tracy took sleeping pills every night after her husband's ten o'clock call."

"Not tonight," Keonig said.

"Obviously. That's interesting, isn't it? Let me see that bottle." It was nearly half full. Shelly read the prescription label and frowned. "Dr. Youngston," he read aloud. "Two pills before retiring. 10–7–59. Keonig, what's the date?"

"It was the twelfth of January at midnight," Keonig answered.

"Dr. Youngston," Shelly mused. "Your wife did see someone outside of this house, Tracy. Who else?"

The man still seemed to be in a state of shock. He groped for words. "I told you—no one."

"At any time—before your marriage."

"I didn't know Linda very long before our marriage. Leo talked me into going to this party—"

"Leo? Leo who?"

"Leo Manfred. We worked together at Flight Research.

107

Look, why don't you stop asking these questions? Why don't you look for that cab?''

"Where can I find Leo Manfred?" Shelly persisted.

"I don't know! At home, I suppose. I lost track of Leo when I went on nights. I don't even know if he's with Flight Research now.''

"But he did know your wife?"

"That was months ago—seven, eight months ago."

"Leo Manfred and Dr. Youngston." Shelly slipped the bottle of pills into his pocket. "Who else, Tracy? Who else knew that your wife would be here alone at ten-thirty? Who might she have gone with without fear?''

"But she was afraid," Keonig protested. "The Petersons said—''

"Who else, Tracy?"

Chester Tracy sank down on the edge of the bed. The kid with his face pressed against the window wanted to cry; but the kid was a man of forty, and so, instead, he took a pack of cigarettes from his pocket, standard brand, no filter tip, pulled out one cigarette and held it between thumb and forefinger, until the thumb clenched white and the cigarette snapped in two. He looked up.

"I can't think!" he protested. "You're the police. Find my wife! Please, find my wife!''

Linda Tracy, white Caucasian, female. Age: 19. Height 5'3". Weight, 110. Blond hair, Hazel eyes. Probably wearing a blue jacket dress, black pumps, and a light tan cashmere coat. Last seen entering a taxi at 1412 North . . .

A description of the missing woman was going out over the police radio before Shelly and Keonig left the Peterson property. Shelly took a turn about the premises, while Keonig used the telephone. It was still a good hour before dawn, and a light fog had wrapped the world in a close, damp blanket. At the side of the tenant house, Shelly found the station wagon, the windshield and windows curtained with moisture. Beyond it, the paved area terminated at an unpaved alleyway. He took a few steps into the alley and peered toward the street lamp at the nearest corner. It was at least four lots distant—darkness and fog prohibited a closer guess—and no backyard taxpayer units such as the Petersons had added were in evidence. This was the route by which Chester Tracy had arrived home—the only other access to the property except the front drive. Underfoot, the stubborn adobe had absorbed most of a none too recent gravel topping, and the pale light from the corner lamp caught in small, wet shallows of leftover rain. Shelly scraped his shoes clean on the parking slab and returned to the car and Keonig.

"It's a break—that cab business," Keonig said. "A cab can be traced."

"I know it can," Shelly mused. "That's what is bothering me."

A cab can be traced, but it takes time. Time to check each office of each company; run down each call sheet; pry out of bed a driver who had worked most of the night. Meanwhile, a sun rises, a city comes awake, the air begins to fill with the aromas of coffee, frying bacon, and, predominantly, carbon monoxide. Shelly couldn't wait. The Southern Area telephone directory listed a Dr. Carl Youngston on Manchester Boulevard—hours: nine to five.

At ten minutes before nine, Mike Shelly waited in the foyer of a handsome new medical building and watched a slender, blond young man in a gray topcoat unlock the slab door leading to Dr. Youngston's office. He stooped to retrieve an advertising folder that had been deposited in the mail slot, and arose pulling a pair of tortoise rimmed glasses from an inner pocket. These he donned in time to bring the full width and height of Mike Shelly into focus.

Surprise didn't seem to unnerve the doctor.

"Do you have an appointment?" he asked.

Shelly's appointment was a badge that bridged all priorities. Inside the office, Dr. Youngston removed his topcoat, straightened a tie that caught the blue of his eyes behind the tortoise rims, and then scrutinized the bottle of sleeping pills Shelly now held in his hand.

"Linda Tracy," he read aloud. " 'Two every night before retiring.' Yes, I remember Mrs. Tracy. Quite a young woman. Quite—" He hesitated. "—attractive," he added.

"You *remember* Mrs. Tracy." Shelly echoed. "Isn't she your patient now?"

"I suppose she is. Her record is in my files. It's just that I haven't seen her for some time."

"Since she lost her baby?"

"Oh, yes. Certainly. Before, at the time, and after."

"She took it hard, then?"

"Every woman takes it hard. Some may seem indifferent, but that's superficial."

"But doesn't a miscarriage affect different women in different ways?"

Dr. Youngston wasn't over thirty-five. His blond hair was clipped close; his clean-shaven face had a military alertness about it.

"What's your problem, Sergeant?" he queried. "Is Mrs. Tracy in trouble?"

"Why do you ask that question?"

"Why is a police officer at my door when I open the office in the morning?"

"It could be Mr. Tracy who's in trouble."

"Mr. Tracy was never my patient. Mrs. Tracy was."

"You're using the past tense again, Doctor."

"All right, Sergeant, I'll take your bait. Has Mrs. Tracy been murdered?"

It was early morning, but the fog had lifted and the sun was shining through the windows. The world was bright, and Dr. Youngston didn't seem a morbid-minded man.

"That's an interesting thought," Shelly mused, "but, so far as the police know, Mrs. Tracy is only the victim of abduction."

"Abduction? What do you mean?"

"I'm not sure. That's why I came to you. A doctor does more than treat the body, doesn't he? You have to understand something of the psychological makeup of the patient."

"I'm merely an obstetrician," Youngston protested.

"Merely? Wouldn't an obstetrician need to know quite a bit about feminine psychology—not to mention family relationships? Now, consider this situation, Doctor. Knowing Mrs. Tracy, and there you have me at an advantage, what would you make of it if I told you that some man, unidentified, had called for her in a taxi last night at ten-thirty while her husband was at work on the night shift. The landlord and his wife, awakened by the sound of the motor outside the window, got out of bed and watched through the window. They saw the taxi waiting. Moments later, heard a man—careful, apparently, not to step into the beam of the headlights—come from the Tracy house at the rear of the lot."

"I'm familiar with the Tracy house at the rear of the lot," Dr. Youngston said, "I was there when Mrs. Tracy lost her child."

"Good. You see the picture, then. Shortly after the man reached the cab, Mrs. Tracy came from the house. She didn't avoid the lights. The landlord and his wife both insist that she looked frightened. She went to the cab, entered it, and the cab drove off."

Youngston had followed the story carefully.

"And hasn't been heard of since, I presume."

"Exactly," Shelly said. "By the way, could I trouble you for a cigarette, Doctor?"

"Sorry," Youngston answered. "I never acquired the habit." He appeared thoughtful for a moment, then asked, "What does the cab driver have to say?"

"We're tracking him down now," Shelly replied. "What I'm interested in is your reaction. What do you think happened last night?"

It was a tough question to spring on a man so early in the morning. Youngston frowned, thoughtfully.

"While Mr. Tracy was at work, did you say?"

"Night shift—five-forty-five to two-forty-five. Calls his wife every night during the ten o'clock coffee break to make sure she's all right.

Dr. Youngston took the pill bottle from Shelly's hand and studied the label again.

"Being a physician," he said, slowly, "my mind may run in a rut; but isn't it possible that the man who came in the cab told Mrs. Tracy that her husband had been injured on the job?"

"Highly possible," Shelly agreed. "But why did he tell her that?"

"She was a very attractive woman," the doctor suggested.

"Is that what you see typed on the prescription label, Doctor?"

Youngston didn't answer with words. Instead, he went to his files. A few minutes later, he returned with the information that Linda Tracy had come to him on the seventh of October complaining of severe nervous tension and an inability to sleep. He had given her a prescription for sixty pills, together with the admonition not to use more than two at a time.

"How many pills would you guess are in that bottle, Doctor?" Shelly asked.

Youngston adjusted his glasses.

"I won't guess," he said. "I'll just ask. How many, Sergeant?"

"Twenty-eight," Shelly said. "That means only thirty-two pills used, or sixteen nights—"

"It's not unusual for a patient to fail to follow instructions," Youngston said.

"—out of better than three months," Shelly concluded. "Has Mrs. Tracy been back since you issued that prescription?"

"No," Youngston said. "If she had, it would have been entered in the files."

"When she came, did she come alone?"

Dr. Youngston hesitated. "No," he said, thoughtfully. "Mr. Tracy was with her. In fact, it was he who made her come. He was always very concerned about her."

"How did he take it when she lost the baby?"

"Hard. No, actually, not too hard. It was Mrs. Tracy's safety that concerned him. He had an almost paternal—"

Youngston paused until silence grew awkward. "—posses-
siveness," he added.

"Did Mrs. Tracy reciprocate?"

Youngston smiled wryly. "With paternal possessive-
ness?"

"You know what I mean. Did she love him?"

"That's a peculiar question, Sergeant."

"But a necessary one, Doctor. For a few months you were
close to this woman—closer than anyone. Closer, even than
her husband in many ways. Did she seem a happy woman?"

"Sergeant, a pregnant woman is every kind of woman.
Happy, unhappy, fearful, miserable—"

"Dr. Youngston, I remind you, for sixteen nights, con-
secutively or otherwise, Linda Tracy took the sleeping pills
you prescribed for her and, presumably, went to sleep. And
yet, her husband told me that he called his wife every night
at ten o'clock just before she took her sleeping pills and went
to bed. Somebody lied, Doctor. Either Chester Tracy lied to
me, or Linda Tracy lied to her husband. That's why I asked
you if the woman who disappeared last night loved her husband."

Dr. Youngston wasn't naïve. People married for many
reasons; occasionally, love. He hesitated a long time before replying.

"I can't answer that," he said.

"Can't, or won't, Doctor?"

"Can't, Sergeant. You need facts, don't you? Ask me
something I can answer factually, and I'll cooperate."

He was adamant. This was the time for diagnosis, analysis, conjecture, or just plain old-fashioned gossip; but Dr.
Youngston had chosen none of these, and there was a hard-
ness about his mouth that was impervious to change. Shelly
recognized defeat when he met it.

"Just one more question," he said. "What was Mrs. Tracy's condition, aside from nervousness, when you last saw
her?"

"Physically—excellent," Youngston said.

"Thank you, Doctor. If you think of anything else—

factual, of course, that might help us, my name is Shelly. Mike Shelly. You can reach me at headquarters.''

Twenty-eight pills in a bottle, and dried mud on her walking shoes. The words made a kind of jingle in Shelly's mind. He was still looking for Linda Tracy—not, of course, in that small room at headquarters where Chester Tracy was pleading for action:

"Haven't you found that cab driver yet? My God, my wife's been gone for nearly twelve hours!''

"We've located the cab company, Mr. Tracy. It's one of the big ones, and it took a while to trace the call sheet. The driver was a man named Berendo—Don Berendo.''

"What does he say?''

"He's off duty. We've sent a couple of men to pick him up.''

"All right, all right! But when are you going to find Linda? My God!''

No, Shelly couldn't take much of Chester Tracy. A man with more control was easier to interview. A man half a head taller than Tracy, wiry but strong. Black curly hair, teeth that gleamed white in an easy smile.

His name was Leo Manfred. He was thirty-ish. He lived in a small apartment over a garage that housed—visible through raised doors—half a section of discarded rental furnishings, a single horse trailer, and a two-year-old convertible with trailer hitch. The interior of the apartment, furnished chiefly by two large couches and a jazz-playing stereo set, was profusely decorated with mounted photos of horses, as well as a small collection of loving cups. Manfred himself was attired in fitted twill pants, a heavy-knit turtleneck sweater, and western boots. Between the white teeth was a rough brier pipe, which he removed at the sight of Shelly's badge. It was still early in the morning, and he hadn't expected a visitor.

"Just got back from the stable," he explained. "Showing

114

a horse I've got to sell to a prospective buyer. A Palomino, good strain. I like to work him out early when he's frisky."

"I thought you were on the day shift," Shelly said.

"What? Where?"

"At Flight Research."

And so the call was official, with Leo Manfred involved enough to have given Sergeant Shelly reason to acquire some background. There was no evident of Manfred's easy smile now.

"Not for a week," he said.

"What happened a week ago?"

"I quit. Life's too short to waste on a job you don't like."

Manfred stepped back to the stereo set and turned down the volume. The jazz continued behind the conversation like a muted heartbeat.

"Low pay?" Shelly queried.

"Good pay," Manfred said. "I just wanted a change. Look, what is this? Did somebody make off with the payroll?"

"Somebody," Shelly answered, "made off with Chester Tracy's wife."

Mike appreciated good jazz, and what was coming from the stereo was very good jazz. It was smooth and cool and well organized, and so was Leo Manfred, who took this information with just a trace of muscular reaction in his face that only an expert could have noticed. And then he waited, because, if he waited, Mike Shelly would have to stop listening to the jazz and tell the story that had previously been told to the only other man known to have been acquainted with Linda Tracy.

"Why have you told me this?" he asked, when Shelly finished.

"Chester Tracy mentioned your name."

"Does he think I made off with Linda?"

Manfred's facial expression was controlled, but his voice wasn't. An unmistakable note of derision had crept into his tone.

"Is something wrong with Linda Tracy?" Shelly asked.

"No comment," Manfred answered.

"In that case, I'll have to ask where you were last night at ten-thirty."

Chester Tracy had named two men who knew his wife. One was a doctor who didn't smoke; the other was a man with a horse to sell who had one forefinger laced tightly around the stem of a brier pipe.

"Now I'm getting it," Manfred said. "I introduced Linda to Chester—he must have told you that."

"He did." Shelly answered.

"And now you want to know what I know about her. Well, I don't. Linda was half of a double date I once went on. I don't think I even knew her last name before she nailed Chester."

"Nailed?" Shelly echoed.

"She was one of those—that's why I gave her to Chester. She was hunting, and Chester had that certain look."

The face of a kid pressed against the window, Shelly thought.

"The potential husband look," Manfred explained. "I don't have it. Most women sense that right away; to some it has to come subtly—like a blow on the head."

"How did it come to Linda?" Shelly asked.

He was getting tired of jazz. The photos of horses mounted on the walls were more interesting. Some of them had Leo Manfred astride the horse, standing beside the horse; one was of Manfred introducing the horse to a beautiful blonde. Both Manfred and the blonde were wearing dark glasses, but both were recognizable. The blonde was Linda Tracy.

"Who was the other half of the blind date?" Shelly prodded. "A Palomino?"

Manfred said nothing for a few seconds. His face was still controlled, but his glands didn't know it. The frown lines on his forehead were getting moist.

"Look," he said, suddenly. "I wasn't even in the city last night. I drove down to San Diego to see about a job I'm angling for. I didn't get back until almost midnight."

"Did you drive alone?"

"Alone? Sure. Sergeant, I knew this girl a couple of weeks before I introduced her to Chester. We went dancing—things like that. Pairing her off with Chester was a joke. He was afraid of women. I had no idea he'd fall for her. My guess is that Linda was just too much woman for Chester. I think she rigged that whole deal last night in order to get away from him."

"Why?" Shelly demanded.

"Love in bloom. Linda was always the romantic type. She had a big imagination."

"She's not the only one," Shelly said dryly. "If Mrs. Tracy wanted to run off with another man, she could have staged a fight with Chester and then disappeared. We could have classed it as just another domestic quarrel and waited seventy-two hours before issuing a Missing Persons bulletin."

It was good jazz, but it ended. Leo Manfred walked to the stereo set and switched it off. For a moment, his back was to Shelly, and in that moment, it seemed to stiffen.

When he turned around, he said, "I was only trying to be helpful, Sergeant."

"Thanks," Shelly answered. "You can be a lot more helpful if you find someone in San Diego, or on the road back, who can verify the story that you were driving home alone at ten-thirty last night."

Don Berendo. He still looked sleepy. A pile of comb-resistant black hair crowded for space on the top of his head, spilling over to his forehead. He hadn't had time to shave before being taken in for questioning, and his beard came out black. He wore a brown leather jacket, and twisted his taxi driver's cap in his hands.

"I picked this guy up at the airport," he said. "He came out of the Inter-Continental waiting room and hailed me just as I was getting ready to pull away after unloading a gent and a lady who were flying to Paris. Must have been all of seventy—both of them, but cute as a couple of kids starting out on a honeymoon. Paris." Berendo's face broke in a sleepy

117

smile. "I bet they have a devil of a time at the Folies Bèrgere."

"The man who came out of the waiting room," Keonig prodded. "What was he like?"

"Him? Let's see. He wore a raincoat—one of those Private Eye kind, and a brown felt hat with the brim snapped down, and dark glasses."

"Dark glasses *and* a raincoat?" Shelly echoed.

"You get all kinds at International, Sergeant."

"How tall was he?" Keonig asked. "How heavy? Fat or thin?"

Berendo scowled. He stared at Keonig; he stared at Shelly. Then he stared at Chester Tracy, who crouched at the edge of his chair listening with his whole body. Suddenly, Berendo brightened.

"He was about my size," he said. "About medium. I didn't get a good look at his face—that hat brim and the glasses."

"Did he have luggage?" Shelly asked.

"No, he didn't. I asked about that. 'It's checked through,' he told me. 'I have to go home. I forgot something.' Then he gave me that address—the place you call Peterson's where this guy, Tracy, lives. He kept telling me to hurry."

"What time was it when you picked him up?"

"Ten after ten. I marked it on my sheet. I got him to the address he gave me before ten-thirty. He told me to wait in the drive with the motor running while he went to the place in the back. He was gone about two minutes. When he came back, I thought we'd go again; but he just opened the back door and stood there smoking a cigarette. A minute or so later, the woman came."

"You saw my wife?" Chester demanded. "How did she look?"

"Scared," Berendo said. "No, there's a better word—shocked."

"As if she'd received bad news?" Shelly suggested.

"Something like that. She got into the cab and the guy after her. I backed out of the drive and started back to the airport, thinking we had a plane to catch and wondering, I'll tell you, how a guy could go off and forget a woman like that at home.''

"Did they talk?" Keonig asked. "Did you hear any conversation?"

Berendo hesitated. "I was pretty busy driving," he said at last. "Wait—there was something. The cigarette. The guy gave her a cigarette. She must have been nervous because she used three matches trying to get a light."

"*She* used the matches?" Shelly repeated. "The man didn't give her a light?"

"No. He didn't even sit near her. He sat on one side of the seat and she sat on the other—all tense. I thought maybe they'd had a fight and that was why he had to go back for her. You know where Airport Boulevard crosses Century— that intersection just before you pull into the airport? Well, I was barreling along, still thinking I had a plane to catch, and I started to speed up so's I'd make the green. This guy leans forward and says, 'Turn left here!' I slam on the brakes, thinking he's kidding. 'Look, Mister,' I started to say; but he comes right back at me. 'I said, turn left here!' Okay, so he's the customer. I turned left."

"Where did you go then?" Shelly asked.

"Just about half a block—to this engineering place. Flight Research. 'Stop here,' he says, and I stopped. The woman got out and the man got out and paid me. 'Shall I wait?' I ask him. 'Don't bother,' he said. I couldn't figure it, but, like I said, you get all kinds."

"Did they go inside?" Keonig queried.

"That's the funny thing," Berendo answered. "I started to pull out into traffic again, but I smelled something burning. I stopped and looked in the back. This woman had dropped her cigarette and the floor mat was smoldering. I stopped and yanked open the back door, and I naturally looked back at where I'd let them out because I was thinking a few choice things I'd like to say, and they were gone."

"What do you mean—gone?"

"What I said—gone! I felt downright spooky."

"Do you mean that they had gone inside the building?" Shelly demanded.

"They couldn't have gone inside the building. It sets way back off the street—one of those real modern places with no windows, just a big glass entrance to a lobby with a reception desk and a row of doors behind it. A couple of months ago, they landscaped in front and put in a long, winding walk of some kind of flagstone, or maybe slate. They put in new grass, the kind you never have to cut, and trees and shrubs so it doesn't look like a factory at all. At night they've got ground lights on the walk, and the lights shining out from that lobby. There was nobody on the walk and nobody in the lobby."

"They might have gone through one of the inner doors," Keonig suggested.

And then Don Berendo smiled sleepily, but knowingly. "That walk goes back a good two hundred feet," he said, "and I hadn't even got pulled away from the curb. What did they use for transportation—rockets?"

There was only one way to check Berendo's story—a trip to Flight Research. It was a little past eleven when Shelly and Keonig arrived. Berendo was right. The walk, slate slabs set in white gravel, formed a huge S curving back to the plate glass entrance. The entire foyer was visible from the street.

"It was dark," Keonig reminded. "The shrubs might have thrown shadows."

"The shrubs might have given shelter," Shelly said.

Halfway to the doors, at the first reverse curve of the walk, a cluster of semi-tropical growth raised a barrier which fanned back to join the edge of the building. Shelly stepped off the walk onto the Dicondra. The growth was tight and cushiony, like a closely woven carpet. It absorbed footprints and sprang back into place. But the foliage, he discovered, was more than decorative. It hid from the street the less scenic tight wire fence which enclosed the loading and parking areas at the side and rear of the building. At first, there seemed to be no break in the fence; then Shelly noticed a small gate, probably for the gardener's use. He started toward it, then stopped. Behind the foliage, there was a break in the grass—a small, round hole about the size of a penny with one side slightly flattened. Nearby, a sprinkler embedded in the earth was leaking, releasing just enough moisture to soften the ground. Shelly's eyes scanned the area. There were no other holes. He continued to the gate, Keonig at his heels, and found it locked. Over a buzzer on the wall of the building was a small sign: "Ring for Admittance." Shelly rang. Moments later, a uniformed guard appeared, demanding I.D. cards and received instead, police badges. The gate opened. From the inside, Shelly turned and examined the lock.

"Can this be set to remain unlocked?" he asked.

"From the inside," the guard answered.

"That's good enough," Shelly said.

They continued past the guard, past the loading platform, and on to where the parking lot fanned out before them in six rows of double-parked vehicles. By this time, a shirt-sleeved official, summoned by the guard, joined them to inquire the nature of their business. His badge announced that he was C. H. Dawson, Supervisor. Dept. E.

"How many employees do you have here?" Shelly asked.

"Four hundred and fifty—approximately," Dawson replied. "Three hundred on the day shift and a hundred and fifty on swing and graveyard."

"Skeleton crews," Keonig suggested.

"Somewhat. You see, we produce high precision equipment for the Air Force. The day shift is largely production, but much of our experimental work demands around the clock schedules. We keep skeleton shop and shipping crew at night, but a fairly complete technical force."

Shelly was still staring at the parking lot.

"Precision equipment," he said. "That means I.D. cards and gate inspection for all employees of all shifts."

"Exactly."

"And no one could enter or leave these premises, by foot or by automobile, who wasn't known to either the guard or the receptionist on duty."

"Not without proper credentials," Dawson replied. "What is the difficulty, officers? We have an Air Force Intelligence officer inside."

"It's nothing like that," Shelly said. And then he paused, reflecting. "Around the clock," he said musingly. "Mr. Dawson, do you have anyone in the plant now who was here all last night?"

Dawson smiled wearily. "Several," he admitted, "including myself. We're running some tests—"

"Do you know an employee named Chester Tracy?"

For a moment it seemed that he'd hit a blank wall, and then Dawson brightened. Chester. Of course he knew Chester. He was in charge of the tool crib, night shift.

"Did you see him last night?"

Dawson was puzzled, but still cooperative. Chester'd spent most of the night in the lab, but had stepped out for a coffee—

"At what time?" Shelly asked.

"Time? We lose all sense of time when we're running tests. No, I do remember. It was eleven. Just eleven. I looked at the clock over the coffee machine, still thinking I might get home by midnight. Well, I'm still here."

"Where was Chester?"

"At the machine. The sugar pull jammed and he loosened it for me. 'It's a dull night,' he said. 'I need something to keep me awake.' I think he was making an excuse for being there when it wasn't time for the regular break. Some shop men never lose their awe of the white collar, even when it's open at the neck and frayed on both sides." And then Dawson paused and seemed to reflect on the total conversation. "I hope Chester isn't in some kind of trouble," he said, "—or his wife."

"Why do you mention his wife?" Keonig asked.

"Because she's not well. I know for a fact that Chester telephones her every night during the ten o'clock break. One night—oh, six weeks or so ago—I found him at the phones, frantic. We had a big wind that night and the telephone wires were down. He explained how nervous she had been since

122

losing their child. He was so upset, I told him to goof off and go home to see how she was taking the storm.''

"Goof off?" Shelly said.

"It was a simple matter for Chester. His work is chiefly at the beginning and the end of the shift. He could duck out the loading exit without being missed.''

"Did he do it?"

"Yes, he did. About forty-five minutes later, I noticed he was back in the crib. I kidded him about not even turning off the motor, and he told me that his wife was asleep and he hadn't wanted to disturb her. Chester's a conscientious worker, Officer. I wouldn't have made such a suggestion to anyone else.''

"He still had to drive past the gateman," Shelly observed.

"Yes, he did."

"Would there be any way of finding out if anyone drove out of your parking lot last night between shift changes.''

There was a way. It took a little time, and left everything as it had been in the first place. Two army officers had left the parking lot, and also the wife of one of the late working technicians who had brought him a dietetic supper. No one else. That left only one question to ask the cooperative Mr. Dawson.

"Did you know a former employee named Leo Manfred?" Shelly inquired.

This time Dawson smiled. "The 'Don Juan' of the drafting board," he said. "Leo was a good man, but he's a drifter. He's left us before. He'll be back when it blows over."

"When what blows over, Mr. Dawson?"

"Whatever made him decide it was time to move on—a woman, probably. Leo loves 'em, but leaves 'em." Then Dawson paused and examined the expressionless faces before him. "I don't suppose it would do any good, if I asked what this inquiry is all about," he added.

Shelly gave him the only possible reply.

"As much good," he said, "as if we asked what you were testing last night."

Back on the sidewalk, Mike Shelly stood for awhile watching the traffic at the intersection in front of the airport entrance. Most of it bound for the airport consisted of taxi cabs. He counted six before Keonig called him back to the radio car. They were wanted at headquarters. Dr. Youngston had come in to make a statement.

Factual. That was the word Shelly had left with Dr. Youngston. He waited alone in a small room. His statement, he prefaced, was confidential.

"This is Sergeant Keonig," Shelly explained. "He's working on the case with me."

"Very well," Youngston said. "I suppose I should have told you this when you called at my office this morning, but I hadn't had the time to absorb the gravity of the situation. Besides, there are moments between a doctor and a patient that are as sacred as those between a confessor and a priest. I told you that I was called to the Tracy home when Mrs. Tracy lost her child. I was called by Mrs. Peterson. It was all over then, but Mrs. Tracy wasn't aware of what had happened. When I told her, she said something that might have a bearing on her disappearance."

"What did she say?" Shelly asked.

"She called out for someone."

"Her husband?"

"Her husband's name is Chester. The name she called was Leo."

Youngston might have said more, but he didn't have the opportunity. There was a sound from the doorway; Youngston, Shelly, Keonig, all turned at once. Chester Tracy stood staring at them with tragic eyes.

"Leo—" he echoed.

"I thought we were alone," Youngston protested.

"He took Linda. Leo. I'll kill him!"

Chester Tracy was in the doorway one instant; gone from it the next. A moment of shocked surprise, and then Shelly led the exodus to the door. The corridor was already empty; the elevator indicator was starting downward.

"Who is Leo?" Keonig demanded. "Where is he?"

124

Leo was a target on the other side of the city. Leo was in a garage apartment Shelly had visited once, and Chester Tracy probably a dozen times. Now the elevator indicator had reached street level, and Tracy would be racing for his station wagon. With a grim face, Shelly watched the indicator crawl upward again.

"Leo," he said, "is where we're going right now!"

On the far side of the garage apartment, the side not visible from the street, a sliding glass door opened onto a small sun deck. Shortly after noon, the sun leaned across the roof and bathed the deck in winter warmth. Leo Manfred sprawled in a low-slung deck chair. He still wore his boots and western pants, but had removed the sweater. He tossed his dark glasses on a nearby cocktail table and closed his eyes. He might have fallen asleep if it weren't for an annoying sound in the driveway below. Finally, it ceased and Leo relaxed. He remained relaxed until a shadow fell across his naked chest. Without benefit of the direct sun, the air was cold. Leo opened his eyes and looked up. Chester Tracy stood over him with a trench coat over his right arm and a brown felt hat in his left hand. He watched Leo's eyes open, and then tossed the hat on his chest in a gesture of contempt.

Leo slid one foot to the floor for leverage.

"Chester—" he said.

The coat slid off Chester's arm. In his hand, he held a gun. There was no time for conversation; only an instant for action. Tossing the hat in Chester's face, Leo lunged forward. Chester had time to fire one shot, wildly, and then Leo's arms were about his body, hurling him back into the room behind the glass doors. When Chester fell, Leo broke free and ran for the front stairway. He had scrambled down to the garage level when suddenly brought up short by the solid substance of Mike Shelly, pistol in hand.

"Drop that gun!" Shelly ordered.

Leo whirled. Chester stood above him at the top of the stairs. He'd retrieved the gun and was leveling it at Leo's head.

"I found the raincoat," he yelled, "and the brown hat—"

"Drop the gun!" Shelly repeated.

"I found 'em—in Leo's closet!"

"Drop it or I'll shoot it out of your hand!"

It wasn't just Mike Shelly facing Chester now; Keonig had come up behind him. Slowly, the gun lowered—then dropped.

"Come down," Shelly said.

Chester obeyed. He came down and stood within a few feet of Leo, while Keonig raced upstairs to find and bring back the hat and coat. At the sight of them, Chester found his voice.

"Make him tell what he's done with my Linda," he demanded. "Make Leo tell!"

"I haven't done anything with Linda," Leo protested. "I was in San Diego—"

"You took her away in a taxi! You always were crazy about Linda!"

Shelly took the hat and coat from Keonig's hands. Both showed signs of a lot of use.

"*I* was crazy about Linda?" Leo howled. "Let's get this straight. Linda was crazy about me! Why do you think she married you, Chester? I'll tell you why. Because she was crazy about me and I wouldn't have her. She married you out of spite—"

Chester no longer had a gun, but he had a body. Before anyone could stop him, he rushed at Leo and hurled him back against the chrome handle of a refrigerator stacked among the landlord's furnishings. Leo groaned and staggered forward, and then the door of the refrigerator slowly opened, bringing Mike Shelly's search to an end. All of the racks had been removed to make room for Linda Tracy's body.

"My God!" Leo gasped. "Oh, my God!"

It was Dr. Youngston who recovered first from the shock of discovery. He went to the body and made a quick examination. Linda Tracy had been struck a blow on the head

"—with the usual blunt instrument," he said. "Dead for at least twelve hours."

"A little longer," Shelly said quietly. "Since about ten-fifty-five last night."

His words sounded strange against the stunned silence which still pervaded the garage.

"How do you know that?" Keonig demanded.

"Because," Shelly answered, "if it takes eighteen minutes to drive from Flight Research to the Tracy house; it must take the same time to drive from the Tracy house to Flight Research. Think back, Keonig. The cab driver told us that he had picked up a man wearing a trench coat, a brown felt hat, and dark glasses at ten minutes past ten in front of the Inter-Continental waiting room at the airport. He drove to the Tracy address, reaching it shortly before ten-thirty, picked up Linda Tracy and drove to Flight Research where he discharged his passengers."

"Where they promptly disappeared," Keonig added. "Completely."

"But they didn't. They stepped behind the shrubbery and started to walk toward the gate in the wide fence, and then—" Shelly handed the coat and hat back to Keonig and went to the body. It was fully clothed—light tan coat, blue suit, black pumps. He wrenched loose the right pump and examined the heel. It was very high and narrow with a tip about the size of a penny with one side flattened. "Dr. Youngston, if a woman wearing a pump such as this were struck a heavy blow, hard enough to kill, from the back, left side, wouldn't the weight of her body fall on the right foot?"

"I suppose it would," Youngston said.

Shelly's thumb pricked at the residue of dried mud on the heel. "The grass on the grounds at Flight Research doesn't leave tracks," he mused, "but there was one small round hole near a leaky sprinkler valve that would just fit this heel. A woman's shoes are very interesting, particularly Mrs. Tracy's. She has a pair of plastic slippers in her closet less than a month old; but the soles are worn down as if she'd been doing a lot of dancing. And she has a pair of walking shoes in that same closet with mud on them. Now there's no mud on the way to the mail box, but there could be mud in the unpaved alley leading to the street.''

Still holding the pump, Shelly made his way past a dazed Leo and a stunned Chester to the trunk of Leo's convertible. He opened it and peered inside. A jack, a tire iron, a spare tire and a folded saddle blanket. He shook out the blanket with one hand and then tossed it back inside the trunk.

''And then,'' he continued, ''there's the matter of the sleeping pills Linda Tracy didn't take—but told her husband she did. What was to stop her, after that ten o'clock call, from slipping out the back way, walking down the alley, and meeting some Prince Charming to take her to the ball? But, like Cinderella, she had a witching hour—three A.M. Before three, when faithful husband returned, she had to be back in bed, asleep.''

''Cinderella slipped up,'' Keonig observed.

''So did Linda Tracy. And so did her killer.''

''I was in San Diego!'' Leo protested. ''I was on the road driving home at ten-fifty-five.''

''What about the night the wind blew down the telephone wires?'' Shelly demanded. ''Where were you then?''

Leo didn't answer. He was still struggling with shock.

''Weren't you waiting in your convertible at the end of the alley—''

''I didn't kill her,'' Leo protested.

''—wearing that trench coat and the brown hat—''

''I went out with her a few times, that's all. Just—just a few times—''

''—under the street lamp where you could be watched by anyone who had cause to be suspicious?''

''I didn't want to go out with her!'' Leo cried. ''I was sick of her. That's why I put in for this job in San Diego.''

''He's lying—'' Chester began.

''No,'' Shelly said, firmly, ''I don't think he is. But rumors fly fast in a small plant, don't they? What did you think when you heard that Leo Manfred had quit and was moving south, Mr. Tracy? Were you afraid he was going to take your wife with him?"

The question caught Chester Tracy by surprise. He blinked stupidly, like a man blinded by sudden light.

"It's Leo's coat," he stammered. "It's Leo's hat—"

"Yes, and your wife had seen both of them often enough to have recognized Leo in an instant if he'd been the man who came for her in the cab. But she couldn't have recognized a new trench coat and a new hat—particularly not if she'd been called at ten o'clock and told her husband had been injured on the job and the company was sending someone after her in a cab. The man who came for her was careful not to talk more than necessary. He sat on the opposite side of the seat. When he gave her a cigarette—not the brand he smoked, but a brand picked up in the airport waiting room where he must have kept the coat and hat in a locker—he let her get her own light. There could be only one reason for such caution."

Shelly stood with the black pump in his hands, and the tense faces of four men before him. But one face was more tense than the others.

"If Linda Tracy hadn't been upset," he added, "she would have recognized the man who came for her, in spite of his disguise. She knew him well enough. He was her husband."

"No!" Tracy protested. "It was Leo—"

"It was meant to sound like Leo when the cab driver told his story, as you knew he would do. That cab bothered me from the beginning. It was too easy to trace. Hadn't you been watching your wife since the night Dawson sent you home to inadvertently discover that she wasn't taking her pills at ten o'clock?"

"I work!" Tracy said. "I work nights!"

"But Dawson showed you a way to get in and out of the plant any time you wanted to without being missed. You knew she was going out with Manfred, and you knew Manfred was moving. You killed your wife, Mr. Tracy."

"No—"

"And made a clumsy attempt to frame Leo Manfred. The

way you pushed him against that refrigerator just now was a little obvious. If Manfred had put your wife's body in there, he wouldn't have stood within twenty feet of it!''

Chester Tracy's station wagon was parked just outside the open garage. Shelly went to it and opened the tailgate. Early in the morning, the windows had been curtained with fog; nothing inside could be seen. But now he found a canvas tarpaulin, old and dirty but spotted with stains the police lab would find interesting.

''Time of death: approximately ten-fifty-five, Doctor,'' he said, ''and then the body was carried to the parking lot until the usual time. After that, Chester Tracy went inside to have a cup of coffee before finishing his shift. But it wasn't a dull night was it, Tracy?''

Shelly turned around and waited for a protest that didn't come. Chester Tracy had lowered his head and was crying, softly.

''Linda,'' he said. ''My Linda—''

He had the face of a kid who had been given the loveliest toy in the shop window—and broken it.

No Comment

·

John Jakes

John Jakes has earned a well-deserved reputation as a contemporary master of the historical novel; his most recent in a long line of bestsellers is California Gold *(1989). But Jakes is also an accomplished writer in other fields, the crime-fiction genre being one of them. "No Comment," his first new short story in many years, is about as far-removed from his panoramic historicals as it is possible to get—a brief, savage indictment of chemical pollution, with its potential effects illustrated in a graphically horrifying fashion. Warning: This story is not for the squeamish.*

The gruesome Slub Canal murders had a long history.

The start of it could be dated 1953. A developer from nearby Buffalo bought some land within sight of the main plant of Metrochemical, Inc., and the waterway for which the tract was eventually named. Young couples, most with husbands employed at Metrochem, snapped up all the houses before they were built; those were the days when a Philco TV, a carport, and a chain link fence consummated the American Dream, and you knew your company would take care of you till you retired or died.

Soon children from the tract houses were playing along the canal bank. Under a slaggy winter sky at twilight, mothers who came to call them in began to notice the slow, sludgelike quality of the canal that had flowed briskly and noisily only a couple of years before, when the lots were being sold. Looking along the canal to the huge tangle of pipes and smokestacks of Metrochem, the mothers could see two large conduits in the bank spilling more sludge. Flames from the stacks snapped like flags, and even on sunny days a deep lavender haze filled the air. No one thought much of it, though.

One night in 1963, Mrs. Sheila Johnson of 22 Crystal Court went into the bedroom belonging to her twins and screamed. Kimmy, the girl, the frail one, slept to the left of the door. Near her bed a small night-light glowed. In the bed, Kimmy's forearm bones glowed. They glowed a faint but unmistakable green through her pale translucent skin. Seven months later—two days after her sixth birthday— Kimmy breathed her last. For the final two months she had screamed almost constantly as the cancer ate her bones away.

By this time the nation was beginning to wake up to the dangers of chemical pollution. Metrochemical, meanwhile, was expanding, increasing production and changing its name to Metrochem World-Wide. A young man named Hollister (Buddy) Wood was promoted from accountant to sales assistant, to broaden his background. He was considered a comer.

Not everyone in the tract worked for MWW. Stan Krasno did not. Stan lived at 36 Sparkling Avenue with his wife and three tiny daughters. Stan's house backed up to Slub Canal. Sometimes on a summer night, getting a beer from the Frigidaire, he could hear turgid bubbles popping on the canal's surface. If he glanced out the window at the right time, he could see the same popping bubbles briefly emit a yellow-green glow. It worried him in an unfocused way.

Stan's wife Helen took a job in the sales literature department at MWW when the last of her three girls entered school. Stan worked in the meat department of the Sav-All Supermart in one of the new Buffalo suburbs creeping out toward Slub Canal. The meat department occupied the right wall as you entered. From behind the work area's one-way glass Stan could see the MWW executives driving to and from work in their company Cadillacs. At this point they did not yet have chauffeurs.

By the late sixties, when MWW was making chemicals for Vietnam, four children and two adults from the tract had died of forms of cancer. Several women held a meeting which Helen Krasno attended. They prepared a sincere if crudely written petition and presented it to the company, requesting an inquiry into possible links between the deaths and the plant's waste-dumping practices. Assistant to the President Buddy Wood returned the petition through the mail, having written on the front page THE COMPANY HAS NO COMMENT.

In the early seventies three more deaths occurred. By now cause and effect were no longer in doubt, at least to the residents of Slub Canal. This caused some agonizing moments in the Krasno household.

The Krasnos were devout Catholics. Stan never missed a Sunday mass and went regularly, compulsively, to confession. *"Bless me, Father . . ."* His list of sins, some real, some fanciful, was always long. Helen had the deep misfortune of believing that the basic teachings of her religion should be practiced universally. She lived by standards of honesty, decency, fairness, personal responsibility, and took it on faith that everyone else did, too. She assumed everyone's word was good, without exception.

Helen also believed in loyalty to her employer. But her ideals, her family, and her neighbors won out. She began to write Congressmen and organize Saturday coffees. She invited a young and hairy environmentalist to sleep on the couch after he addressed a group in the living room. She took a night school course in better letter writing, and bought a book on improving telephone skills. Finally the government sent investigators to Slub Canal. At this point Helen lost her job. It was claimed that she misdirected a huge shipment of sales literature to the Bangkok branch when it was urgently needed in Frankfurt.

Stan Krasno expressed his outrage to his bowling buddies. One of the best of them, Chief of Police Milt Dubofsky, a pal since high school, warned him, "Don't do anything rash. I'd have to haul you in and knock a confession out of you and then you'd be on your way to jail." He way only half-joking.

There were six more harrowing cancer deaths in the next three years. Buddy Wood, now president of MWW, turned aside questions from teams of TV and newspaper reporters who swarmed into Slub Canal, photographing the green-brown "water" which now hardly moved at all. While Buddy Wood certainly didn't own the company, he was a large stockholder thanks to his option programs, and he had become the target of the anger of Slub Canal householders, including Stan Krasno. Chopping or packaging meat, Stan would stare out through the one-way glass, watch Buddy Wood's silver stretch whisk by and angrily recall that Helen couldn't even get work as a domestic, cleaning the homes of the executives of MWW; as soon as someone learned her name, the door closed in her face.

The news media practically camped in Slub Canal. Buddy Wood, now plump and middle-aged, was occasionally photographed coming out the gate in his silver limo; he wore rimless bifocals at this point in life, and dyed his hair dark brown to promote a youthful image, as so many businessmen did. He never smiled for cameras.

The day the government announced its twenty-million-dollar suit against MWW for violations of environmental laws, Buddy Wood issued a statement from his office before dashing off to Scottsdale on the company jet with his wife Chrissy. Buddy was scheduled to address a conference of high-level corporate executives on the subject of the dangers of executive stress. Chrissy carried their tennis rackets and her ankle-length mink coat. The departing statement consisted of two words. "No comment."

That was all you ever heard from the company, Stan Krasno thought as he sat in front of his flickering TV that evening, a beer can in one hand and the lights turned off to hide the increasing shabbiness of the deteriorating house. That was all you heard, "no comment," or "the company declines comment," or "spokesmen for the company declined comment," or "the New York attorneys representing the company declined comment at this time. . . ." Stan belched and stood and listened because he thought he'd heard a sound. Yes, there it was again. A bubble went *pop* in Slub Canal. The smell made him gag.

Stan slouched to the door of the bedroom where his teen-age daughter, Cherylanne, slept; the other girls were grown and gone, Babette married, Lynne Marie in cosmetology school. Stan opened the door, looked in, and practically tore the phone off the wall before he got Helen on the line; she was night manager at the local Señor Speedy Taco Hacienda.

"She's green, her bones are green, I can see 'em," Stan screamed into the phone.

Ten and a half months later, lying mewling in a pool of her own green diarrhea, Cherylanne died at three-ten A.M. In the adjoining bedroom Helen was likewise dying; she expired a week after her daughter's burial. Stan was hysterical most of that night.

Next day he summoned reporters from the Buffalo media and accused MWW of murdering his wife and child. This provoked a surprising personal appearance by Buddy Wood on evening news shows. Looking grave and correct in his seven hundred dollar custom-tailored suit, the lights reflecting off his rimless glasses, he said:

"At this point in time we have no comment other than to extend the sympathy of the entire Metrochem family to Mr. Krasno in his hour of loss. We will of course launch a thorough and objective investigation. Beyond that, I must say again that we cannot comment at this time. Now if you'll excuse me, I have to make a flight out of JFK to Zurich this evening for a conference on the merger announced last week. I have no further comment." Off camera, his wife Chrissy waited with their skis. The camera caught a glimpse of her and, at home, Stan went wild.

"No comment, no comment," he screamed. "Fucking coward. Fucking CRIMINAL. Always hiding, hiding behind your fucking lawyers and your fucking hired help to save your fucking profits and your fucking greedy ass." Stan no longer believed in the carport-and-chain-link dream, or that MWW, or any other company, would take care of an ordinary Joe unless it served some cold-blooded purpose.

DEADLY DOINGS

Ten days later the Woods returned to their suburban Buffalo home, severely jet-lagged and exhausted. At five-fourteen in the morning, alarms went off in the central office of the security service which looked after their property. The service automatically dialed the local police, who rushed to the site of the alarm. They found the huge house broken into on the first floor. Upstairs, in the enormous master bedroom suite (two complete baths and his-and-hers walk-in closets in which you could hold a small dinner party) they found carnage.

Buddy and Chrissy Wood had been stabbed to death through their night clothes. Many cuts were visible on both bodies, but his had been mutilated. The bedding was blood-soaked; the walls resembled huge wet abstract paintings done in red. In the warm ashes in the bedroom hearth, a detective discovered something black and meaty. It turned out to be most of Buddy Wood's tongue.

When Chief Milt Dubofsky got the call, he was only mildly surprised. He'd watched his bowling buddy Stan slowly come apart following his wife's firing and then her death a week after their daughter's. "The poor son of a bitch," the chief said, strapping on his hip holster with considerable reluctance. He drove to the shoebox house on Sparkling Avenue with two deputies. Guns drawn, they knocked at the front door.

"Stan? This is Milt. Got to talk to you."

From inside came a weird gargling noise.

"Stan, if you come out peaceably, you won't get hurt. But you've got to come out. We've got to talk about what you did."

The noise again, a kind of moist glottal choking sound. Chief Milt Dubofsky cautiously tested the door.

Not locked. Unhappily, he gestured his deputies forward with his gun.

They found Stan seated in an old armchair in his living room. The arms of the chair were soaked with blood. Pools of it glistened under his shoes. Stan was still alive—barely—with a delirious smile on his bloodstained mouth. He made another of those weird gagging sounds, as if to demonstrate that he couldn't speak. One of the deputies turned away to be sick.

"Stan, you got to tell me—" But Stan was shaking his head. Grinning, very pleased, he pointed to his bloody mouth with the butcher knife in his right hand. Then the Chief saw the bloody object lying in Stan's lap. What he had done to Wood, he had done to himself.

The Unicorn's Daughter

•

Edward D. Hoch

Simon Ark is one of several series characters created by Edward D. Hoch, the dean of modern writers of short crime fiction, and one of the most unusual the genre has yet produced. Ark claims to be a two thousand-year-old Coptic priest on an unending mission to seek out and destroy the devil's earthly handiwork; as a result, his investigations, while on the one hand formal detective stories, are also spiced with elements of fantasy and mysticism—a blend that is reminiscent of G.K. Chesterton's Father Brown. Ark's exploits have appeared in numerous anthologies and in three collections: City of Brass *(1971),* The Judges of Hades *(1971), and* The Quests of Simon Ark *(1984). The manuscript of a strange "adult fairy tale" entitled* The Unicorn's Daughter *is the subject of the adventure which follows.*

The man's name was Harvey Cross and he sat across the desk from me much as hundreds of other authors and would-be authors had in the years I'd been a senior editor at Neptune Books. In those first minutes of our meeting he wasn't especially different from those others. Slim and just a bit boyish, with a trace of a stutter, he clutched the thick manuscript to his chest and said, "I wanted to try Neptune with it first because you published Simon Ark's book."

"That was more than ten years ago," I reminded him. "If it's something occult we wouldn't really be interested at the present time." I was beginning to regret having agreed to see him. He could just as well have left his manuscript with my secretary, the practice followed with most other unsolicited submissions. But there'd been something in his voice on the phone that interested me. Seeing him now, I couldn't remember what it had been.

"Oh, it's not an occult book. Not in the true sense of the word. It's—I suppose you'd call it an adult fairy tale, about a strange place in the forest and a strange girl who lives there."

"I don't really think—"

"At least give it a reading!"

"All right, Mr. Cross. Why don't you leave it with my secretary? She'll—"

I was interrupted by the flashing of the intercom. I flipped a switch and heard Martha Scane, our publicity director, say, "This is Martha. Could I see you for a few moments when you're free?"

Harvey Cross had gotten out of his chair and was walking to the window. "Right, Martha," I acknowledged and flipped the switch.

I started to turn toward my visitor when I heard the shattering of glass and saw him going through the window.

"Cross!" I shouted, but it was too late.

I sat stunned for a second, then ran to the big broken window and peered out at the street twenty-eight stories below. I could see cars stopping and people gathering.

My secretary ran in. "What was that crash?"

"Put me through to the police, Irene! A man just jumped through the window!"

"Was it that Cross fellow?"

"I'm afraid so." I saw his manuscript in a corner of my desk and I glanced at the title page. *The Unicorn's Daughter* by Harvey Cross. It was all that was left of him now. I noticed the return address in the upper left-hand corner. It was a box number in Catskill, New York.

Others crowded into my office as word of the tragedy spread. "Terrible," Ash Gregory from the Art Department said, patting my shoulder. "Who was he, some nut?"

"I don't really know," I admitted. "Just an author trying to sell his book."

Martha Scane came in, her blond hair flying. "My God! Did he jump while I was talking to you?"

"Just about. I didn't really see it happen. He walked over to the window, and when I looked around he was going through the glass."

I told the police the same thing. They shook their heads and I got the impression they thought Harvey Cross had been less than rational. By the time they left and everyone else cleared out of my office, I was still a bit unnerved. The building's maintenance people placed a sheet of plywood over the window until it could be replaced in the morning and the lack of a familiar angle of illumination further depressed me. I told Irene I'd work the rest of the day at home.

I was halfway out the door when I remembered the dead man's manuscript. I went back to my office for it but it wasn't on the desk. I wondered if the police had taken it without telling me, or if someone else had picked it up while my office was crowded.

On the way out I stopped at my secretary's desk. "Irene, send a memo around—ask if anyone inadvertently took a manuscript from my office today. The title is *The Unicorn's Daughter* and the author is Harvey Cross."

"The man who jumped?"

"That's right. The man who jumped."

When the manuscript didn't reappear by Friday afternoon my curiosity got the better of me. The newspaper accounts of Cross's spectacular leap from my office window had given his address as a furnished apartment in Brooklyn, and had listed no family. But he'd given me that box number in Catskill. Suddenly I was curious enough to pursue it.

That afternoon I phoned Simon Ark at the Institute for Medieval Studies where he'd been pursuing some esoteric research project for several months. He seemed pleased to hear from me. "Ah, my friend, I read about the bizarre event at your office."

"Bizarre is right. That's not the half of it, Simon." I told him about the vanished manuscript.

"Could one of your employees plan to sell it to another publisher, perhaps as his own?"

"That would presuppose it had some value. As near as I can tell, Harvey Cross never published a thing. I can't believe the manuscript has any value at all, except perhaps as the final ravings of a troubled mind."

"But you didn't read it."

"No," I admitted.

"What do you plan to do about it?"

"He mentioned you, Simon. Before he jumped he said he came to Neptune Books because we'd published Simon Ark."

"Hardly a recommendation, my friend. The book wasn't one of your better sellers."

"He implied his book might have the same mystic quality that led us to publish it—though he denied it was an occult book."

"I repeat my question. What do you plan to do about it?"

"Well, the address on the manuscript was a box number in Catskill. That's a two-hour drive up the Hudson. I thought I might go up there tomorrow morning, arriving before the post office closes at noon. Do you want to come along?"

"A drive in the country is tempting," he admitted. "The dust of old books is thick in my throat these days."

At home that night I invited my wife Shelly to join us. But with the passing years she's taken an increasing dislike to Simon and, as I expected, she refused. "One of these days he's going to get you killed on one of these foolish expeditions," she predicted.

"This one was my idea," I pointed out.

"It's about that man who jumped from your window, isn't it?"

"Yes," I admitted. "I can't just let it rest, Shelly."

She sighed and said simply, "Try to be careful."

After living with me for twenty-six years she knew there was nothing more she could say.

DEADLY DOINGS

* * *

It was a fine warm Saturday in early June, a perfect day for our journey up the Hudson. Simon had shed his traditional black garb for gray slacks and a dark-blue jacket. It wasn't much of an improvement but it helped. Though he often claimed to be two thousand years old, on that day he would have passed for a reasonably vigorous seventy-five.

"What do you expect to find here?" he asked as we pulled up in front of the post office.

"Cross didn't drive all this way to pick up his mail. If he had a box here it means he lived near here at least part of the time. The police might be willing to dismiss this whole business, but I'm not. After all, he jumped out of my window."

Luckily I'd remembered the box number correctly. The postal clerk checked his records and informed me, "We have notice that Harvey Cross is recently deceased."

"That's correct. What's being done with his mail?"

"His sister discontinued the box and instructed us to forward the mail directly to her. I guess he used to live with her."

"Here in Catskill?" The newspaper had mentioned no sister, anywhere.

"Not far from here. A town called Olympus. It's over toward the mountains about fifteen miles. I suppose that's how it got its name, though there's no Mount Olympus there."

I showed him my business card. "Look, it's important I contact Cross's sister about a manuscript he submitted to us. I need her address."

He thought it over and replied, "I suppose I could give you that. It's Hazel Phoenix, Hillside Road, Olympus."

I wrote it down and thanked him. Back in the car I told Simon what I'd learned. "It's not far. Let's drive over and see the sister. Maybe she can tell us something about the dead man."

"By all means," he agreed, and for the first time I detected a glimmer of interest in his eyes.

"I'm afraid there won't be any devils for you to chase," I said.

"Don't be too sure, my friend. At Olympus we may find gods, and where there are gods there could be devils as well."

It took us some time to find the home of Hazel Phoenix. As its name implied, Hillside Road ran along the side of a hill. The area was on the northeastern rim of the Catskills, and although the hills weren't as steep as those we could see in the distance they were still formidable.

The house sat back some distance from the road, almost hidden among the trees. It might have been the forest Harvey Cross said he'd written about. I wondered if he'd written the book while living in this house.

We parked at the end of the long driveway and had a closer look at the place. It was a small house that had been added onto in a seemingly haphazard manner. The overall impression was as if the original structure had sprouted wings—or tentacles—to spread itself over the surrounding landscape. "The gingerbread house gone wild," Simon commented.

At first no one answered the big brass knocker, but as we were about to turn away we heard the sound of a power saw from somewhere behind the house. We walked around back, past a cinder block garage, and found a slim young woman cutting through some small logs.

"That's hard work for a woman," I said, regretting the chauvinistic greeting almost at once.

She turned off the saw and eyed us uncertainly. "What can I do for you?"

"We're looking for Hazel Phoenix."

"You've found her." She set down the saw and wiped her hands on the legs of her jeans. I introduced Simon and myself and she shook hands, though I thought her eyes hardened at the mention of my name.

"Mrs. Phoenix, we came about your brother, Harvey Cross."

"Yes?"

"You may have recognized my name. It was my office he jumped from."

"Yes, I know." Her expression didn't change. She was a fairly attractive woman, around thirty, with the sort of face I wanted to see break out in a smile. But I wasn't giving her anything to smile about.

"Before he died, Harvey brought me the manuscript of a novel he'd written. It was called *The Unicorn's Daughter.* Unfortunately, the manuscript was mislaid during the confusion following his death. I'm sure it'll turn up, but in the meantime I wonder if you might have a carbon copy of it I could read. I feel I owe it to your brother."

She rolled the sleeves of her shirt higher on her slim arms and squinted at me in the sunlight. "It seems to me you owe him a lot more than that, mister. It seems to me you're responsible for his suicide."

"No, I assure you I'm not. We'd only just begun to talk. Nothing much had been said, and certainly nothing to cause his sudden decision to jump out the window."

"Well, I know nothing about his manuscript."

"Did he work on it while he was living here?"

"Who told you he lived here?" she asked sharply.

"The man at the post office mentioned it. He gave me your address."

"Well, he misunderstood. My brother lived in New York. He came here only occasionally for a visit."

"I see. Do you live here with your husband?"

"I'm not married."

"Oh. I thought, since your name was different from your brother's—"

"I'm not married," she repeated, offering no further explanation, and bent to pick up the power saw.

"Thank you for your help, Miss Phoenix," I muttered, and we turned away.

"Odd sort," Simon commented as we walked back to the car.

"That's for sure."

"Did you notice the names on the mailbox out by the road?"

"No," I admitted.

"Take a look."

I did and saw there were two names printed on a small piece of paper which had been taped to the box. A. GRIFFIN and H. PHOENIX. "So she's living here with some guy," I said as we got in the car.

"Perhaps."

"Or some girl."

"Are you in a hurry to get back, my friend?"

"Not especially."

"This case, if we could call it that, interests me. I'd like to drive around the neighborhood and ask a few questions."

"About Harvey Cross?"

"No, about A. Griffin and Hazel Phoenix."

There were no close neighbors along Hillside Road, and when we finally stopped at a house nearly a mile away an elderly couple there professed to know nothing about their distant neighbors. We had better luck at a small grocery store at the next crossroads. It was called Buraq's Country Store and the owner, Sam Buraq, a stocky man in his thirties, with a short beard, talked to us.

"Hazel Phoenix? Sure, she shops here. Lives there alone most of the time, but this fellow Griffin comes up and spends the weekends. I guess he works in New York and doesn't want to make that two-hour drive every night."

"What's he like?" I asked.

"About her age, I guess. Early thirties. Quiet fellow. Some sort of artist, I think."

"If he comes up on weekends he should be here today," I pointed out.

"He is. I seen him drive past not ten minutes ago. Had somebody with him in the car, but I didn't see who it was."

"What kind of car?"

"A blue Ford, the one he always drives. He was headin'

up toward the house. If you came that way you must have passed him."

I thanked him and we went back to my car. "What do you think, Simon? Should we try Hazel Phoenix one more time?"

"It might prove interesting," he agreed. "This is interesting country."

We were about halfway back along the road when I spotted the blue Ford parked on the shoulder. It was empty. I pulled up just ahead of it and we got out. "Where could they have gone from here?" I said. "There's nothing but woods."

"Let's take a look," Simon suggested.

We walked a few feet into the woods and were enveloped by twilight. It was an eerie, silent place and I wanted to turn back at once. "Maybe he's in here with some girl," I said.

"Quiet," Simon cautioned, raising his hand. "Do you hear something?"

There was a breaking of the underbrush somewhere nearby, as if someone was running through the woods. We paused, frozen in our tracks, as the sound grew nearer. Then suddenly we saw a man crash into view ahead of us. His face and chest were covered with blood, and for an instant I didn't recognize him, but he seemed to know me. "God, Simon!"

"Quickly! He needs help!"

The man had collapsed on the ground. He reached out a trembling hand and spoke my name.

Then I saw it was Ash Gregory, the artist from my office. "Ash, what happened? What are you doing here?"

He was trying to speak, but there was blood in his mouth. "Took—took manuscript from your office. Had to know—"

"Cross's manuscript? *You* took it?"

He nodded. "They—all—wanted it."

I could see now he'd been stabbed several times about the face and chest. "Who did this to you?"

"I—she—unicorn's daughter—help her."

"Why did Cross kill himself?"

"Because she—"

But that was all he said before he died there in the forest, a long way from Manhattan.

* * *

Simon and I looked quickly through his car before going for the police. There was no sign of Cross's manuscript. The killer might have taken it. But there was also a good chance it was back in New York. If so, we had to find it.

When the police arrived we told them as little as possible. I didn't want to be held up there all day and we didn't know very much anyway. They seemed to attribute the killing to some hitchhiker Gregory had picked up and put out an alarm to watch for hitchhikers in the area. But one of the local police, a sheriff's deputy named Toby Chimera, thought it an odd coincidence that I'd traveled all this distance to find the body of a man I worked with in Manhattan.

I thought it an odd coincidence too, and I tried to explain it away with a lie. "I recognized his car," I said. "He'd told me he sometimes drove up this way on weekends, so when I saw the car pulled off the road I thought he might be in some sort of trouble and I pulled off too."

"Still seems to be quite a coincidence," Chimera said, scratching his cheek. "We'll probably want to talk with you again. And you too, Mr. Ark."

"I'm available," Simon informed him. And then he said an odd thing. "Mr. Chimera, you know this part of the state. Are there many goats in the area? And snakes?"

"Well, sure—some of the farmers raise goats. And the Catskills are full of snakes."

"But no lions, I imagine."

The deputy's face hardened suddenly. "No, no lions." He left us and walked back to his car.

"What was that all about?" I asked Simon.

"This is a strange area. I was only trying to establish exactly how strange."

"Strange enough to have goats and snakes, but not lions?"

"I'll explain later."

When we got back to Manhattan I discovered I didn't know Ash Gregory's address, and there were too many A. Gregory listings in the phone book. I wasn't even sure he lived in Manhattan. I tried phoning my secretary Irene but it was already Saturday evening, and when she didn't answer I figured she was out with her boyfriend and I tried Martha Scane from publicity.

She was surprised to hear my voice and I told her as quickly as possible the tragic news about Ash Gregory. "I can't believe it!" she said, her voice breaking. "Not Ash!"

"I'm sorry I had to tell you like this, Martha. I know you were a friend of his and that's why I called. I need to know his address."

"He lived down in Greenwich Village," she replied, and gave me the address on Christopher Street. "Do the police have any idea who killed him?"

"They think it might have been a hitchhiker. If I hear anything more I'll let you know."

"He lived in the Village," I told Simon. "Let's get going."

"Do you plan on breaking and entering?" he asked with a slight smile.

"I plan on finding that manuscript, if it's there to be found."

We parked on the street about a block away from the address Martha had given me. It was eight o'clock, but not yet dark, as we mounted the steps and I rang the bell under A. Gregory's name. When no one answered we entered the vestibule through the unlocked door and moved down the dim hallway to his apartment at the rear of the first floor. I don't know how I intended to get in but that problem was solved when we saw that the lock had been forced and the wood around it splintered.

"Hardly the sort of thing the police would do," Simon whispered.

I pushed the door open cautiously and at once we heard the muffled sounds of a search in progress. Drawers were being pulled open and papers were being rifled. We must have made some slight noise because suddenly the sounds ceased and a figure in black appeared in a doorway across the living room from us.

As the figure moved, so did I, springing forward to grab one leg as it darted toward a window. We went down together with a thud and then I saw that my captive was a woman.

"What are you doing here?" I demanded.

She sat up, rubbing her shoulder where she'd hit the floor, and I had my first real look at her. She appeared to be in her thirties, and she had long black hair and brown eyes. The black slacks and sweater gave her the appearance of a sneak thief, but her face seemed open and almost innocent. "I might ask you the same thing," she countered, shifting her gaze to Simon in the doorway. "Are you police?"

"No. I worked with Ash. We found him today just before he died."

That didn't surprise her. She'd known he was dead. "I came here to collect some things of mine," she said. "My name's Kate Talos. Ash was a friend."

"How'd you know he was dead?"

"I heard it on the news."

It was possible, but I couldn't immediately check it. While I questioned her, Simon peered at the paintings on the walls. "He had a great interest in mythology," he observed.

"He painted those himself," Kate Talos said, getting to her feet and brushing herself off. I switched on the light in order to see them better.

There were seven paintings in all, and I recognized Ash's distinctive style from the jacket illustrations he'd done for some of our books. One showed a man of brass guarding an island, another a unicorn with a small naked girl at its side. There was a great bird, its wings spread wide, rising from smoldering ashes, and another winged creature with a lion's body. One painting showed a beast that seemed to have a fire-breathing lion's head, the body of a sheep or goat, and a serpent's tail. There was a dragon too. And the final painting showed a winged horse with the face of a woman and a peacock's tail. Studying them, I began to wonder how well I'd really known Ash Gregory.

"We may not need Harvey Cross's manuscript," Simon

said. "These may tell us what we want to know. What do you think, Miss Talos?"

"I don't know what you're talking about. I don't know anything about a manuscript."

"Where is the child, Miss Talos?"

"What child?"

"The unicorn's daughter. The one in that painting."

"The painting was just his imagination."

"I don't think so." Simon took a step toward her. "Two of the seven are already dead, aren't they? Do you want more to die? Do you want the child to die?"

"No one would harm her," she blurted out, and then tried to backtrack. "If this child you speak of even exists."

"You're playing a dangerous game, Miss Talos. Who sent you here to search for the manuscript?"

"No one." She was defiant once more. "I'm leaving now. Don't try to stop me."

"Only your conscience will stop you, and I pray that it does. Otherwise, the death of that child could be on your head."

She hurried out the door, running from Simon and me, and maybe from herself.

"What was that all about?" I asked him.

"Only she can tell us. I hope she will."

"And the manuscript?"

"Is here in this apartment, most likely. If the killer had removed it from Gregory's body Kate Talos wouldn't have been here searching for it."

We took up the search where she had abandoned it, but found nothing. Two hours later I was about to give it up. "Simon, it's only a matter of time before the Olympus police contact the New York police and ask them to check this place. If we're here when they arrive they'll think we broke in the door."

"Yes, it's odd the police haven't turned up before this." He had that knowing look on his face that often infuriates me. "It's almost as if they were being kept away until the apartment could be searched."

"Well, she searched it and we've searched it. There's no manuscript here," I said.

"Don't be too sure."

"It was about an inch and a half thick, Simon—a good three hundred and fifty pages. There's nowhere it could be hidden we haven't looked."

He stood in the center of the room, gazing around. "Your mistake, my friend, is in regarding it as a complete unit, like a book. Think of it as three hundred fifty separate pages."

"What?"

He strode to the closest of the seven paintings and lifted it from the wall. There, taped to the back of the painting, was a thickness of typewritten sheets. "You see? Divide it into seven parts, tape it to the backs of these paintings, and each part becomes less than a quarter-inch thick—hardly noticeable with the thickness of these frames."

"How did you know?"

"Because the paintings are the key to everything. They became the logical hiding place when the rest of the apartment turned up nothing."

We quickly assembled the manuscript and Simon sat down at the kitchen table to read it. "What about the police?" I asked.

"They won't be coming. We're safe here."

"How do you know?"

But he didn't answer. He was already engrossed in the book. I joined him and tried reading some of it, but my eyelids soon grew heavy. Harvey Cross had not been a great prose stylist, and the world of literature, at least, had lost nothing by his untimely death.

Simon read through the night while I dozed on the couch. When he roused me it was near dawn, but he seemed as fresh as if he'd just awakened. "How was it, Simon?" I asked. "As bad as the first twenty pages?"

"It had a story to tell."

"The girl living in the forest has already been done," I reminded him, "in *Green Mansions*."

"But this girl is only a child of seven, and a flashback later in the manuscript tells how she came to be there."

"I know. She's the unicorn's daughter."

He started to speak, but a noise at the door distracted him. Moving quickly across the room, he yanked it open and Kate Talos all but fell in. She took a deep breath and said, "I came back."

"At five in the morning?" Simon said. "For another look for the manuscript?"

"No. I was hoping you might still be here. I want to take you to her."

"The child?"

She nodded. "If it's not too late."

"Do you think it might be?"

"As you pointed out, two people have died already. I've been awake all night thinking about that."

I had to interrupt. "Will one of you please tell me what's going on?"

"There will be time for that on the road," Simon said. "We're driving back to Olympus."

The Sunday-morning traffic along the Hudson seemed surprisingly light until I remembered it was not yet seven o'clock. As I drove, Simon and Kate Talos talked.

"How did you know there were seven?" she asked Simon.

"Because Gregory had done seven paintings. I recognized several of the names, of course, and it was not difficult to connect each name with its painting. It was reasonable to assume there were seven of you in all."

"And the child?"

"It was painted realistically in the portrait of the unicorn, not symbolized as the rest of you were. That told me there was a real child, and it also told me the subject of Harvey Cross's manuscript was more truth than fiction."

I saw her nod in the rearview mirror. "Ash loved the child. He had to portray her as she really was."

"Would somebody please tell me what this is all about?" I asked.

"The story begins a long time ago," Simon replied, "more than ten years ago, in that era of war protests and alternate life-styles and the heavy use of drugs by the counterculture. Harvey Cross's manuscript tells all about it. Seven people—four men and three women—went to live in a commune in the Catskills. They adopted the names of mythical creatures, perhaps because the commune was located near the village of Olympus and somehow they imagined themselves to be like those ancient Greek gods. But over the years there was a falling-out. One man left the commune completely and was cursed by some who remained. A woman bore a child by one of the other men and decided it should run wild in the woods and grow up as a free creature. The commune members fed the little girl, but there was no thought of sending her to school or allowing her to mingle with other children."

"The unicorn's daughter," I said.

"Exactly. Harvey Cross was the one who left the commune, but he kept his ties with at least one member. You, Miss Talos?"

"Yes," she admitted. "I did see Harvey after he left. We all did, really, except for Unicorn. Occasionally Harvey even went back and stayed at the house with Phoenix, but never when Griffin was there on weekends. He was afraid of Griffin, because of the child."

"Griffin was the child's father?"

"Yes. Isn't that in the manuscript?"

"Not in so many words, but it seemed likely."

"Would you mind telling me who this Griffin is?" I asked.

"That should be obvious, my friend. The name on the mailbox in Olympus was *A. Griffin*, just as the name on that apartment was *A. Gregory*. And the portrait of the little girl was so lovingly detailed it seemed more likely to be the painter's daughter than someone else's daughter. Griffin and Gregory were the same person. That's why he appeared in Olympus only on weekends—because he was employed at

Neptune Books during the week. The identification shouldn't surprise you, since Mr. Buraq at the store told us Griffin had passed by in his blue Ford—the car Gregory was driving."

The girl seemed surprised. "So you know Buraq too."

"Oh, yes. We know almost all of them." And he said to me, "Some of the seven adopted their mythical names for permanent use. Others, like Unicorn and Griffin and Dragon, found the names more suitable within the confines of the commune. Back in the city they kept their own names."

"What are the names?" I'd been so interested in the conversation that I hadn't realized we'd almost reached our destination. It was not yet eight o'clock.

"The seven creatures portrayed in Gregory's paintings. The bird rising from the ashes signified Hazel Phoenix. The man of brass guarding the island of Crete was Miss Talos here. Ash Gregory was Griffin, the winged creature with the lion's body. Sam Buraq, at the store where we stopped, was an Islamic beast, the winged horse with the face of a woman and a peacock's tail. I think by process of elimination we can conclude that Harvey Cross was Dragon before he deserted the commune and started writing his book. As for the remaining two—"

"There are cars at the house," Kate Talos said, pointing ahead of us.

"That is good," Simon Ark decided. "The commune is assembled for the last act."

"They won't let you take the child," Kate warned.

"We'll see."

Simon led the way to the door of the gingerbread house while Kate Talos and I trailed along. They must have seen our approach, because Hazel Phoenix greeted us and said, "Well, Kate—another traitor in our midst?"

"He found the manuscript, Hazel. He knows all about it. I didn't have to tell him a thing."

We stepped into the living room and I saw Sam Buraq sitting in a chair. The curtains blocking the adjoining room stirred and another man stepped in, holding a revolver in his hand. I recognized Toby Chimera, the sheriff's deputy we'd met the previous day.

"Thank God, you're here, Sheriff," I began. "These people are—"

"My friend," said Simon, "Mr. Chimera knows who these people are. Mr. Chimera is one of them."

"What?"

"Chimera—the fire-breathing monster with a lion's head, the body of a goat, and the tail of a serpent. Don't you remember my asking him about those creatures yesterday? The New York police never came to Gregory's apartment last night because Chimera delayed notifying them of the murder until Miss Talos had time to search for the manuscript."

"You know a great deal," Chimera said. "Too much."

"We came for the child," Simon told him. "You can't leave her to grow up in the woods like some sort of animal."

"That's none of your business," Hazel Phoenix told him.

"It's everyone's business. It's the law's business when two people are killed."

"Cross committed suicide," Sam Buraq reminded us.

"But Ash Gregory didn't. He was murdered because he'd finally seen the light and decided to rescue his daughter."

I was standing near the window looking out on the backyard that ran down to the woods and thought I saw a movement at their edge. "The law will deal with Gregory's murder," Chimera was saying.

"As a man of the law you must make a choice, Mr. Chimera," Simon told him. "You must serve your friends *or* uphold the law—you cannot do both. You can no longer cover up what goes on here. None of you are gods and you never were. Perhaps in truth you are more like the beasts whose names you bear." He turned to Phoenix. "The war is over now and the revolution never happened. It's time to come home with the rest of us."

Her face hardened as she stared at Simon. "Shoot him, Toby," she said.

"Simon! There's a child in the woods!" My shout brought

them running to the window in time to see a little girl in raggedy clothing vanish into the underbrush.

"We must hurry," Simon Ark urged, "before she gets away."

I didn't know if a bullet might stop us, but they let us go.

Simon didn't move fast and by the time we reached the edge of the woods the child was gone from sight. We went further in, searching for her. "We'll never find her," I said after a few minutes.

"Yes, we will. She's not afraid of people. Cross's manuscript said she liked strangers."

We hurried on into the deepest part of the forest until at last we came to a little clearing by a brook. And then we saw her, playing down by the water. The unicorn's daughter.

"Six of them, Simon. The four in the house and the two that are dead. We never got to the seventh. We never got to Unicorn."

The little girl turned at the sound of my voice and smiled up at us. "Who are you?" she asked. "Are you the wise Wufniks from the desert lands?"

"We are your new friends," Simon told her, kneeling in the grass by her side. "We have come to take you away with us."

"No, you won't!" a voice behind us said.

We turned and I saw the woman who stood at the edge of the woods, clad in jeans and a shirt. Though I'd never seen her in anything but her office dresses, I recognized Martha Scane at once.

Her head was down, sighting along the barrel of the shotgun pointed at us. At that angle it might almost have been a unicorn's horn protruding from her forehead.

"Get away from them, Lilith!" she shouted to the child, and the little girl obeyed instantly, running for cover in the woods.

"Martha—" I started to say.

She fired once, and the blast from the shotgun thudded into the ground near Simon. I saw little specks of blood appear on his hand.

Her second shot came like an echo of the first, almost drowning out the simultaneous crack of a revolver. But this shot was wide to the left, and then I saw the blood on Martha Scane's shirt.

She fell on her face in the soft grass, still clutching the shotgun.

Toby Chimera came out of the woods holding his service revolver. I saw that he was crying as he walked to her body, but I knew he had made his choice at last.

It was much later that day when Simon and I finally drove back to New York. The little girl, Lilith, would find foster parents to care for her and the four we'd left at the house would go their own ways when the investigation was completed.

"She did it all for the child," Simon explained as we drove. "In some misguided way she thought she was protecting Lilith from the world. She'd threatened to destroy Harvey Cross many times before, and when he heard her voice come over that intercom in your office he must have thought she was a true demon. He'd never known where she or Ash worked, you see, and he'd unwittingly brought his manuscript to the very publisher who employed her. It must have been an overwhelming rush of sheer despair that made him leap through your window to his death."

"And his death brought matters to a head."

Simon nodded. "Ash Gregory began to realize that his daughter had to be removed from the commune. She wasn't a goddess—only a child. He and Martha must have argued about it driving up yesterday. She got him to stop the car—perhaps by pretending to see Lilith in the woods—and then stabbed him to death. She had to keep the child at all costs, to raise her as a daughter of nature."

"And you knew it was Martha all along?"

"The way you described the event to me, only her voice on the intercom could have affected Harvey Cross so quickly. And doesn't it seem reasonable that if Gregory was the child's father, then the mother—and Gregory's killer—who was

157

driving up with him from New York, might be someone who worked with him during the week?"

"I can't believe the coincidence that brought Cross to the same publisher where they worked," I said. It was early evening now, and the lights of Manhattan were coming into view across the Hudson.

"Oh, it was no coincidence, my friend. Harvey Cross was lured to your office by the same conscious urge that brought Martha Scane and Ash Gregory there as employees in the first place. Don't you see it yet? These seven people believed in the old Roman and Greek gods. They established their commune in a place called Olympus and took the names of mythical creatures. It was not coincidence but a logical choice that brought them to a publisher named Neptune Books."

The Small Assassin

·

Ray Bradbury

Ray Bradbury's stories of mystery, terror, and the macabre compare in quality to his mainstream and science-fiction tales and to his poetry. Such collections as Dark Carnival *(1948),* October Country *(1955), and* Memory of Murder *(1984)—and his only mystery novel,* Death is a Lonely Business *(1985)— are testimony to his ability to baffle and terrify with the best in the business. "The Small Assassin," which first appeared in the pulp* Dime Mystery *in 1946, is among the best of his short chillers and contains a liberal dose of cauld grue.*

Just when the idea occurred to her that she was being murdered she could not tell. There had been little subtle signs, little suspicions for the past month; things as deep as sea tides in her, like looking at a perfectly calm stretch of tropic water, wanting to bathe in it and finding, just as the tide takes your body, that monsters dwell just under the surface, things unseen, bloated, many-armed, sharp-finned, malignant, and inescapable.

A room floated around her in an effluvium of hysteria. Sharp instruments hovered, and there were voices and people in sterile white masks.

My name, she thought, what is it?

Alice Leiber. It came to her. David Leiber's wife. But it gave her no comfort. She was alone with these silent, whispering white people and there was great pain and nausea and death-fear in her.

I am being murdered before their eyes. These doctors, these nurses, don't realize what hidden thing has happened

to me. David doesn't know. Nobody knows except me and—
the killer, the little murderer, the small assassin.

I am dying and I can't tell them now. They'd laugh and
call me one in delirium. They'll see the murderer and hold
him and never think him responsible for my death. But here
I am, in front of God and man, dying, no one to believe my
story, everyone to doubt me, comfort me with lies, bury me
in ignorance, mourn me, and salvage my destroyer.

Where is David? she wondered. In the waiting room,
smoking one cigarette after another, listening to the long
tickings of the very slow clock?

Sweat exploded from all of her body at once, and with it
an agonized cry. Now. Now! Try and kill me, she screamed.
Try, try, but I won't die! I won't!

There was a hollowness. A vacuum. Suddenly the pain
fell away. Exhaustion, and dusk came around. It was over.
Oh, God! She plummeted down and struck a black nothingness which gave way to nothingness and nothingness and
another and still another. . . .

Footsteps. Gentle, approaching footsteps.

Far away, a voice said, "She's asleep. Don't disturb her."

An odor of tweeds, a pipe, a certain shaving lotion. David
was standing over her. And beyond him the immaculate smell
of Dr. Jeffers.

She did not open her eyes. "I'm awake," she said quietly.
It was a surprise, a relief, to be able to speak, not to be dead.

"Alice," someone said, and it was David beyond her
closed eyes, holding her tired hands.

Would you like to meet the murderer, David? she thought.
I hear your voice asking to see him, so there's nothing but
for me to point him out to you.

David stood over her. She opened her eyes. The room
came into focus. Moving a weak hand, she pulled aside a
coverlet.

The murderer looked up at David Leiber with a small, red-
faced, blue-eyed calm. Its eyes were deep and sparkling.

"Why!" cried David Leiber, smiling. "He's a *fine* baby!"

The Small Assassin

* * *

Dr. Jeffers was waiting for David Leiber the day he came to take his wife and new child home. He motioned Leiber to a chair in his office, gave him a cigar, lit one for himself, sat on the edge of his desk, puffing solemnly for a long moment. Then he cleared his throat, looked David Leiber straight on, and said, "Your wife doesn't like her child, Dave."

"What!"

"It's been a hard thing for her. She'll need a lot of love this next year. I didn't say much at the time, but she was hysterical in the delivery room. The strange things she said—I won't repeat them. All I'll say is that she feels alien to the child. Now, this may simply be a thing we can clear up with one or two questions." He sucked on his cigar another moment, then said, "Is this child a 'wanted' child, Dave?"

"Why do you ask?"

"It's vital."

"Yes. Yes, it is a 'wanted' child. We planned it together. Alice was so happy, a year ago, when—"

"Mmmm—that makes it more difficult. Because if the child was unplanned, it would be a simple case of a woman hating the idea of motherhood. That doesn't fit Alice." Dr. Jeffers took his cigar from his lips, rubbed his hand across his jaw. "It must be something else, then. Perhaps something buried in her childhood that's coming out now. Or it might be the simple temporary doubt and distrust of any mother who's gone through the unusual pain and near death that Alice has. If so, then a little time should heal that. I thought I'd tell you, though, Dave. It'll help you be easy and tolerant with her if she says anything about—well—about wishing the child had been born dead. And if things don't go well, the three of you drop in on me. I'm always glad to see old friends, eh? Here, take another cigar along for—ah—for the baby."

It was a bright spring afternoon. Their car hummed along wide, tree-lined boulevards. Blue sky, flowers, a warm wind. Dave talked a lot, lit his cigar, talked some more. Alice

161

answered directly, softly, relaxing a bit more as the trip progressed. But she held the baby not tightly or warmly or motherly enough to satisfy the queer ache in Dave's mind. She seemed to be merely carrying a porcelain figurine.

"Well," he said at last, smiling. "What'll we name him?"

Alice Leiber watched green trees slide by. "Let's not decide yet. I'd rather wait until we get an exceptional name for him. Don't blow smoke in his face." Her sentences ran together with no change of tone. The last statement held no motherly reproof, no interest, no irritation. She just mouthed it and it was said.

The husband, disquieted, dropped the cigar from the window. "Sorry," he said.

The baby rested in the crook of his mother's arm, shadows of sun and trees changing his face. His blue eyes opened like fresh blue spring flowers. Moist noises came from the tiny pink, elastic mouth.

Alice gave her baby a quick glance. Her husband felt her shiver against him.

"Cold?" he asked.

"A chill. Better raise the window, David."

It was more than a chill. He rolled the window slowly up.

Suppertime.

Dave had brought the child from the nursery, propped him at a tiny, bewildered angle, supported by many pillows, in a newly purchased high chair.

Alice watched her knife and fork move. "He's not high-chair size," she said.

"Fun having him here, anyway," said Dave, feeling fine. "Everything's fun. At the office too. Orders up to my nose. If I don't watch myself I'll make another fifteen thousand this year. Hey, look at Junior, will you? Drooling all down his chin!" He reached over to wipe the baby's mouth with his napkin. From the corner of his eye he realized that Alice wasn't even watching. He finished the job.

"I guess it wasn't very interesting," he said, back again

162

at his food. "But one would think a mother'd take some interest in her own child!"

Alice jerked her chin up. "Don't speak that way! Not in front of him! Later, if you must."

"Later?" he cried. "In front of, in back of, what's the difference?" He quieted suddenly, swallowed, was sorry. "All right. Okay. I know how it is."

After dinner she let him carry the baby upstairs. She didn't tell him to; she *let* him.

Coming down, he found her standing by the radio, listening to music she didn't hear. Her eyes were closed, her whole attitude one of wondering, self-questioning. She started when he appeared.

Suddenly she was at him, against him, soft, quick; the same. Her lips found him, kept him. He was stunned. Now that the baby was gone, upstairs, out of the room, she began to breathe again, live again. She was free. She was whispering, rapidly, endlessly.

"Thank you, thank you, darling. For being yourself, always. Dependable, so very dependable!"

He had to laugh. "My father told me, 'Son, provide for your family!' "

Wearily, she rested her dark, shining hair against his neck.

"You've overdone it. Sometimes I wish we were just the way we were when we were first married. No responsibilities, nothing but ourselves. No—no babies."

She crushed his hand in hers, a supernatural whiteness in her face.

"Oh, Dave, once it was just you and me. We protected each other, and now we protect the baby, but get no protection from it. Do you understand? Lying in the hospital I had time to think a lot of things. The world is evil—"

"Is it?"

"Yes. It is. But laws protect us from it. And when there aren't laws, then love does the protecting. You're protected from my hurting you, by my love. You're vulnerable to me, of all people, but love shields you. I feel no fear of you, because love cushions all your irritations, unnatural instincts, hatreds, and immaturities. But—what about the baby? It's too young to know love, or a law of love, or anything, until we teach it. And in the meantime we're vulnerable to it."

"Vulnerable to a baby?" He held her away and laughed gently.

"Does a baby know the difference between right and wrong?" she asked.

"No. But it'll learn."

"But a baby is so new, so amoral, so conscience-free." She stopped. Her arms dropped from him and she turned swiftly.

"That noise? What was it?"

Leiber looked around the room. "I didn't hear—"

She stared at the library door. "In there," she said slowly.

Leiber crossed the room, opened the door, and switched the library lights on and off. "Not a thing." He came back to her. "You're worn out. To bed with you—right now."

Turning out the lights together they walked slowly up the soundless hall stairs, not speaking. At the top she apologized. "My wild talk, darling. Forgive me. I'm exhausted."

He understood, and said so.

She paused, undecided, by the nursery door. Then she fingered the brass knob sharply, walked in. He watched her approach the crib much too carefully, look down, and stiffen as if she'd been struck in the face. "David!"

Leiber stepped forward, reached the crib.

The baby's face was bright red and very moist; his small pink mouth opened and shut, opened and shut; his eyes were a fiery blue. His hands flew about in the air.

"Oh," said Dave, "he's just been crying."

"Has he?" Alice Leiber seized the crib railing to balance herself. "I didn't hear him."

"The door was closed."

"Is that why he breathes so hard, why his face is red?"

"Sure. Poor little guy. Crying all alone in the dark. He can sleep in our room tonight, just in case he cries."

"You'll spoil him," his wife said.

Leiber felt her eyes follow as he rolled the crib into their bedroom. He undressed silently, sat on the edge of the bed. Suddenly he lifted his head, swore under his breath, snapped his fingers. "Damn it! Forgot to tell you. I must fly to Chicago Friday."

"Oh, David." Her voice was lost in the room.

"I've put this trip off for two months, and now it's so critical I just *have* to go."

"I'm afraid to be alone."

"We'll have the new cook by Friday. She'll be here all the time. I'll only be gone a few days."

"I'm afraid. I don't know of what. You wouldn't believe me if I told you. I guess I'm crazy."

He was in bed now. She darkened the room; he heard her walk around the bed, throw back the cover, slide in. He smelled the warm woman-smell of her next to him. He said, "If you want me to wait a few days, perhaps I could—"

"No," she said, unconvinced. "You go. I know it's important. It's just that I keep thinking about what I told you. Laws and love and protection. Love protects you from me. But the baby—" She took a breath. "What protects you from him, David?"

Before he could answer, before he could tell her how silly it was, speaking of infants, she switched on the bed light abruptly.

"Look," she said, pointing.

The baby lay wide-awake in its crib, staring straight at him, with deep, sharp blue eyes.

The lights went out again. She trembled against him.

"It's not nice being afraid of the thing you birthed." Her whisper lowered, became harsh, fierce, swift. "He tried to kill me! He lies there, listens to us talking, waiting for you to go away so he can try to kill me again! I swear it!" Sobs broke from her.

"Please," he kept saying, soothing her. "Stop it, stop it. Please."

She cried in the dark for a long time. Very late she relaxed, shakingly, against him. Her breathing came soft, warm, regular, her body twitched its worn reflexes, and she slept.

He drowsed.

And just before his eyes lidded wearily down, sinking him into deeper and deeper tides, he heard a strange little sound of awareness and awakeness in the room.

The sound of small, moist, pinkly elastic lips.

The baby.

And then—sleep.

In the morning the sun blazed. Alice smiled.

David Leiber dangled his watch over the crib. "See, baby? Something bright. Something pretty. Sure. Sure. Something bright. Something pretty."

Alice smiled. She told him to go ahead, fly to Chicago, she'd be very brave, no need to worry. She'd take care of baby. Oh, yes, she'd take care of him, all right.

The airplane went east. There was a lot of sky, a lot of sun and clouds and Chicago running over the horizon. Dave was dropped into the rush of ordering, planning, banqueting, telephoning, arguing in conference. But he wrote letters each day and sent telegrams to Alice and the baby.

On the evening of his sixth day away from home he received the long-distance phone call. Los Angeles.

"Alice?"

"No, Dave. This is Jeffers speaking."

"Doctor!"

"Hold on to yourself, son. Alice is sick. You'd better get the next plane home. It's pneumonia. I'll do everything I can, boy. If only it wasn't so soon after the baby. She needs strength."

Leiber dropped the phone into its cradle. He got up, with no feet under him, and no hands and no body. The hotel room blurred and fell apart.

"Alice," he said, blindly starting for the door.

The propellers spun about, whirled, fluttered, stopped; time and space were put behind. Under his hand David felt the doorknob turn, under his feet the floor assumed reality, around him flowed the walls of a bedroom, and in the late afternoon sunlight Dr. Jeffers stood, turning from a window, as Alice lay waiting in her bed, something carved from a fall of winter snow. Then Dr. Jeffers was talking, talking continuously, gently, the sound rising and falling through the lamplight, a soft flutter, a white murmur of voice.

"You wife's too good a mother, Dave. She worried more about the baby than herself. . . ."

Somewhere in the paleness of Alice's face there was a sudden constriction that smoothed itself out before it was realized. Then, slowly, half-smiling, she began to talk, and she talked as a mother should about this, that, and the other thing, the telling detail, the minute-by-minute and hour-by-hour report of a mother concerned with a dollhouse world and the miniature life of that world. But she could not stop; the spring was wound tight, and her voice rushed on to anger, fear, and the faintest touch of revulsion, which did not change Dr. Jeffers's expression, but caused Dave's heart to match the rhythm of this talk that quickened and could not stop:

"The baby wouldn't sleep. I thought he was sick. He just lay, staring, in his crib, and late at night he'd cry. So loud, he'd cry, and he'd cry all night and all night. I couldn't quiet him, and I couldn't rest."

Dr. Jeffers's head nodded slowly, slowly. "Tired herself right into pneumonia. But she's full of sulfa now and on the safe side of the whole damn thing."

David felt ill. "The baby, what about the baby?"

"Fit as a fiddle; cock of the walk!"

"Thanks, Doctor."

The doctor walked off away and down the stairs, opened the front door faintly, and was gone.

"David!"

He turned to her frightened whisper.

"It was the baby again." She clutched his hand. "I try to lie to myself and say that I'm a fool, but the baby knew I was weak from the hospital, so he cried all night every night, and when he wasn't crying he'd be much too quiet. I knew if I switched on the light he'd be there, staring up at me."

David felt his body close in on itself like a fist. He remembered seeing the baby, feeling the baby, awake in the dark, awake very late at night when babies should be asleep. Awake and lying there, silent as thought, not crying, but watching from its crib. He thrust the thought aside. It was insane.

Alice went on. "I was going to kill the baby. Yes, I was. When you'd been gone only a day on your trip I went to his room and put my hands about his neck; and I stood there, for a long time, thinking, afraid. Then I put the covers up over his face and turned him over on his face and pressed him down and left him that way and ran out of the room.

He tried to stop her.

"No, let me finish," she said hoarsely, looking at the wall. "When I left his room I thought, It's simple. Babies smother every day. No one'll ever know. But when I came back to see him dead, David, he was alive! Yes, alive, turned over on his back, alive and smiling and breathing. And I couldn't touch him again after that. I left him there and I didn't come back, not to feed him or look at him or do anything. Perhaps the cook tended to him. I don't know. All I know is that his crying kept me awake, and I thought all through the night, and walked around the rooms, and now I'm sick." She was almost finished now. "The baby lies there and thinks of ways to kill me. Simple ways. Because he knows I know so much about him. I have no love for him; there is no protection between us; there never will be."

She was through. She collapsed inward on herself and finally slept. David Leiber stood for a long time over her, not able to move. His blood was frozen in his body; not a cell stirred anywhere, anywhere at all.

The next morning there was only one thing to do. He did it.

He walked into Dr. Jeffers's office and told him the whole thing, and listened to Jeffers's tolerant replies:

"Let's take this thing slowly, son. It's quite natural for mothers to hate their children, sometimes. We have a label for it—ambivalence. The ability to hate while loving. Lovers hate each other, frequently. Children detest their mothers—"

Leiber interrupted. "I never hated my mother."

"You won't admit it, naturally. People don't enjoy admitting hatred for their loved ones."

"So Alice hates her baby."

"Better say she has an obsession. She's gone a step further than plain, ordinary ambivalence. A cesarean operation brought the child into the world and almost took Alice out of it. She blames the child for her near death and her pneumonia. She's projecting her troubles, blaming them on the handiest object she can use as a source of blame. We *all* do it. We stumble into a chair and curse the furniture, not our own clumsiness. We miss a golf stroke and damn the turf or our club, or the make of ball. If our business fails we blame the gods, the weather, our luck. All I can tell you is what I told you before. Love her. Finest medicine in the world. Find little ways of showing your affection, give her security. Find ways of showing her how harmless and innocent the child is. Make her feel that the baby was worth the risk. After a while, she'll settle down, forget about death, and begin to love the child. If she doesn't come around in the next month or so, ask me. I'll recommend a good psychiatrist. Go on along now, and take that look off your face."

When summer came, things seemed to settle, become easier. Dave worked, immersed himself in office detail, but found much time for his wife. She in turn took long walks, gained strength, played an occasional light game of badminton. She rarely burst out anymore. She seemed to have rid herself of her fears.

Except on one certain midnight when a sudden summer wind swept around the house, warm and swift, shaking the trees like so many shining tambourines. Alice wakened, trembling, and slid over into her husband's arms, and let him console her and ask her what was wrong.

She said, "Something's here in the room, watching us."

He switched on the light. "Dreaming again," he said. "You're better, though. Haven't been troubled for a long time."

She sighed as he clicked off the light again, and suddenly she slept. Her held her, considering what a sweet, weird creature she was, for about half an hour.

He heard the bedroom door sway open a few inches.

There was nobody at the door. No reason for it to come open. The wind had died.

He waited. It seemed like an hour he lay silently in the dark.

Then, far away, wailing like some small meteor dying in the vast inky gulf of space, the baby began to cry in his nursery.

It was a small, lonely sound in the middle of the stars and the dark and the breathing of this woman in his arms and the wind beginning to sweep through the trees again.

Leiber counted to one hundred slowly. The crying continued.

Carefully disengaging Alice's arm he slipped from bed, put on his slippers, robe, and moved quietly from the room.

He'd go downstairs, he thought, fix some warm milk, bring it up, and—

The blackness dropped out from under him. His foot slipped and plunged. Slipped on something soft. Plunged into nothingness.

He thrust his hands out, caught frantically at the railing. His body stopped falling. He held. He cursed.

The "something soft" that had caused his feet to slip rustled and thumped down a few steps. His head rang. His heart hammered at the base of his throat, thick and shot with pain.

Why do careless people leave things strewn about a house? He groped carefully with his fingers for the object that had almost spilled him headlong down the stairs.

His hand froze, startled. His breath went in. His heart held one or two beats.

The thing he held in his hand was a toy. A large, cumbersome patchwork doll he had bought as a joke, for—

For the baby.

Alice drove him to work the next day.

She slowed the car halfway downtown, pulled to the curb,

170

and stopped it. Then she turned on the seat and looked at her husband.

"I want to go away on a vacation. I don't know if you can make it now, darling, but if not, please let me go alone. We can get someone to take care of the baby, I'm sure. But I just have to get away. I thought I was growing out of this—this *feeling*. But I haven't. I can't stand being in the room with him. He looks up at me as if he hates me too. I can't put my finger on it; all I know is I want to get away before something happens."

He got out on his side of the car, came around, motioned to her to move over, got in. "The only thing you're going to do is see a good psychiatrist. And if he suggests a vacation, well, okay. But this can't go on; my stomach's in knots all the time." He started the car. "I'll drive the rest of the way."

Her head was down; she was trying to keep back tears. She looked up when they reached his office building. "All right. Make the appointment. I'll go talk to anyone you want, David."

He kissed her. "Now you're talking sense, lady. Think you can drive home okay?"

"Of course, silly."

"See you at supper, then. Drive carefully."

"Don't I always? Bye."

He stood on the curb, watching her drive off, the wind taking hold of her long, dark, shining hair. Upstairs, a minute later, he phone Jeffers and arranged an appointment with a reliable neuro-psychiatrist.

The day's work went uneasily. Things fogged over, and in the fog he kept seeing Alice lost and calling his name. So much of her fear had come over to him. She actually had him convinced that the child was in some ways not quite natural.

He dictated long, uninspired letters. He checked some shipments downstairs. Assistants had to be questioned and kept going. At the end of the day he was exhausted, his head throbbed, and he was very glad to go home.

On the way down in the elevator he wondered, What if I

171

told Alice about the toy—that patchwork doll—I slipped on on the stairs last night? Lord, wouldn't *that* back her off? No, I won't ever tell her. Accidents are, after all, accidents.

Daylight lingered in the sky as he drove home in a taxi. In front of the house he paid the driver and walked slowly up the concrete walk, enjoying the light that was still in the sky and the trees. The white colonial front of the house looked unnaturally silent and uninhabited, and then he remembered this was Thursday and the hired help they were able to obtain from time to time were all gone for the day.

He took a deep breath of air. A bird sang behind the house. Traffic moved on the boulevard a block away. He twisted the key in the door. The knob turned under his fingers, oiled, silent.

The door opened. He stepped in, put his hat on the chair with his briefcase, started to shrug out of his coat, when he looked up.

Late sunlight streamed down the stairwell from the window near the top of the hall. Where the sunlight touched it took on the bright color of the patchwork doll sprawled at the bottom of the stairs.

But he paid no attention to the toy.

He could only look, and not move, and look again at Alice.

Alice lay in a broken, grotesque, pallid gesturing and angling of her thin body at the bottom of the stairs, like a crumpled doll that doesn't want to play anymore, ever.

Alice was dead.

The house remained quiet, except for the sound of his heart.

She was dead.

He held her head in his hands, he felt her fingers. He held her body. But she wouldn't live. She wouldn't even try to live. He said her name, out loud, many times, and he tried, once again, by holding her to him, to give her back some of the warmth she had lost, but that didn't help.

He stood up. He must have made a phone call. He didn't remember. He found himself suddenly upstairs. He opened the nursery door and walked inside and stared blankly at the crib. His stomach was sick. He couldn't see very well.

The baby's eyes were closed, but his face was red, moist with perspiration, as if he'd been crying long and hard.

"She's dead," said Leiber to the baby. "She's dead."

Then he started laughing low and soft and continuously for a long time until Dr. Jeffers walked in out of the night and slapped him again and again across his face.

"Snap out of it! Pull yourself together!"

"She fell down the stairs, Doctor. She tripped on a patch-work doll and fell. I almost slipped on it the other night myself. And now—"

The doctor shook him.

"Doc, Doc, Doc," said Dave hazily. "Funny thing. Funny. I—I finally thought of a name for the baby."

The doctor said nothing.

Leiber put his head back in his trembling hands and spoke the words. "I'm going to have him christened next Sunday. Know what name I'm giving him? I'm going to call him Lucifer."

It was eleven at night. A lot of strange people had come and gone through the house, taking the essential flame with them—Alice.

David Leiber sat across from the doctor in the library.

"Alice wasn't crazy," he said slowly. "She had good reason to fear the baby."

Jeffers exhaled. "Don't follow after her! She blamed the child for her sickness, now you blame it for her death. She stumbled on a toy, remember that. You can't blame the child."

"You mean Lucifer?"

"Stop calling him that!"

Leiber shook his head. "Alice heard things at night, mov-ing in the halls. You want to know what made those noises, Doctor? They were made by the baby. Four months old, moving in the dark, listening to us talk. Listening to every word!" He held to the sides of the chair. "And if I turned the lights on, a baby is so small. It can hide behind furniture, a door, against a wall—below eye level."

"I want you to stop this!" said Jeffers.

"Let me say what I think or I'll go crazy. When I went to Chicago, who was it kept Alice awake, tiring her into pneumonia? The baby! And when Alice didn't die, then he tried killing me. It was simple; leave a toy on the stairs, cry in the night until your father goes downstairs to fetch your milk and stumbles. A crude trick, but effective. It didn't get me. But it killed Alice dead."

David Leiber stopped long enough to light a cigarette. "I should have caught on. I'd turn on the lights in the middle of the night, many nights, and the baby'd be lying there, eyes wide. Most babies sleep all the time. Not this one. He stayed awake, thinking."

"Babies don't think."

"He stayed awake doing whatever he *could* do with his brain, then. What in hell do we know about a baby's mind? He had every reason to hate Alice; she suspected him for what he was—certainly not a normal child. Something—different. What do you know of babies, Doctor? The general run, yes. You know, of course, how babies kill their mothers at birth. Why? Could it be resentment at being forced into a lousy world like this one?"

Leiber leaned toward the doctor tiredly. "It all ties up. Suppose that a few babies out of all the millions born are instantaneously able to move, see, hear, think, like many animals and insects can. Insects are born self-sufficient. In a few weeks most mammals and birds adjust. But children take years to speak and to learn to stumble around on their weak legs.

"But suppose one child in a billion is—strange? Born perfectly aware, able to think, instinctively. Wouldn't it be a perfect setup, a perfect blind for anything the baby might want to do? He could pretend to be ordinary, weak, crying, ignorant. With just a *little* expenditure of energy he could crawl about a darkened house, listening. And how easy to place obstacles at the top of stairs. How easy to cry all night and tire a mother into pneumonia. How easy, right at birth, to be so close to the mother that *a few deft maneuvers might cause peritonitis*!''

"For God's sake!" Jeffers was on his feet. "That's a repulsive thing to say!"

"It's a repulsive thing I'm speaking of. How many mothers have died at the birth of their children? How many have suckled strange little improbabilities who cause death one way or another? Strange, red little creatures with brains that work in a bloody darkness we can't even guess at. Elemental little brains, warm with racial memory, hatred, and raw cruelty, with no more thought than self-preservation. And self-preservation in this case consisted of eliminating a mother who realized what a horror she had birthed. I ask you, Doctor, what is there in the world more selfish than a baby? Nothing!"

Jeffers scowled and shook his head helplessly.

Leiber dropped his cigarette down. "I'm not claiming any great strength for the child. Just enough to crawl around a little, a few months ahead of schedule. Just enough to listen all the time. Just enough to cry late at night. That's enough, more than enough."

Jeffers tried ridicule. "Call it murder, then. But murder must be motivated. What motive had the child?"

Leiber was ready with the answer. "What is more at peace, more dreamfully content, at ease, at rest, fed, comforted, unbothered, than an unborn child? Nothing. It floats in a sleepy, timeless wonder of nourishment and silence. Then suddenly it is asked to give up its berth, is forced to vacate, rushed out into a noisy, uncaring, selfish world where it is asked to shift for itself, to hunt, to feed from the hunting, to seek after a vanishing love that once was its unquestionable right, to meet confusion instead of inner silence and conservative slumber! And the child *resents* it! Resents the cold air, the huge spaces, the sudden departure from familiar things. And in the tiny filament of brain the only thing the child knows is selfishness and hatred because the spell has been rudely shattered. Who is responsible for this disenchantment,

175

this rude breaking of the spell? The mother. So here the new child has someone to hate with all its unreasoning mind. The mother has cast it out, rejected it. And the father is no better; kill him too! He's responsible in *his* way!''

Jeffers interrupted. ''If what you say is true, then every woman in the world would have to look on her baby as something to dread, something to wonder about.''

''And why not? Hasn't the child a perfect alibi? A thousand years of accepted medical belief protects him. By all natural accounts he is helpless, not responsible. The child is born hating. And things grow worse instead of better. At first the baby gets a certain amount of attention and mothering. But then as time passes, things change. When very new, a baby has the power to make parents do silly things when it cries or sneezes, jump when it makes a noise. As the years pass, the baby feels even that small power slip rapidly, forever away, never to return. Why shouldn't it grasp all the power it can have? Why shouldn't it jockey for position while it has all the advantages? In later years it would be too late to express its hatred. *Now* would be the time to strike.''

Leiber's voice was very soft, very low.

''My little boy baby, lying in his crib nights, his face moist and red and out of breath. From crying? No. From climbing slowly out of his crib, from crawling long distances through darkened hallways. My little boy baby. I want to kill him.''

The doctor handed him a water glass and some pills. ''You're not killing anyone. You're going to sleep for twenty-four hours. Sleep'll change your mind. Take this.''

Leiber drank down the pills and let himself be led upstairs to his bedroom, crying, and felt himself being put to bed. The doctor waited until he was moving into sleep, then left the house.

Leiber, alone, drifted down, down.

He heard a noise. ''What's—what's *that*?'' he demanded feebly.

Something moved in the hall.

David Leiber slept.

* * *

176

Very early the next morning Dr. Jeffers drove up to the house. It was a good morning, and he was here to drive Leiber to the country for a rest. Leiber would still be asleep upstairs. Jeffers had given him enough sedative to knock him out for at least fifteen hours.

He rang the doorbell. No answer. The servants were probably not up. Jeffers tried the front door, found it open, stepped in. He put his medical kit on the nearest chair.

Something white moved out of sight at the top of the stairs. Just a suggestion of a movement. Jeffers hardly noticed it.

The smell of gas was in the house.

Jeffers ran upstairs, crashed into Leiber's bedroom.

Leiber lay motionless on the bed, and the room billowed with gas, which hissed from a released jet at the base of the wall near the door. Jeffers twisted it off, then forced up all the windows and ran back to Leiber's body.

The body was cold. It had been dead quite a few hours.

Coughing violently, the doctor hurried from the room, eyes watering. Leiber hadn't turned on the gas himself. He *couldn't* have. Those sedatives had knocked him out, he wouldn't have wakened until noon. It wasn't suicide. Or was there the faintest possibility?

Jeffers stood in the hall for five minutes. Then he walked to the door of the nursery. It was shut. He opened it. He walked inside and to the crib.

The crib was empty.

He stood swaying by the crib for half a minute, then he said something to nobody in particular.

"The nursery door blew shut. You couldn't get back into your crib where it was safe. You didn't plan on the door blowing shut. A little thing like a slammed door can ruin the best of plans. I'll find you somewhere in the house, hiding, pretending to be something you are not." The doctor looked dazed. He put his hand to his head and smiled palely. "Now I'm talking like Alice and David talked. But I can't take any chances. I'm not sure of anything, but I can't take chances."

He walked downstairs, opened his medical bag on the chair, took something out of it, and held it in his hands.

Something rustled down the hall. Something very small and very quiet. Jeffers turned rapidly.

I had to operate to bring you into this world, he thought. Now I guess I can operate to take you out of it. . . .

He took half a dozen slow, sure steps forward into the hall. He raised his hand into the sunlight.

"See, baby! Something bright—something pretty!"

A scalpel.

Double Edge

•

Robert J. Randisi

*No one has done more to promote the subgenre of American private-detective fiction than Robert J. Randisi. He is the founder of the Private Eye Writers of America, and thus far has edited three well-received volumes of original stories by PWA's members—*The Eyes Have it *(1984),* Mean Streets *(1986), and* An Eye for Justice *(1988). A prolific writer of both mysteries and Westerns, Randisi has created three successful fictional private eyes of his own: Henry Po, an investigator for the New York State Racing Club* (The Disappearance of Penny); *Manhattan-based Miles Jacoby* (The Steinway Collection, Full Contact); *and Brooklyn-based Nick Delvecchio* (No Exit from Brooklyn). *"Double Edge" features Delvecchio in a case involving a man whose double-edged anger leads him to irrationally abuse his wife.*

1

I have done laundry in laundromats when being there was a bachelor's delight. In fact, up to about six months ago there were these three girls who were roommates living in the neighborhood, and they used to take turns doing the laundry. In the summer, those girls would come in dressed in shorts and halter tops, and in the winter—when they took off their coats—they'd be wearing tight jeans and leg warmers. I mean, during that time I looked *forward* to doing the laundry. But they only lived there for a few months and then moved on, and the laundry went back to being a chore.

As a whole, the regular people who used this laundromat—

which was right on the corner of my block of Sackett Street
in downtown Brooklyn—were pretty nice, but they were no
great shakes to look at. Mrs. Goldstein was a woman in her
late fifties who sort of adopted me—telling me what detergent
to use, and what fabric softener, and "Oye, boychick, don't
wash those in cold water!"—but she resembled the front end
of a battleship; big "Mad Dog" Bolinsky, a bruiser who
worked for the department of sanitation, looked like the *whole*
battleship; Mr. Quinn, the Greek grocer, was in his late fifties also, and Mrs. Goldstein knew he was a widower just as
he knew she was a widow.

And then there was Sam. Her real name was Samantha
Karson, but she published her romance novels under the name
"Kit Karson"—when she sold them, that is. Kit lived across
the hall from me and once in a blue moon took time away
from her typewriter to take in a movie with me, or to do her
laundry. She wasn't the neatest person in the world, but she
was pretty and easy to get along with.

When Linda Kellogg first walked into the laundromat, nobody spoke to her beyond saying hello because that wasn't
the way things were done. If she came back again, indicating
that she might become a regular, then everyone would make
an effort to get to know her. Mrs. Goldstein, of course, would
make the initial approach, and then the introductions.

I noticed a few other things, though, that first day: Linda
Kellogg wore a wedding ring, she had a bruise alongside her
left eye, and as she was putting her clothes into the machine
I saw a blouse with some blood on it. When she turned my
way at one point I saw that her lip was split on the right side.
This could all have been a result of anything from a mugging
to a family dispute, and I really didn't give it a second thought
after leaving the laundromat.

The second time she came I found out her name—from
Mrs. Goldstein, of course. During the course of the next few
weeks she came every Friday—which was my regular day—
and Mrs. Goldstein busied herself getting all the dope.

Linda usually had a small bruise here or there when she
me—she *could* have been clumsy—but finally one Friday

I noticed her talking to Mrs. Goldstein and crying. And that was when nice Mrs. Goldstein dragged her over to me.

"This quiet fella is Nick Delvecchio, Linda. He's a nice enough boy to be Jewish," Mrs. Goldstein said, which was the highest praise she could have given anyone. Then she added, "And he's the best private eye in Brooklyn," which was, at best, a dubious distinction.

"Hello," Linda said meekly.

"We've met in passing," I said.

"Linda has a problem, Nick," Mrs. Goldstein said, "and I told her you could help her."

"Is that a fact? What kind of problem?" I asked, looking at the mouse beneath her right eye.

I hated domestic cases.

"Tell him, dearie," Mrs. Goldstein urged Linda Kellogg.

Linda looked from Mrs. Goldstein to me a couple of times and I said, "Mrs. Goldstein, isn't your machine finished?"

"What?" The older woman looked behind her. Her wash was still being swirled about inside the machine. But never let it be said that Mrs. Goldstein couldn't take a hint.

"Hmm," she said, giving me the eye. "You help her, Nick. She's a nice girl."

"We'll see, Mrs. Goldstein."

"Hmm," she said again, and went back to her machine and her book.

"She's a nice old busybody," I told Linda.

"She's a nice woman."

"Do you want to tell me about it, or do you want to just make her think you're telling me?"

"I think I'll talk to you, Mr. Delvecchio. Even if you can't help me it might do me some good."

"All right," I said. "You don't mind if I fold my shirts while we talk, do you?"

"Oh," she said, as if the thought of a man folding his own belongings surprised her, "I'll do that."

She walked to my pile of laundry and began to talk and fold at the same time.

Put succinctly, it seemed that over the past few months—

since they moved to this neighborhood—her husband had taken to beating her up on occasion. It always seemed to take place after he came home from work, even if she had cooked him his favorite dinner.

"Some nights he's fine, very loving," she said, "and other nights the slightest thing will set him off. I can't understand it."

"Do you know of any problems he might be having, either with family or his business?"

"No. He has no brothers or sisters, no aunts or uncles. Both his parents are dead."

"Do you think he might have a girlfriend?"

She looked at me with shock. "I *never* thought of that."

Was she on the level? Could she be that innocent?

"Linda, what is it you want me to do if not to find out about a girlfriend?"

"I—I want you to find out what is making him so angry. If he didn't come home angry, then he wouldn't have any reason to hit me."

"Have you thought about leaving him?"

"And go where? I have no family. I barely have any friends. I wouldn't have anyplace to go, Mr. Delvecchio. Besides, I love him. Will you help me?"

She finished folding my laundry and stared at me, waiting for my answer.

Helpless before the tragic look in her eyes I said, "I'll try '

"Thank you, Mr. Delvecchio, thank you."

I smiled halfheartedly and said, "Call me Nick."

2

Linda Kellogg's husband's name was Dan, and he worked as a dispatcher for a trucking firm with an office on Metropolitan Avenue in the Greenpoint section of Brooklyn. According to Linda, the position was a promotion for him, and the raise in salary was what enabled them to move to a better neighborhood. If they considered downtown Brooklyn a better neighborhood, I hated to think where they'd been living before.

I followed Dan Kellogg to and from work for a week and I found out nothing except that he didn't have a girlfriend—which, for all I knew, might have been what was making him so angry. All he ever did was go home, sometimes stopping in a bar first, usually the same one. I followed him into the bar and watched him sit alone each time and drink a beer. One for the road before going home, I guessed.

I spoke to Linda after the week was up and she told me that Dan hadn't laid a finger on her since she hired me. I asked if she thought he knew about me and she said she was sure he didn't. She asked me to please stay on the case for a little while longer and I agreed.

After another week there was still no indication that *anything* was bothering Dan Kellogg, and still no sign of a girlfriend, either. So I figured the problem had resolved itself. I felt guilty taking a fee from Linda Kellogg, and when she asked me how much she owed me, I charged her for one week instead of two. We severed our business relationship in the same place it had started, the laundromat.

After Linda left that day, Mrs. Goldstein came over. "Did you help her, Nicky?"

"I tried, Mrs. Goldstein, but I couldn't find out anything."

"You must have done something good, Nicky. The brute hasn't touched her in two weeks."

"I think the problem just solved itself."

Looking doubtful she said, "Mark my words, boychick. Problems very rarely solve themselves. Somebody usually has to solve them."

"I'll remember that," I said, and left with my clean laundry.

The following week I walked into the laundromat and got the dirtiest look from Mrs. Goldstein she could muster.

"So, Mister Smart-Guy?" she asked, folding her arms across her ample chest.

"So what, Mrs. Goldstein?"

"What have you got to say for yourself?"

"About what?"

"Linda Kellogg."

"Mrs. Goldstein," I said, "could we stop playing twenty questions and just get down to the nitty gritty?"

"Sure, tough-guy private eye talk you can do," she said, accusingly, "but when it comes to helping a little girl whose husband beats her up and puts her in the hospital—"

"Wait a minute," I said. "Are you telling me that Linda Kellogg is in the hospital?"

"That's what I said."

"What hospital?" I asked, putting my laundry basket down on her machine.

"That one near Atlantic Avenue."

"Long Island College Hospital?"

"That's the one."

"Mrs. Goldstein, will you do my laundry and hold it for me?"

"Are you going to the hospital?"

"Yes."

"Then I'll do your laundry, Mister Private Eye. You go and do what you should have done before, give that brute what-for."

I wasn't about to give her husband "what-for," but I did want to talk to Linda Kellogg. I wasn't feeling very good at that moment.

Linda was sharing a room with three other women. I pulled the curtain all the way around her bed so that we could have some privacy. I was glad not to find her husband there.

"He's at work," she said. "He said he'll come up later."

"Tell me what happened?"

She didn't look too bad, although her face was bruised and swollen so that she had to speak out of the corner of her mouth. Most of the damage had been done to the rib area, where he had broken two of them.

"I fell," she said.

"Linda, this is me you're talking to."

184

She looked directly at me and lied, and I had the feeling that she was trying to tell me something *by* lying to me.

"I fell," she said.

For some reason, she didn't want to admit—even to me—that her husband had hospitalized her.

"Who called for an ambulance?"

"Dan did."

"Did anyone call the police?"

"No police," she said, shaking her head.

"Linda, he could have killed you—"

"I want to hire you again," she said. "Find out what's making him so angry, Nick. Please!"

"I'll find out, all right," I said, "but I've already been paid and I didn't accomplish anything. This time it's on the house."

She closed her eyes and said, "Thank you."

When I left her she seemed to be asleep. I wondered what she had told the doctor about how she'd received her injuries.

I figured there was only one way I was going to find out what was making Dan Kellogg so violent. And that was to ask him.

3

Dan Kellogg's place of business was on Metropolitan Avenue, in an industrial area of Greenpoint, and I cabbed it there from the hospital.

Greenpoint is a funny section of Brooklyn, because in order to get there from some parts of the borough, you've got to go into *Queens* and then come *back* into Brooklyn. My driver, however, simply jumped onto the BQE—the Brooklyn-Queens Expressway—at the Atlantic Avenue entrance and jumped off at the McGuiness Boulevard exit, which left us just a few blocks from our destination.

When I got there I asked somebody where to find Dan Kellogg and was directed to the dispatcher's booth.

The man in the booth was a burly gent of about thirty, with thick brown hair and a mustache. It was the first time I had been closer to Dan Kellogg than fifty feet.

"Kellogg?" I said, leaning my head in the window.

"Just a sec," he said. He held a short conversation with someone over the radio, then turned to me and said, "Can I help you?"

"I'd like to talk to you if you can get relieved."

"Relieved?" he said, laughing. "Mister, you know how many trucks I'm juggling? I can't get just anybody to relieve me. What's it about?"

"It's about your wife."

"Linda?" he asked, frowning. "You from the hospital?"

"No," I said. "I'm investigating her 'accident.' "

His eyes widened momentarily, and then he licked his lips.

"There's a lounge down the hall," he said then. "Wait for me there, huh?"

"Sure."

There was another man in the lounge, but when I entered he left. It took Kellogg about five minutes to find somebody to relieve him.

"Why are the police interested in my wife's accident?" he asked, sitting next to me on a worn leather couch. "Did somebody say something . . . ?"

"About what, Mr. Kellogg?" I asked, prodding him.

"Nothing," he muttered. "What do you want to know?"

"I want to know how your wife received her injuries."

"Didn't the hospital tell you?"

"I want you to tell me."

"She fell . . . while changing a light bulb."

"Really?"

"Yes . . . really," he said. "That's what happened."

"Can I see your hands, Mr. Kellogg?"

"What for?"

"I'm curious."

"Look," Kellogg said, standing up and keeping his hands behind him, "I don't know what you're after, but I think I want to see your identification."

"That won't be necessary, Mr. Kellogg," I said, standing up. He was about my height, but he had me by twenty pounds. Still, I was pretty sure I could take him. Men who beat up on women can very rarely handle another man. "I'm not a policeman, and I never said I was."

His face turned red. He forgot about his hands and allowed them come into sight, and I could see that both hands had skinned knuckles. "Who the hell are you?"

"Somebody who'd like to know what kind of man takes out his anger on a woman," I said. "And not just any woman, but his wife."

His hands closed into fists, but he held them at his side as he snapped, "Get out of here!"

"You beat up your wife, Mr. Kellogg," I said, taking out one of my business cards. "You know it, and I know it." I tucked the card into his shirt pocket and said, "I'm going to prove it, and I'm going to find out why, but for now just know this. If you touch that woman again, I'm personally going to break you in half."

4

I started tailing Kellogg again, but still to no avail. The day Linda got out of the hospital, he picked her up, brought her flowers, and took her home. They looked very cozy.

I went home that night and did something I hadn't done in a few days. I read the papers, going back three days. I was flipping through the news section when my eye was caught by a story on page three. It was about a truck hijacking, and the truck was one of the company's that Dan Kellogg worked for. The paper was dated the day he last abused his wife.

I picked up the phone and called Linda Kellogg, assuming—and hoping—that Dan Kellogg was at work. He was. I asked her if she could remember the last few dates that Dan had taken out his anger on her. She thought a few moments, checked a calendar, and gave me four dates that she thought were right.

"Tell me something else, Linda. You said the first beating took place after you moved here, right?"

"Yes."

"Did it also coincide with Dan's new job?"

"Well, of course. We moved here because he got the promotion."

"All right."

"Nick, have you found out something?"

"I don't know yet. I'll give you a call."

I hung up and left, heading for the main Brooklyn library near Grand Army Plaza. There I checked the files for the newspapers on the days after Dan Kellogg abused his wife. In each paper there was a report of a truck hijacking, and in two of the four cases, the trucks were from Dan Kellogg's company.

And he was the new dispatcher. How difficult would it be for him to give somebody information on what a particular truck was carrying, and then to set up a hijacking?

I made photocopies of the stories and left the library. It was dark, and I started walking so I could think. There was one thing that bothered me. Of the five hijackings I had read about, only three involved trucks that belonged to Kellogg's firm. If Kellogg was involved, then what about the other two? And why, after each hijacking, did he go home angry enough to beat his wife? Could he have been involved against his will? Was *that* what was making him so angry?

When I got home I called Linda again and asked her if her husband was home from work yet. He wasn't.

"Did you find out—"

"I have to find him first, Linda, and then I can answer your question. I'll call."

I had followed Kellogg enough times after work to know where he might be.

On more than one occasion he had dropped into the same bar on the way home, a place on Fourth Avenue. I took a cab over there and went inside looking for him. He was seated at the bar, with a mug of beer in front of him. I slid onto the stool next to him and said, "Hi, Danny, boy."

"What are you doing here?"

"I came to talk to you."

"Well, I don't want to talk to you."

"I think you'd better."

He turned his head and looked at me. I had never seen such empty eyes before.

"Look, friend, I know you're trying to help Linda, but you don't know—"

"I know more than you think."

"Like what?"

"Like about the hijackings."

Surprise brought him off his stool. "You think you know about that, huh?" he demanded. "Big shot p.i., huh?" He faced me, clenching his hands angrily.

"You want to try me, Kellogg?"

"Yeah," he said, and hit me.

The blow didn't hurt that much, but it sure as hell surprised me. And it knocked me off my stool and onto the floor.

"Come on," Kellogg said, standing over me, "get up. Let's see how tough you are."

"Take it easy," I said. I was seeing the Dan Kellogg that his wife saw. "What the hell is making you so mad?"

"I thought you knew."

Yeah, I thought I knew, too. But I'd also had him pegged as a wife beater who'd back away from a real fight. I could be wrong as often as I was right.

I got to my feet and said, "Wait a second—" but he swung again. I stepped away from it. "Kellogg—" I said, but he wasn't listening. The emptiness that had been in his eyes had been replaced by rage. He advanced on me and swung a third time.

I stepped *inside* this blow and landed one of my own to his belly. He was softer than he looked there, and all of the air—and fight—went out of him. He fell to the floor on his butt, gasping for air.

I glanced around the bar. What few people were there decided that the fight was over and looked away.

"You want a beer?" the bartender asked me.

"Why not?"

By the time he brought my beer Kellogg had his breath back.

"I'm gonna help you up," I said. "If you swing at me again we're gonna go all the way. Got it?"

"Yeah," he said hoarsely.

I helped him up and onto his stool again, then took the one next to him.

"What do you know about those hijackings?" he asked.

"It wasn't hard to figure. The last five times you hit Linda were days following a hijacking, and the hijackings started after you got promoted to dispatcher."

"Yeah," he said. "It's easy for me to let them know which trucks to hit, where and when."

"Two of the trucks weren't yours, though."

"That's no problem. I talk to dispatchers from other firms. I can get information."

"Why are you doing it?"

He didn't answer that right away. He said, "Look, I admit that I've . . . hit Linda a couple of times, but this last time, when she went to the hospital . . . it wasn't me. I swear it wasn't."

"Sure. She fell screwing in a light bulb."

"No . . . it was Harry."

"Who's Harry?"

"Her cousin, Harry Sullivan."

"Her own cousin beat her up?"

"That's right."

"Why?"

"It was a message to me."

"Wait," I said. "Are you telling me that this cousin Harry is involved in the hijackings?"

"You're getting it now," he said. "When he found out from Linda that I'd been promoted, he came to see me. He's got a record, see, and he saw my promotion as a chance for him and his friends to make some money."

"And they got you to go along by threatening Linda?"

"That, and he said he'd tell my boss I was passing information, just to get me fired."

"Nice family."

"He's a bum," he said, and I was tempted to tell him that

he was, too. This Harry threatens to hurt Linda, so Kellogg goes along with the hijackings—and then *he* hurts Linda.

"Did you tell Linda?"

"No, but after this last hijacking I tried to pull out, and Harry went to see her."

"So now she knows?"

"Yes."

"Why didn't she say something?"

"Hey, he's her family."

One thing I had to say for Linda Kellogg, she was loyal to the men in her family, even if it was misplaced loyalty. Still, she had come to me—looking for somebody to make things right.

"And you let this bum get away with knocking your wife around?"

"Yeah," he said, wrapping his hand around his beer mug, "yeah, I did . . . but no more."

"You ready to turn them in?"

"How? I'd have to turn myself in."

"We'll talk to the police together. I know a lieutenant named Wager who would be very interested in hearing your story."

"And then what?"

"And then they'll set something up with you, to catch the hijackers in the act."

"Will I go to jail?"

"I doubt it. You were coerced, and you'll cooperate. I don't think you'll go to jail." I leaned closer to him and said, "*I'll* see that you go to jail, though, if you ever lay a hand on Linda again."

He said he wouldn't and for Linda's sake I hoped he was telling the truth. In his anger and frustration he had lashed out at the easiest prey available, but deep down there was another anger, this one directed at his wife. It was *her* cousin who was forcing him to do these things, so it had to be *her* fault.

His was a double-edged anger, carved out of frustration and guilt. I could help with some of it, but the rest was up

DEADLY DOINGS

to him. He still had to come to terms with the fact that he was a man who battered his wife because of something *he* couldn't handle.

Chinese Puzzle

•

Ed McBain

*Before he created his hugely successful 87th Precinct series
in 1956, Ed McBain (Evan Hunter) was a frequent contributor to the mystery and detective magazines under a variety
of names. Not surprisingly, the best of his early crime stories
are embryonic 87th-style police procedurals; "Chinese Puzzle" is one—a clever tale in which a Chinese woman named
Mary Chang suddenly fulfills the prophecy of an unidentified
telephone voice telling her she is about to die. Other of
McBain's early procedurals and suspense stories can be
found in such fine collections as* The Jungle Kids *(1956) and*
The McBain Brief *(1984).*

The girl slumped at the desk just inside the entrance doorway of the small office. The phone lay uncradled, just the
way she'd dropped it. An open pad of telephone numbers
rested just beyond reach of her lifeless left hand.

The legend on the frosted glass door read *Gotham Lobster
Company*. The same legend was repeated on the long row of
windows facing Columbus Avenue, and the sun glared hotly
through those windows, casting the name of the company
onto the wooden floor in shadowed black.

Mr. Godrow, President of Gotham Lobster, stood before
those windows now. He was a big man with rounded shoulders and a heavy paunch. He wore a gray linen jacket over
his suit pants, and the pocket of the jacket was stitched with
the word *Gotham*. He tried to keep his meaty hands from
fluttering, but he wasn't good at pretending. The hands wan-

dered restlessly, and then exploded in a gesture of impatience.

"Well, aren't you going to do something?" he demanded.

"We just got here, Mr. Godrow," I said. "Give us a little . . ."

"The police are supposed to be so good," he said petulantly. "This girl drops dead in my office and all you do is stand around and look. Is this supposed to be a sightseeing tour?"

I didn't answer him. I looked at Donny, and Donny looked back at me, and then we turned our attention to the dead girl. Her left arm was stretched out across the top of the small desk, and her body was arched crookedly, with her head resting on the arm. Long black hair spilled over her face, but it could not hide the contorted, hideously locked grin on her mouth. She wore a tight silk dress, slit on either side in the Oriental fashion, buttoned to the throat. The dress had pulled back over a portion of her right thigh, revealing a roll-gartered stocking. The tight line of her panties was clearly visible through the thin silk of her dress. The dead girl was Chinese, but her lips and face were blue.

"Suppose you tell us what happened, Mr. Godrow," I said.

"Freddie can tell you," Godrow answered. "Freddie was sitting closer to her."

"Who's Freddie?"

"My boy," Godrow said.

"Your son?"

"No, I haven't any children. My boy. He works for me."

"Where is he now, sir?"

"I sent him down for some coffee. After I called you." Godrow paused, and then reluctantly said, "I didn't think you'd get here so quickly."

"Score one for the Police Department," Donny murmured.

"Well, you fill us in until he gets back, will you?" I said.

"All right," Godrow answered. He said everything grudgingly, as if he resented our presence in his office, as if this whole business of dead bodies lying around should never have been allowed to happen in his office. "What do you want to know?"

"What did the girl do here?" Donny asked.

"She made telephone calls."

"Is that all?"

"Yes. Freddie does that, too, but he also runs the addressing machine. Freddie . . ."

"Maybe you'd better explain your operation a little," I said.

"I sell lobsters," Godrow said.

"From this office?" Donny asked skeptically.

"We take the orders from this office," Godrow explained, warming up a little. It was amazing the way they always warmed up when they began discussing their work. "My plant is in Boothbay Harbor, Maine."

"I see."

"We take the orders here, and then the lobsters are shipped down from Maine, alive of course."

"I like lobsters," Donny said. "Especially lobster tails."

"Those are not lobsters," Godrow said indignantly. "Those are crawfish. African rock lobster. There's a big difference."

"Who do you sell to, Mr. Godrow?" I asked.

"Restaurants. That's why Mary worked for me."

"Is that the girl's name? Mary?"

"Yes, Mary Chang. You see, we do a lot of business with Chinese restaurants. Lobster Cantonese, you know, like that. They buy small lobsters usually, and in half-barrel quantities for the most part, but they're good steady customers."

"And Miss Chang called these Chinese restaurants, is that right?"

"Yes. I found it more effective that way. She spoke several Chinese dialects, and she inspired confidence, I suppose. At any rate, she got me more orders than any Occidental who ever held the job."

"And Freddie? What does he do?"

"He calls the American restaurants. We call them every morning. Not all of them each morning, of course, but those we feel are ready to reorder. We give them quotations, and we hope they'll place orders. We try to keep our quotes low. For example, our Jumbos today were going for—''

"How much did Miss Chang receive for her duties, Mr. Godrow?''

"She got a good salary.''

"How much?''

"Why? What difference does it make?''

"It might be important, Mr. Godrow. How much?''

"Forty-five a week, plus a dollar-fifty commission on each barrel order from a new customer.'' Godrow paused. ''Those are good wages, Mr. . . .''

"Parker. Detective-Sergeant Ralph Parker.''

"Those are good wages, Sergeant Parker.'' He paused again. ''Much more than my competitors are paying.''

"I wouldn't know about that, Mr. Godrow, but I'll take your word for it. Now . . .''

A shadow fell across the floor, and Godrow looked up and said, ''Ah, Freddie, it's about time.''

2.

I turned to the door, expecting to find a sixteen-year-old kid maybe. Freddie was not sixteen, nor was he twenty-six. He was closer to thirty-six, and he was a thin man with sparse hair and a narrow mouth. He wore a rumpled tweed suit and a stained knitted tie.

"This is my boy,'' Godrow said. ''Freddie, this is Detective-Sergeant Parker and . . .''

"Katz,'' Donny said. ''Donald Katz.''

"How do you do?'' Freddie said.

"Since you're here,'' I said, ''suppose you tell us what happened this morning, Freddie.''

"Mr. Godrow's coffee . . .'' Freddie started apologetically.

"Yes, yes, my coffee,'' Godrow said. Freddie brought it to his desk, put it down, and then fished into his pocket for some silver which he deposited alongside the paper container. Godrow counted the change meticulously, and then took the lid from the container and dropped in one lump of sugar. He opened his top drawer and put the remaining lump of sugar into a small jar there.

"What happened this morning, Freddie?" I asked.

"Well, I got in at about nine, or a little before," he said.

"Were you here then, Mr. Godrow?"

"No. I didn't come in until nine-thirty or so."

"I see. Go on, Freddie."

"Mary . . . Miss Chang was here. I said good morning to her, and then we got down to work."

"I like my people to start work right away," Godrow said. "No nonsense."

"Was Miss Chang all right when you came in, Freddie?"

"Yes. Well, that is . . . she was complaining of a stiff neck, and she seemed to be very jumpy, but she started making her phone calls, so I guess she was all right."

"Was she drinking anything?"

"Sir?"

"Was she drinking anything?"

"No, sir."

"Did she drink anything all the while you were here?"

"No, sir. I didn't see her, at least."

"I see." I looked around the office and said, "Three phones here, is that right?"

"Yes," Godrow answered. "One extension for each of us. You know how they work. You push a button on the face of the instrument, and that's the line you're on. We can all talk simultaneously that way, on different lines."

"I know how it works," I said. "What happened then, Freddie?"

"We kept calling, that's all. Mr. Godrow came in about nine-thirty, like he said, and we kept on calling while he changed to his office jacket."

"I like to wear this jacket in the office," Godrow explained. "Makes me feel as if I'm ready for the day's work, you know."

"Also saves wear and tear on your suit jacket," Donny said.

Godrow seemed about to say something, but I beat him to the punch. "Did you notice anything unusual about Miss Chang's behavior, Mr. Godrow?"

"Well, yes, as a matter of fact. As Freddie told you, she was quite jumpy. I dropped a book at one point, and she almost leaped out of her chair."

"Did *you* see her drink anything?"

"No."

"All right, Freddie, what happened after Mr. Godrow came in?"

"Well, Mary started making another phone call. This was at about nine-thirty-five. She was behaving very peculiar by this time. She was twitching and well . . . she was having . . . well, like spasms. I asked her if she was all right, and she flinched when I spoke, and then she went right on with her call. I remember the time because I started a call at about the same time. You see, we have to get our orders in the morning if Boothbay is to deliver the next morning. That means we're racing against the clock, sort of, so you learn to keep your eye on it. Well, I picked up my phone and started dialing, and then Mary started talking Chinese to someone on her phone. She sits at the desk right next to mine, you see, and I can hear everything she says."

"Do you know who she was calling?"

"No. She always dials . . . dialed . . . the numbers and then started talking right off in Chinese. She called all the Chinese restau—"

"Yes, I know. Go on."

"Well, she was talking on her phone, and I was talking on mine, and all of a sudden she said in English, 'No, why?' "

"She said this in English?"

"Yes."

"Did you hear this, Mr. Godrow?"

"No. My desk is rather far away, over here near the windows. But I heard what she said next. I couldn't miss hearing that. She yelled it out loud."

"What was that, sir?"

198

"She said 'Kill me? No! No!' "

"What happened then?"

"Well," Freddie said, "I was still on the phone. I looked up, and I didn't know *what* was going on. Mary started to shove her chair back, and then she began . . . shaking all over . . . like . . . like . . ."

"The girl had a convulsion," Godrow put in. "If I'd known she was predisposed toward . . ."

"Did she pass out?"

"Yes," Freddie said.

"What did you do then?"

"I didn't know what to do."

"Why didn't you call a doctor?"

"Well, we did, after the second convulsion."

"When was that?"

"About . . . oh I don't know . . . ten, fifteen minutes later. I really don't know."

"And when the doctor came, what did he say?"

"Well, he didn't come," Freddie said apologetically.

"Why not? I thought you called him."

"The girl died after the second convulsion," Godrow said. "Good Lord, man, she turned blue, you saw her. Why should I pay a doctor for a visit when the girl was dead? I canceled the call."

"I see."

"It's obvious she was predisposed toward convulsions, and whoever spoke to her on the phone frightened her, bringing one on," Godrow said. "He obviously told her he was going to kill her or something."

"This is all very obvious, is it, Mr. Godrow?" I asked.

"Well, of course. You can see the girl is blue. What else . . ."

"Lots of things," I said. "Lots of things could have caused her coloration. But only one thing would put that grin on her face."

"What's that?" Godrow asked.

"Strychnine poisoning," I said.

3.

When we got back to Homicide I put a call through to Mike Reilly. The coroner had already confirmed my suspicions, but I wanted the official autopsy report on it. Mike picked up the phone on the third ring and said, "Reilly here."

"This is Ralph," I said. "What've you got on the Chinese girl?"

"Oh. Like you figured, Ralph. It's strychnine, all right."

"No question?"

"None at all. She sure took enough of the stuff. Any witnesses around when she went under?"

"Yes, two."

"She complain of a stiff neck, twitching, spasms?"

"Yes."

"Convulsions?"

"Yes."

"Sure, that's all strychnine. Yeah, Ralph. And her jaws locked the way they are, that grin. And the cyanotic coloring of lips and face. Oh, no question. Hell, I could have diagnosed this without taking a test."

"What else did you find, Mike?"

"She didn't have a very big breakfast, Ralph. Coffee and an English muffin."

"Have any idea when she got the strychnine?"

"Hard to say. Around breakfast, I suppose. You're gonna have a tough nut with strychnine, Ralph."

"How so?"

"Tracing it, I mean. Hell, Ralph, they sell it by the can. For getting rid of animal pests."

"Yeah. Well, thanks, Mike."

"No trouble at all. Drop in anytime."

He hung up, and I turned to Donny, who had already started on a cup of coffee.

"Strychnine, all right."

"What'd you expect?" he said. "Malted milk?"

"So where now?"

"Got a check on the contents of the girl's purse from the

lab. Nothing important. Lipstick. Some change. Five-dollar bill, and three singles. Theater stubs.''

"For where?"

"Chinese theater in Chinatown."

"Anything else?"

"Letter to a sister in Hong Kong."

"In Chinese?"

"Yes."

"And?"

"That's it. Oh yes, a program card. She was a transfer student at Columbia. Went there nights."

"So what do you figure, Donny?"

"I figure some bastard slipped the strychnine to her this morning before she came to work. Maybe a lover, how do I know? She called him later to say hello. She talks Chinese on the phone, so who can tell whether she's calling a restaurant or her uncle in Singapore? The guy all at once says, 'You know why you're feeling so punk, honey?' So she *is* feeling punk. She's got a stiff neck, and her reflexes are hypersensitive, and she's beginning to shake a little. She forgets she's supposed to be talking to a Chinese restaurant owner. She drops the pose for a minute and says 'No, why?' in English. The boyfriend on the other end says, 'Here's why, honey. I gave you a dose of strychnine when I saw you this morning. It's going to kill you in about zero minutes flat.' The kid jumps up and screams 'Kill me? No! No!' Curtain. The poison's already hit her."

"Sounds good," I said. "Except for one thing."

"Yeah?"

"Would the poisoner take a chance like that? Tipping her off on the phone?"

"Why not? He probably knew how long it would take for the poison to kill her."

"But why would she call him?"

"Assuming it was a him. How do I know? Maybe she didn't call anybody special. Maybe the joker works at one of the Chinese restaurants she always called. Maybe she met him every morning for Chop Suey, and then he went his way

201

and she went hers. Or maybe she called . . . Ralph, she could have called anyone."

"No. Someone who spoke Chinese. She spoke Chinese to the party in the beginning."

"Lots of Chinese in this city, Ralph."

"Why don't we start with the restaurants? This book was open on her desk. Two pages showing. She could have been talking to someone at any one of the restaurants listed on those pages—assuming she opened the book to refer to a number. If she called a sweetheart, we're up the creek."

"Not necessarily," Donny said. "It'll just take longer, that's all."

4.

There were a lot of Chinese restaurants listed on those two pages. They were not listed in any geographical order. Apparently, Mary Chang knew the best times to call each of the owners, and she'd listed the restaurant numbers in a system all her own. So where the first number on the list was in Chinatown, the second was up on Fordham Road in the Bronx. We had a typist rearrange the list according to location, and then we asked the skipper for two extra men to help with the legwork. He gave us Belloni and Hicks, yanking them off a case that was ready for the DA anyway. Since they were our guests, so to speak, we gave them the easy half of the list, the portion in Chinatown where all the restaurants were clustered together and there wouldn't be as much hoofing to do. Donny and I took the half that covered Upper Manhattan and the Bronx.

A Chinese restaurant in the early afternoon is something like a bar at that time. There are few diners. Everyone looks bleary-eyed. The dim lights somehow clash with the bright sunshine outside. It's like stepping out of reality into something unreal and vague. Besides, a lot of the doors were locked solid, and when a man can't speak English it's a little difficult to make him understand what a police shield means.

It took a lot of time. We pounded on the doors first, and

then we talked to whoever's face appeared behind the plate glass. We showed shields, we gestured, we waited for someone who spoke English. When the doors opened, we told them who we were and what we wanted. There was distrust, a natural distrust of cops, and another natural distrust of Westerners.

"Did Gotham Lobster call you this morning?"

"No."

"When did Gotham call you?"

"Yes'day. We take one ba'l. One ba'l small."

"Who did you speak to at Gotham?"

"Ma'y Chang."

And on to the next place, and the same round of questions, and always no luck, always no call from Gotham or Mary Chang. And then we hit a place on the Grand Concourse where the waiter opened the door promptly. We told him what we wanted, and he hurried off to the back of the restaurant while we waited by the cash register. A young Chinese in an impeccable blue suit came out to us in about five minutes. He smiled and shook hands and then said, "I'm David Loo. My father owns the restaurant. May I help you?"

He was a good-looking boy of about twenty, I would say. He spoke English without a trace of singsong. He was wearing a white button-down shirt with a blue and silver striped silk tie. A small Drama Masks tie-clasp held the tie to the shirt.

"I'm Detective-Sergeant Parker, and this is my partner, Detective-Sergeant Katz. Do you know Mary Chang?"

"Chang? Mary Chang? Why, no, I . . . oh, do you mean the girl who calls from Gotham Lobster?"

"Yes, that's her. Do you know her?"

"Oh yes, certainly."

"When did you see her last?"

"See her?" David Loo smiled. "I'm afraid I've never seen her. I spoke to her on the phone occasionally, but that was the extent of our relationship."

"I see. When did you speak to her last?"

"This morning."

"What time was this?"

"Oh, I don't know. Early this morning."

"Can you try to pinpoint the time?"

David Loo shrugged. "Nine, nine-fifteen, nine-thirty. I really don't know." He paused. "Has Miss Chang done something?"

"Can you give us a closer time than that, Mr. Loo? Mary Chang was poisoned this morning, and it might be . . ."

"Poisoned? My God!"

"Yes. So you see, any help you can give us would be appreciated."

"Yes, yes, I can understand that. Well, let me see. I came to the restaurant at about . . . nine-ten it was, I suppose. So she couldn't have called at nine, could she?" David Loo smiled graciously, as if he were immensely enjoying this game of murder. "I had some coffee, and I listened to the radio back in the kitchen, and . . ." Loo snapped his fingers. "Of course," he said. "She called right after that."

"Right after what?"

"Well, I listen to swing a lot. WNEW is a good station for music, you know. Do you follow bop?"

"No. Go on."

"Well, WNEW has a newsbreak every hour on the half hour. I remember the news coming on at nine-thirty, and then as the newscaster signed off, the phone rang. That must have been at nine-thirty-five. The news takes five minutes, you see. As a matter of fact, I always resent that intrusion on the music. If a person likes music, it seems unfair . . ."

"And the phone rang at nine-thirty-five, is that right?"

"Yes, sir, I'm positive."

"Who answered the phone?"

"I did. I'd finished my coffee."

"Was it Mary Chang calling?"

"Yes."

"What did she say?"

"She said, 'Gotham Lobster, good morning.' I said good morning back to her—she's always very pleasant on the phone—and . . ."

"Wasn't she pleasant *off* the phone?"

"Well, I wouldn't know. I only spoke to her on the phone."

"Go on."

"She gave me a quotation then and asked if I'd like some nice lobster."

"Was this in Chinese?"

"Yes. I don't know why she spoke Chinese. Perhaps she thought I was the chef."

"What did you do then?"

"I asked her to hold on, and then I went to find the chef. I asked the chef if he needed any lobster, and he said we should take a half barrel. So I went back to the phone. But Miss Chang was gone by that time." Loo shrugged. "We had to order our lobsters from another outfit. Shame, too, because Gotham has some good stuff."

"Did you speak to her in English at all?"

"No. All Chinese."

"I see. Is that customary? I mean, do you usually check with the chef after she gives her quotation?"

"Yes, of course. The chef is the only one who'd know. Sometimes, of course, the chef himself answers the phone. But if he doesn't, we always leave the phone to check with him."

"And you didn't speak to her in English at all?"

"No, sir."

"And you didn't know her, other than through these phone conversations?"

"No, sir."

"Ever have breakfast with her?" Donny asked.

"Sir?"

"Did you ever . . ."

"No, of course not. I told you I didn't know her personally."

"All right, Mr. Loo, thank you very much. We may be back."

"Please feel free to return," he said a little coldly.

We left the restaurant, and outside Donny said, "So?"

"So now we know who she was speaking to. What do you think of him?"

"Educated guy. Could conceivably run in the same circles as a Columbia student. And if he *did* poison her this morning and then tell her about it on the phone, it's a cinch he'd lie his goddamned head off."

"Sure. Let's check Miss Chang's residence. Someone there might know whether or not Loo knew her better than he says he did."

5.

Mary Chang, when she was alive, lived at International House near the Columbia campus, on Riverside Drive. Her roommate was a girl named Frieda who was a transfer student from Vienna. The girl was shocked to learn of Miss Chang's death. She actually wept for several moments, and then she pulled herself together when we started questioning her.

"Did she have any boyfriends?"

"Yes. A few."

"Do you know any of their names?"

"I know *all* of their names. She always talked about them."

"Would you let us have them, please."

Frieda reeled off a list of names, and Donny and I listened. Then Donny asked, "A David Loo? Did he ever come around?"

"No, I don't think so. She never mentioned a David Loo."

"Never talked about him at all?"

"No."

"That list you gave us—all Chinese names. Did she ever date any American boys?"

"No. Mary was funny that way. She didn't like to go out with Americans. I mean, she liked the country and all, but I guess she figured there was no future in dating Occidentals." Frieda paused. "She was a pretty girl, Mary, and a very happy one, always laughing, always full of life. A lot of

American boys figured her for . . . an easy mark, I suppose. She . . . she sensed this. She wouldn't date any of them.''

"Did they ask her?"

"Oh, yes, all the time. She was always very angry when an American asked her for a date. It was sort of an insult to her. She . . . she knew what they wanted."

"Where'd she eat breakfast?"

"Breakfast?"

"Yes. Where'd she eat? Who'd she eat with?"

"I don't know. I don't remember ever seeing her eat breakfast."

"She didn't eat breakfast?"

"I don't think so. We always left here together in the morning. I have a job, too, you see. I work at Lord and Taylor's. I'm . . ."

"Yes, you left here together?"

"To take the subway. She never stopped to eat."

"Coffee?" I asked. "An English muffin? Something?"

"No, not when I was with her."

"I see. What subway did you take?"

"The Broadway line."

"Where did she get off?"

"At Seventy-Second Street."

"What time did she get off the subway usually?"

"At about nine, or maybe a few minutes before. Yes, just about nine."

"But she didn't stop for breakfast."

"No. Mary was very slim, very well built. I don't think she ate breakfast in the morning."

"She ate breakfast *this* morning," I said. "Thank you, Miss. Come on, Donny."

6.

There was an Automat on West Seventy-Second Street, a few doors from Broadway. Mary Chang wouldn't have gone to the Automat because Mary Chang had to be at work at nine, and she got off the train at nine. We walked down the street, all the way up to the building that housed the offices of Gotham Lobster, close to Columbus Avenue. There was a luncheonette on the ground floor of that building. Donny and I went inside and took seats at the counter, and then we ordered coffee.

When our coffee came, we showed the counter man our buzzers. He got scared all at once, the way some people will get scared when a cop shows his shield.

"Just a few questions," we told him.

"Sure, sure," he said. He gulped. "I don't know why . . ."

"You know any of the people who work in this building?"

"Sure, most of 'em. But . . . ."

"Did you know Mary Chang?"

He seemed immensely relieved. "Oh, her. There's some trouble with her, ain't there? She got shot, or stabbed, or something, didn't she?"

"Did you know her?"

"I seen her around, yeah. Quite a piece, you know? With them tight silk dresses, slit up there on the side." He smiled. "You ever seen her? Man, I go for them Chinese broads."

"Did she ever eat here?"

"No."

"Breakfast?"

"No."

"She never stopped here in the morning for coffee?"

"No, why should she do that?"

"I don't know. You tell me."

"Well, what I mean, he always come down for the coffee, you know."

I felt Donny tense beside me.

"Who?" I asked. "Who came down for the coffee?"

"Why, Freddie. From the lobster joint. Every morning like clockwork, before he went upstairs. Two coffees, one heavy on the sugar. That Chinese broad liked it sweet. Also a jelly donut and a toasted English. Sure, every morning."

"You're sure about this?"

"Oh yes, sure. The boss didn't know nothing about it, you

know. Mr. Godrow. He don't go for that junk. They always had their coffee before he come in in the morning."

"Thanks," I said. "Did Freddie come down for the coffee this morning?"

"Sure, every morning."

7.

We left the luncheonette and went upstairs. Freddie was working the addressing machine when we came in. The machine made a hell of a clatter as the metal address plates fed through it. We said hello to Mr. Godrow and then walked right to the machine. Freddie fed postcards and stepped on the foot lever and the address plates banged onto the cards and then dropped into the tray below.

"We've got an idea, Freddie," I said.

He didn't look up. He kept feeding postcards into the machine. The cards read MAINE LIVE LOBSTERS AT FANTASTIC PRICES!

"We figure a guy who kept asking Mary Chang out, Freddie. A guy who constantly got refused."

Freddie said nothing.

"You ever ask her out, Freddie?"

"Yes," he said under the roar of the machine.

"We figure she drove the guy nuts, sitting there in her tight dresses, drinking coffee with him, being friendly, but never anything more, never what he wanted. We figured he got sore at all the Chinese boys who could date her just because they were Chinese. We figure he decided to do something about it. Want to hear more, Freddie?"

"What is this?" Godrow asked. "This is a place of business, you know. Those cards have to . . ."

"You went down for your customary coffee this morning, Freddie."

"Coffee?" Godrow asked. "What coffee? Have you been . . ."

"Only this time you dumped strychnine into Mary Chang's. She took her coffee very sweet, and that probably

209

helped to hide the bitter taste. Or maybe you made some comment about the coffee being very bitter this morning, anything to hide the fact that you were poisoning her.''

"No . . ." Freddie said.

"She drank her coffee and ate her English muffin, and then—the way you did every morning—you gathered up the cups and the napkins and the crumbs and whatever, and you rushed out with them before Mr. Godrow arrived. Only this time, you were disposing of evidence. Where'd you take them? The garbage cans on Columbus Avenue? Do they collect the garbage early, Freddie?''

"I . . . I . . ."

"You knew the symptoms. You watched, and when you thought the time was ripe, you couldn't resist boasting about what you'd done. Mary was making a call. You also knew how these calls worked because you made them yourself. There was usually a pause in the conversation while someone checked with the chef. You waited for that pause, and then you asked Mary if she knew why she was feeling so ill. You asked her because you weren't making a call, Freddie, you were plugged in on her extension, listening to her conversation. She recognized your voice, and so she answered you in English. You told her then, and she jumped up, but it was too late, the convulsion came. Am I right, Freddie?''

Freddie nodded.

"You'd better come with us," I said.

"I . . . I still have to stamp the quotations on these," Freddie said.

"Mr. Godrow will get along without you, Freddie," I said. "He'll get himself a new boy."

"I . . . I'm sorry," Freddie said.

"This is terrible," Godrow said.

"Think how Mary Chang must have felt," I told him, and we left.

The Key

•

Isaac Asimov

Isaac Asimov writes mysteries and science fiction with equal enthusiasm and facility, and when he chooses to combine the two genres, the results usually draw raves from his readers. "The Key" is one such hybrid—a detective puzzle story with the Moon as its essential setting and a member of the American Division of the Terrestrial Bureau of Investigation as its sleuth. Asimov, who has more than 1400 books of fiction and nonfiction to his credit, is the creator of the popular Black Widowers mysteries, as well as such science-fiction crime novels as The Caves of Steel *(1954) and* The Naked Sun *(1957), both of which feature the first robot detective.*

Karl Jennings knew he was going to die. He had a matter of hours to live and much to do.

There was no reprieve from the death sentence, not here on the Moon, not with no communications in operation.

Even on Earth there were a few fugitive patches where, without radio handy, a man might die without the hand of his fellow man to help him, without the heart of his fellow man to pity him, without even the eye of his fellow man to discover the corpse. Here on the Moon, there were few spots that were otherwise.

Earthmen knew he was on the Moon, of course. He had been part of a geological expedition—no, selenological expedition! Odd, how his Earth-centered mind insisted on the "geo-."

Wearily he drove himself to think, even as he worked. Dying though he was, he still felt that artificially imposed clarity of thought. Anxiously he looked about. There was nothing to see. He was in the dark of the eternal shadow of the northern interior of the wall of the crater, a blackness relieved only by the intermittent blink of his flash. He kept that intermittent, partly because he dared not consume its power source before he was through and partly because he dared not take more than the minimum chance that it be seen.

On his left hand, toward the south along the nearby horizon of the Moon, was a crescent of bright white Sunlight. Beyond the horizon, and invisible, was the opposite lip of the crater. The Sun never peered high enough over the lip of his own edge of the crater to illuminate the floor immediately beneath his feet. He was safe from radiation—from that at least.

He dug carefully but clumsily, swathed as he was in his spacesuit. His side ached abominably.

The dust and broken rock did not take up the "fairy castle" appearance characteristic of those portions of the Moon's surface exposed to the alternation of light and dark, heat and cold. Here, in eternal cold, the slow crumbling of the crater wall had simply piled fine rubble in a heterogeneous mass. It would not be easy to tell there had been digging going on.

He misjudged the unevenness of the dark surface for a moment and spilled a cupped handful of dusty fragments. The particles dropped with the slowness characteristic of the Moon and yet with the appearance of a blinding speed, for there was no air resistance to slow them further still and spread them out into a dusty haze.

Jennings's flash brightened for a moment, and he kicked a jagged rock out of the way.

He hadn't much time. He dug deeper into the dust.

A little deeper and he could push the Device into the depression and begin covering it. Strauss must not find it.

Strauss!

The other member of the team. Half-share in the discovery. Half-share in the renown.

If it were merely the whole share of the credit that Strauss had wanted, Jennings might have allowed it. The discovery was more important than any individual credit that might go with it. But what Strauss wanted was something far more, something Jennings would fight to prevent.

One of the few things Jenning was willing to die to prevent.

And he was dying.

They had found it together. Actually, Strauss had found the ship; or, better, the remains of the ship; or, better still, what just conceivably might have been the remains of something analogous to a ship.

"Metal," said Strauss, as he picked up something ragged and nearly amorphous. His eyes and face could just barely be seen through the thick lead glass of the visor, but his rather harsh voice sounded clearly enough through the suit radio.

Jennings came drifting over from his own position half a mile away. He said, "Odd! There is no free metal on the Moon."

"There shouldn't be. But you know well enough they haven't explored more than one percent of the Moon's surface. Who knows what can be found on it?"

Jennings grunted assent and reached out his gauntlet to take the object.

It was true enough that almost anything might be found on the Moon for all anyone really knew. Theirs was the first privately financed selenographic expedition ever to land on the Moon. Till then, there had been only government-conducted shotgun affairs, with half a dozen ends in view. It was a sign of the advancing space age that the Geological Society could afford to send two men to the Moon for selenological studies only.

Strauss said, "It looks as though it once had a polished surface."

"You're right," said Jennings. "Maybe there's more about."

They found three more pieces, two of trifling size and one a jagged object that showed traces of a seam.

"Let's take them to the ship," said Strauss.

They took the small skim boat back to the mother ship.

They shucked their suits once on board, something Jennings at least was always glad to do. He scratched vigorously at his ribs and rubbed his cheeks till his light skin reddened into welts.

Strauss eschewed such weakness and got to work. The laser beam pock-marked the metal and the vapor recorded itself on the spectrograph. Titanium-steel, essentially, with a hint of cobalt and molybdenum.

"That's artificial, all right," said Strauss. His broad-boned face was as dour and as hard as ever. He showed no elation, although Jennings could feel his own heart begin to race.

It may have been the excitement that trapped Jennings into beginning, "This is a development against which we must steel ourselves—" with a faint stress on "steel" to indicate the play on words.

Strauss, however, looked at Jennings with an icy distaste, and the attempted set of puns was choked off.

Jennings sighed. He could never swing it, somehow. Never could! He remembered at the University— Well, never mind. The discovery they had made was worth a far better pun than any he could construct for all Strauss's calmness.

Jennings wondered if Strauss could possibly miss the significance.

He knew very little about Strauss, as a matter of fact, except by selenological reputation. That is, he had read Strauss's papers and he presumed Strauss had read his. Although their ships might well have passed by night in their University days, they had never happened to meet until after both had volunteered for this expedition and had been accepted.

In the week's voyage, Jennings had grown uncomfortably aware of the other's stocky figure, his sandy hair and china-blue eyes and the way the muscles over his prominent jaw-bones worked when he ate. Jennings, himself, much slighter in build, also blue-eyed, but with darker hair, tended to withdraw automatically from the heavy exudation of the other's power and drive.

Jennings said, "There's no record of any ship ever having landed on this part of the Moon. Certainly none has crashed."

"If it were part of a ship," said Strauss, "it should be smooth and polished. This is eroded and, without an atmosphere here, that means exposure to micrometeor bombardment over many years."

Then he *did* see the significance. Jennings said, with an almost savage jubilation, "It's a nonhuman artifact. Creatures not of Earth once visited the Moon. Who knows how long ago?"

"Who knows?" agreed Strauss dryly.

"In the report—"

"Wait," said Strauss imperiously. "Time enough to report when we have something to report. If it was a ship, there will be more to it than what we now have."

But there was no point in looking further just then. They had been at it for hours, and the next meal and sleep were overdue. Better to tackle the whole job fresh and spend hours at it. They seemed to agree on that without speaking.

The Earth was low on the eastern horizon, almost full in phase, bright and blue-streaked. Jennings looked at it while they ate and experienced, as he always did, a sharp homesickness.

"It looks peaceful enough," he said, "but there are six billion people busy on it."

Strauss looked up from some deep inner life of his own and said, "Six billion people ruining it!"

Jennings frowned. "You're not an Ultra, are you?"

Strauss said, "What the hell are you talking about?"

Jennings felt himself flush. A flush always showed against his fair skin, turning it pink at the slightest upset of the even tenor of his emotions. He found it intensely embarrassing.

He turned back to his food, without saying anything.

For a whole generation now, the Earth's population had held steady. No further increase could be afforded. Everyone admitted that. There were those, in fact, who said that "no higher" wasn't enough; the population had to drop. Jennings himself sympathized with that point of view. The globe of the Earth was being eaten alive by its heavy freight of humanity.

But *how* was the population to be made to drop? Randomly, by encouraging the people to lower the birth rate still further, as and how they wished? Lately there had been the slow rise of a distant rumble which wanted not only a population drop but a selected drop—the survival of the fittest, with the self-declared fit choosing the criteria of fitness.

Jennings thought: I've insulted him, I suppose.

Later, when he was almost asleep, it suddenly occurred to him that he knew virtually nothing of Strauss's character. What if it were his intention to go out now on a foraging expedition of his own so that he might get sole credit for—?

He raised himself on his elbow in alarm, but Strauss was breathing heavily, and even as Jennings listened, the breathing grew into the characteristic burr of a snore.

They spent the next three days in a single-minded search for additional pieces. They found some. They found more than that. They found an area glowing with the tiny phosphorescence of Lunar bacteria. Such bacteria were common enough, but nowhere previously had their occurrence been reported in concentration so great as to cause a visible glow.

Strauss said, "An organic being, or his remains, may have been here once. He died, but the micro-organisms within him did not. In the end they consumed him."

"And spread perhaps," added Jennings. "That may be the source of Lunar bacteria generally. They may not be native at all but may be the result of contamination instead—eons ago."

"It works the other way, too," said Strauss. "Since the bacteria are completely different in very fundamental ways from any Earthly form of micro-organism, the creatures they parasitized—assuming this was their source—must have been fundamentally different too. Another indication of extraterrestrial origin."

The trail ended in the wall of a small crater.

"It's a major digging job," said Jennings, his heart sinking. "We had better report this and get help."

"No," said Strauss somberly. "There may be nothing to get help for. The crater might have formed a million years after the ship had crashlanded."

"And vaporized most of it, you mean, and left only what we've found?"

Strauss nodded.

Jennings said, "Let's try anyway. We can dig a bit. If we draw a line through the finds we've made so far and just keep on . . ."

Strauss was reluctant and worked half-heartedly, so that it was Jennings who made the real find. Surely that counted! Even though Strauss had found the first piece of metal, Jennings had found the artifact itself.

It *was* an artifact—cradled three feet underground under the irregular shape of a boulder which had fallen in such a way that it left a hollow in its contact with the Moon's surface. In that hollow lay the artifact, protected from everything for a million years or more; protected from radiation, from micrometeors, from temperature change, so that it remained fresh and new forever.

Jennings labeled it at once the Device. It looked not remotely similar to any instrument either had ever seen, but then, as Jennings said, why should it?

"There are no rough edges that I can see," he said. "It may not be broken."

"There may be missing parts, though."

"Maybe," said Jennings, "but there seems to be nothing movable. It's all one piece and certainly oddly uneven." He noted his own play on words, then went on with a not-altogether-successful attempt at self-control. "*This* is what we need. A piece of worn metal or an area rich in bacteria is only material for deduction and dispute. But this is the real thing—a Device that is clearly of extraterrestrial manufacture."

It was on the table between them now, and both regarded it gravely.

Jennings said, "Let's put through a preliminary report, now."

"No!" said Strauss, in sharp and strenuous dissent. "Hell, no!"

"Why not?"

"Because if we do, it becomes a Society project. They'll swarm all over it and we won't be as much as a footnote when all is done. No!" Strauss looked almost sly. "Let's do all we can with it and get as much out of it as possible before the harpies descend."

Jennings thought about it. He couldn't deny that he too wanted to make certain that no credit was lost. But still—

He said, "I don't know that I like to take the chance, Strauss." For the first time he had an impulse to use the man's first name, but fought it off. "Look, Strauss," he said, "it's not right to wait. If this is of extraterrestrial origin, then it must be from some other planetary system. There isn't a place in the Solar System, outside the Earth, that can possibly support an advanced life form."

"Not proven, really," grunted Strauss, "but what if you're right?"

"Then it would mean that the creatures of the ship had interstellar travel and therefore had to be far in advance, technologically, of ourselves. Who knows what the Device can tell us about their advanced technology. It might be the key to—who knows what. It might be the clue to an unimaginable scientific revolution."

"That's romantic nonsense. If this is the product of a technology far advanced over ours, we'll learn nothing from it. Bring Einstein back to life and show him a microprotowarp and what would he make of it?"

"We can't be certain that we won't learn."

"So what, even so? What if there's a small delay? What if we assure credit for ourselves? What if we make sure that we ourselves go along with this, that we don't let go of it?"

"But Strauss"—Jennings felt himself moved almost to tears in his anxiety to get across his sense of the importance of the Device—"what if we crash with it? What if we don't make it back to Earth? We can't risk this thing." He tapped it then, almost as though he were in love with it. "We should report it now and have them send ships out here to get it. It's too precious to—"

At the peak of his emotional intensity, the Device seemed to grow warm under his hand. A portion of its surface, half-hidden under a flap of metal, glowed phosphorescently.

Jennings jerked his hand away in a spasmodic gesture and the Device darkened. But it was enough; the moment had been infinitely revealing.

He said, almost choking, "It was like a window opening into your skull. I could see into your mind."

"I read yours," said Strauss, "or experienced it, or entered into it, or whatever you choose." He touched the Device in his cold, withdrawn way, but nothing happened.

"You're an Ultra," said Jennings angrily. "When I touched this"— And he did so. "It's happening again. I see it. Are you a madman? Can you honestly believe it is humanly decent to condemn almost all the human race to extinction and destroy the versatility and variety of the species?"

His hand dropped away from the Device again, in repugnance at the glimpses revealed, and it grew dark again. Once more, Strauss touched it gingerly and again nothing happened.

Strauss said, "Let's not start a discussion, for God's sake. This thing is an aid to communication—a telepathic amplifier. Why not? The brain cells each have their electric potentials. Thought can be viewed as a wavering electromagnetic field of microintensities—"

Jennings turned away. He didn't want to speak to Strauss. He said, "We'll report it now. I don't give a damn about credit. Take it all. I just want it out of our hands."

For a moment Strauss remained in a brown study. Then he said, "It's more than a communicator. It responds to emotion and it amplifies emotion."

"What are you talking about?"

"Twice it started at your touch just now, although you'd

been handling it all day with no effect. It still has no effect when I touch it.''

"Well?"

''It reacted to you when you were in a state of high emotional tension. That's the requirement for activation, I suppose. And when you raved about the Ultras while you were holding it just now, I felt as you did, for just a moment.''

"So you should."

"But, listen to me. Are you sure *you're* so right. There isn't a thinking man on Earth that doesn't know the planet would be better off with a population of one billion rather than six billion. If we used automation to the full—as now the hordes won't allow us to do—we could probably have a completely efficient and viable Earth with a population of no more than, say, five million. Listen to me, Jennings. Don't turn away, man.''

The harshness in Strauss's voice almost vanished in his effort to be reasonably winning. "But we can't reduce the population democratically. You know that. It isn't the sex urge, because uterine inserts solved the birth control problem long ago; you know that. It's a matter of nationalism. Each ethnic group wants other groups to reduce themselves in population first, and I agree with them. I want my ethnic group, *our* ethnic group, to prevail. I want the Earth to be inherited by the elite, which means by men like ourselves. We're the true men, and the horde of half apes who hold us down are destroying us all. They're doomed to death anyway; why not save ourselves?''

"No," said Jennings strenuously. "No one group has a monopoly on humanity. Your five million, trapped in a humanity robbed of its variety and versatility, would die of boredom—and serve them right.''

"Emotional nonsense, Jennings. You don't believe that. You've just been trained to believe it by our damn-fool equalitarians. Look, this Device is just what we need. Even if we can't build any others or understand how this one works, this one Device might do. If we could control or influence the minds of key men, then little by little we can superimpose our views on the world. We already have an organization. You must know that if you've seen my mind. It's better motivated and better designed than any other organization on Earth. The brains of mankind flock to us daily. Why not you too? This instrument is a key, as you see, but not just a key to a bit more knowledge. It is a key to the final solution of men's problems. Join us! Join us!'' He had reached an earnestness that Jennings had never heard in him.

Strauss's hand fell on the Device, which flickered a second or two and went out.

Jennings smiled humorlessly. He saw the significance of that. Strauss had been deliberately trying to work himself into an emotional state intense enough to activate the Device and had failed.

"You can't work it," said Jennings. "You're too darned supermanishly self-controlled and can't break down, can you?" He took up the Device with hands that were trembling, and it phosphoresced at once.

"Then *you* work it. Get the credit for saving humanity."

"Not in a hundred million years," said Jennings, gasping and barely able to breathe in the intensity of his emotion. "I'm going to report this now."

"No," said Strauss. He picked up one of the table knives. "It's pointed enough, sharp enough."

"You needn't work so hard to make your point," said Jennings, even under the stress of the moment conscious of the pun. "I can see your plans. With the Device you can convince anyone that I never existed. You can bring about an Ultra victory."

Strauss nodded. "You read my mind perfectly."

"But you won't," gasped Jennings. "Not while I hold this." He was willing Strauss into immobility.

Strauss moved raggedly and subsided. He held the knife out stiffly and his arm trembled, but he did not advance.

Both were perspiring freely.

Strauss said between clenched teeth, "You can't keep it—up all—day."

The sensation was clear, but Jennings wasn't sure he had

the words to describe it. It was, in physical terms, like holding a slippery animal of vast strength, one that wriggled incessantly. Jennings had to concentrate on the feeling of immobility.

He wasn't familiar with the Device. He didn't know how to use it skillfully. One might as well expect someone who had never seen a sword to pick one up and wield it with the grace of a musketeer.

"Exactly," said Strauss, following Jennings's train of thought. He took a fumbling step forward.

Jennings knew himself to be no match for Strauss's mad determination. They both knew that. But there was the skim boat. Jennings had to get away. With the Device.

But Jennings had no secrets. Strauss saw his thought and tried to step between the other and the skim boat.

Jennings redoubled his efforts. Not immobility, but unconsciousness. Sleep, Strauss, he thought desperately. Sleep!

Strauss slipped to his knees, heavy-lidded eyes closing.

Heart pounding, Jennings rushed forward. If he could strike him with something, snatch the knife—

But his thoughts had deviated from their all-important concentration on sleep, so that Strauss's hand was on his ankle, pulling downward with raw strength.

Strauss did not hesitate. As Jennings tumbled, the hand that held the knife rose and fell. Jennings felt the sharp pain, and his mind reddened with fear and despair.

It was the very access of emotion that raised the flicker of the Device to a blaze. Strauss's hold relaxed as Jennings silently and incoherently screamed fear and rage from his own mind to the other.

Strauss rolled over, face distorted.

Jennings rose unsteadily to his feet and backed away. He dared do nothing but concentrate on keeping the other unconscious. Any attempt at violent action would block out too much of his own mind force, whatever it was; too much of his unskilled bumbling mind force that could not lend itself to really effective use.

He backed toward the skim boat. There would be a suit on board—bandages—

The skim boat was not really meant for long-distance runs. Nor was Jennings, any longer. His right side was slick with blood despite the bandages. The interior of his suit was caked with it.

There was no sign of the ship itself on his tail, but surely it would come sooner or later. Its power was many times his own; it had detectors that would pick up the cloud of charge concentration left behind by his ion-drive reactors.

Desperately Jennings had tried to reach Luna Station on his radio, but there was still no answer, and he stopped in despair. His signals would merely aid Strauss in pursuit.

He might reach Luna Station bodily, but he did not think he could make it. He would be picked off first. He would die and crash first. He wouldn't make it. He would have to hide the Device, put it away in a safe place, *then* make for Luna Station.

The Device . . .

He was not sure he was right. It might ruin the human race, but it was infinitely valuable. Should he destroy it altogether? It was the only remnant of nonhuman intelligent life. It held the secrets of an advanced technology; it was an instrument of an advanced science of the mind. Whatever the danger, consider the value—the potential value—

No, he must hide it so that it could be found again—but only by the enlightened Moderates of the government. Never by the Ultras . . .

The skim boat flickered down along the northern inner rim of the crater. He knew which one it was, and the Device could be buried here. If he could not reach Luna Station thereafter, either in person or by radio, he would have to at least get away from the hiding spot; well away, so that his own person would not give it away. And he would have to leave *some* key to its location.

He was thinking with an unearthly clarity, it seemed to him. Was it the influence of the Device he was holding? Did it stimulate his thinking and guide him to the perfect message? Or was it the hallucination of the dying, and would none of it make any sense to anyone? He didn't know, but he had no choice. He had to try.

For Karl Jennings knew he was going to die. He had a matter of hours to live and much to do.

H. Seton Davenport of the American Division of the Terrestrial Bureau of Investigation rubbed the star-shaped scar on his left cheek absently. "I'm aware, sir, that the Ultras are dangerous."

The Division Head, M. T. Ashley, looked at Davenport narrowly. His gaunt cheeks were set in disapproving lines. Since he had sworn off smoking once again, he forced his groping fingers to close upon a stick of chewing gum, which he shelled, crumpled, and shoved into his mouth morosely. He was getting old, and bitter, too, and his short iron gray mustache rasped when he rubbed his knuckles against it.

He said, "You don't know how dangerous. I wonder if anyone does. They are small in numbers, but strong among the powerful who, after all, are perfectly ready to consider themselves the elite. No one knows for certain who they are or how many."

"Not even the Bureau?"

"The Bureau is held back. We ourselves aren't free of the taint, for that matter. Are you?"

Davenport frowned. "I'm not an Ultra."

"I didn't say you were," said Ashley. "I asked if you were free of the taint. Have you considered what's been happening to the Earth in the last two centuries? Has it never occurred to you that a moderate decline in population would be a good thing? Have you never felt that it would be wonderful to get rid of the unintelligent, the incapable, the insensitive, and leave the rest. *I* have, damn it."

"I'm guilty of thinking that sometimes, yes. But considering something as a wish-fulfillment idea is one thing, but planning it as a practical scheme of action to be Hitlerized through is something else."

The Key

"The distance from wish to action isn't as great as you think. Convince yourself that the end is important enough, that the danger is great enough, and the means will grow increasingly less objectionable. Anyway, now that the Istanbul matter is taken care of, let me bring you up to date on this matter. Istanbul was of no importance in comparison. Do you know Agent Ferrant?"

"The one who's disappeared? Not personally."

"Well, two months ago, a stranded ship was located on the Moon's surface. It had been conducting a privately financed selenographic survey. The Russo-American Geological Society, which had sponsored the flight, reported the ship's failure to report. A routine search located it without much trouble within a reasonable distance of the site from which it had made its last report.

"The ship was not damaged but its skim boat was gone and with it one member of the crew. Name—Karl Jennings. The other man, James Strauss, was alive but in delirium. There were no signs of physical damage to Strauss, but he was quite insane. He still is, and that's important."

"Why?" put in Davenport.

"Because the medical team that investigated him reported neurochemical and neuroelectrical abnormalities of unprecedented nature. They'd never seen a case like it. Nothing human could have brought it about."

A flicker of a smile crossed Davenport's solemn face. "You suspect extraterrestrial invaders?"

"Maybe," said the other, with no smile at all. "But let me continue. A routine search in the neighborhood of the stranded ship revealed no signs of the skim boat. Then Luna Station reported receipt of weak signals of uncertain origin. They had been tabbed as coming from the western rim of Mare Imbrium, but it was uncertain whether they were of human origin or not, and no vessel was believed to be in the vicinity. The signals had been ignored. With the skim boat in mind, however, the search party headed out for Imbrium and located it. Jennings was aboard, dead. Knife wound in one side. It's rather surprising he had lived as long as he did.

"Meanwhile the medicos were becoming increasingly disturbed at the nature of Strauss's babbling. They contacted the Bureau and our two men on the Moon—one of them happened to be Ferrant—arrived at the ship.

"Ferrant studied the tape recordings of the babblings. There was no point in asking questions, for there was, and is, no way of reaching Strauss. There is a high wall between the universe and himself—probably a permanent one. However, the talk in delirium, although heavily repetitious and disjointed, can be made to make sense. Ferrant put it together like a jigsaw puzzle.

"Apparently Strauss and Jennings had come across an object of some sort which they took to be of ancient and non-human manufacture, an artifact of some ship wrecked eons ago. Apparently it could somehow be made to twist the human mind."

Davenport interrupted. "And it twisted Strauss's mind? Is that it?"

"That's exactly it. Strauss was an Ultra—we can say 'was' for he's only technically alive—and Jennings did not wish to surrender the object. Quite right, too. Strauss babbled of using it to bring about the self-liquidation, as he called it, of the undesirable. He wanted a final, ideal population of five million. There was a fight in which only Jennings, apparently, could handle the mind-thing, but in which Strauss had a knife. When Jennings left, he was knifed, but Strauss's mind had been destroyed."

"And where was the mind-thing?"

"Agent Ferrant acted decisively. He searched the ship and the surroundings again. There was no sign of anything that was neither a natural Lunar formation nor an obvious product of human technology. There was nothing that could be the mind-thing. He then searched the skim boat and its surroundings. Again nothing."

"Could the first search team, the ones who suspected nothing—could they have carried something off?"

"They swore they did not, and there is no reason to suspect them of lying. Then Ferrant's partner—"

"Who was he?"

"Gorbansky," said the District Head.

"I know him. We've worked together."

"I know you have. What do you think of him?"

"Capable and honest."

"All right. Gorbansky found something. Not an alien artifact. Rather, something most routinely human indeed. It was an ordinary white three-by-five card with writing on it, spindled, and in the middle finger of the right gauntlet. Presumably Jennings had written it before his death and, also presumably, it represented the key to where he had hidden the object."

"What reason is there to think he had hidden it?"

"I said we had found it nowhere."

"I mean, what if he had destroyed it, as something too dangerous to leave intact?"

"That's highly doubtful. If we accept the conversation as reconstructed from Strauss's ravings—and Ferrant built up what seems a tight word-for-word record of it—Jennings thought the mind-thing to be of key importance to humanity. He called it 'the clue to an unimaginable scientific revolution.' He wouldn't destroy something like that. He would merely hide it from the Ultras and try to report its whereabouts to the government. Else why leave a clue to its whereabouts?"

Davenport shook his head, "you're arguing in a circle, chief. You say he left a clue because you think there is a hidden object, and you think there is a hidden object because he left a clue."

"I admit that. Everything is dubious. Is Strauss's delirium meaningful? Is Ferrant's reconstruction valid? Is Jennings's clue really a clue? Is there a mind-thing, or a Device, as Jennings called it, or isn't there? There's no use asking such questions. Right now, we must act on the assumption that there is such a Device and that it must be found."

"Because Ferrant disappeared?"

"Exactly."

"Kidnapped by the Ultras?"

"Not at all. The card disappeared with him."

"Oh—I see."

"Ferrant has been under suspicion for a long time as a secret Ultra. He's not the only one in the Bureau under suspicion either. The evidence didn't warrant open action; we can't simply lay about on pure suspicion, you know, or we'll gut the Bureau from top to bottom. He was under surveillance."

"By whom?"

"By Gorbansky, of course. Fortunately Gorbansky had filmed the card and sent the reproduction to the headquarters on Earth, but he admits he considered it as nothing more than a puzzling object and included it in the information sent to Earth only out of a desire to be routinely complete. Ferrant— the better mind of the two, I suppose—did see the significance and took action. He did so at great cost, for he has given himself away and has destroyed his future usefulness to the Ultras, but there is a chance that there will be no need for future usefulness. If the Ultras control the Device—"

"Perhaps Ferrant has the Device already."

"He was under surveillance, remember. Gorbansky swears the Device did not turn up anywhere."

"Gorbansky did not manage to stop Ferrant from leaving with the card. Perhaps he did not manage to stop him from obtaining the Device unnoticed, either."

Ashley tapped his fingers on the desk between them in an uneasy and uneven rhythm. He said at last, "I don't want to think that. If we find Ferrant, we may find out how much damage he's done. Till then, we must search for the Device. If Jennings hid it, he must have tried to get away from the hiding place. Else why leave a clue? It wouldn't be found in the vicinity."

"He might not have lived long enough to get away."

Again Ashley tapped. "The skim boat showed signs of having engaged in a long, speedy flight and had all but crashed at the end. That is consistent with the view that Jennings was trying to place as much space as possible between himself and some hiding place."

"Can you tell from what direction he came?"

"Yes, but that's not likely to help. From the condition of the side vents, he had been deliberately tacking and veering."

Davenport sighed. "I suppose you have a copy of the card with you."

"I do. Here it is." He flipped a three-by-five replica toward Davenport. Davenport studied it for a few moments. It looked like this:

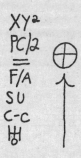

Davenport said, "I don't see any significance here."

"Neither did I, at first, nor did those I first consulted. But consider. Jennings must have thought that Strauss was in pursuit; he might not have known that Strauss had been put out of action, at least, not permanently. He was deadly afraid, then, that an Ultra would find him before a Moderate would. He dared not leave a clue too open. This"—and the Division Head tapped the reproduction—"must represent a clue that is opaque on the surface but clear enough to anyone sufficiently ingenious."

"Can we rely on that?" asked Davenport doubtfully. "After all, he was a dying, frightened man, who might have been subjected to this mind-altering object himself. He need not have been thinking clearly, or even humanly. For instance, why didn't he make an effort to reach Luna Station? He ended half a circumference away almost. Was he too twisted to think clearly? Too paranoid to trust even the Station? Yet he must have tried to reach them at first since they picked up signals. What I'm saying is that this card, which looks as though it is covered with gibberish, *is* covered with gibberish."

Ashley shook his head solemnly from side to side, like a tolling bell. "He was in panic, yes. And I suppose he lacked the presence of mind to try to reach Luna Station. Only the need to run and escape possessed him. Even so, this can't be gibberish. It hangs together too well. Every notation on the card can be made to make sense, and the whole can be made to hang together."

"Where's the sense, then?" asked Davenport.

"You'll notice that there are seven items on the left side and two on the right. Consider the left-hand side first. The third one down looks like an equals sign. Does an equals sign mean anything to you, anything in particular?"

"An algebraic equation."

"That's general. Anything particular?"

"No."

"Suppose you consider it as a pair of parallel lines?"

"Euclid's fifth postulate?" suggested Davenport, groping.

"Good! There is a crater called Euclides on the Moon— the Greek name of the mathematician we call Euclid."

Davenport nodded. "I see your drift. As for F/A, that's force divided by acceleration, the definition of mass by Newton's second law of motion—"

"Yes, and there is a crater called Newton on the Moon also."

"Yes, but wait awhile, the lowermost item is the astronomic symbol for the planet Uranus, and there is certainly no crater—or any other lunar object, so far as I know—that is named Uranus."

"You're right there. But Uranus was discovered by William Herschel, and the H that makes up part of the astronomic symbol is the initial of his name. As it happens, there is a crater named Herschel on the Moon—three of them, in fact, since one is named for Caroline Herschel, his sister, and another for John Herschel, his son.''

Davenport thought awhile, then said, ''PC/2—Pressure times half the speed of light. I'm not familiar with that equation.''

''Try craters. Try P for Ptolemaeus and C for Copernicus.''

''And strike an average? Would that signify a spot exactly between Ptolemaeus and Copernicus?''

''I'm disappointed, Davenport,'' said Ashley sardonically. ''I thought you knew your history of astronomy better than that. Ptolemy, or Ptolemaeus in Latin, presented a geocentric picture of the Solar System with the Earth at the center, while Copernicus presented a heliocentric one with the Sun at the center. One astronomer attempted a compromise, a picture halfway between that of Ptolemy and Copernicus—''

''Tycho Brahe!'' said Davenport.

''Right. And the crater Tycho is the most conspicuous feature on the Moon's surface.''

''All right. Let's take the rest. The C-C is a common way of writing a common type of chemical bond, and I think there is a crater named Bond.''

''Yes, named for an American astronomer, W.C. Bond.''

''The item on top, XY^2. Hmm. XYY. An X and two Y's. Wait! Alfonso X. He was the royal astronomer in medieval Spain who was called Alfonso the Wise. X the Wise. XYY. The crater Alphonsus.''

''Very good. What's SU?''

''That stumps me, chief.''

''I'll tell you one theory. It stands for Soviet Union, the old name for the Russian Region. It was the Soviet Union that first mapped the other side of the Moon, and maybe it's a crater there. Tsiolkovsky, for instance. You see, then, the symbols on the left can each be interpreted as standing for a crater: Alphonsus, Tycho, Euclides, Newton, Tsiolkovsky, Bond, Herschel.''

''What about the symbols on the right-hand side?''

"That's perfectly transparent. The quartered circle is the astronomic symbol for the Earth. An arrow pointing to it indicates that Earth must be directly overhead."

"Ah," said Davenport, "the Sinus Medii—the Middle Bay—over which the Earth is perpetually at zenith. That's not a crater, so it's on the right-hand side, away from the other symbols."

"All right," said Ashley. "The notations all make sense, or they can be made to make sense, so there's at least a good chance that this isn't gibberish and that it is trying to tell us something. But what? So far we've got seven craters and a noncrater mentioned, and what does that mean? Presumably, the Device can only be in one place."

"Well," said Davenport heavily, "a crater can be a huge place to search. Even if we assume he hugged the shadow to avoid Solar radiation, there can be dozens of miles to examine in each case. Suppose the arrow pointing to the symbol for the Earth defines the crater where he hid the Device, the place from which Earth can be seen nearest the zenith."

"That's been thought of, old man. It cuts out one place and leaves us with seven pinpointed craters, the southernmost extremity of those north of the Lunar equator and the northernmost of those south. But which of the seven?"

Davenport was frowning. So far, he hadn't thought of anything that hadn't already been thought of. "Search them all," he said brusquely.

Ashley crackled into brief laughter. "In the weeks since this has all come up, we've done exactly that."

"And what have you found?"

"Nothing. We haven't found a thing. We're still looking, though."

"Obviously one of the symbols isn't interpreted correctly."

"Obviously!"

"You said yourself there were three craters named Herschel. The symbol SU, if it means Soviet Union and therefore the other side of the Moon, can stand for any crater on the other side: Lomonosov, Jules Verne, Joliot-Curie, any of them. For that matter, the symbol of the Earth might stand for the crater Atlas, since he is pictured as supporting the Earth in some versions of the myth. The arrow might stand for the Straight Wall.''

"There's no argument there, Davenport. But even if we get the right interpretation for the right symbol, how do we recognize it from among all the wrong interpretations, or from among the right interpretations of the wrong symbols? Somehow there's got to be something that leaps up at us from this card and gives us so clear a piece of information that we can tell it at once as the real thing from among all the red herrings. We've all failed and we need a fresh mind, Davenport. What do you see here?''

"I'll tell you one thing we could do," said Davenport reluctantly. "We can consult someone I— Oh, my God!" He half rose.

Ashley was all controlled excitement at once. "What do you see?''

Davenport could feel his hand trembling. He hoped his lips weren't. He said, "Tell me, have you checked on Jennings's past life?''

"Of course.''

"Where did he go to college?''

"Eastern University.''

A pang of joy shot through Davenport, but he held on. That was not enough. "Did he take a course in extraterrology?''

"Of course, he did. That's routine for a geology major.''

"All right, then, don't you know who teaches extraterrology at Eastern University?''

Ashley snapped his fingers. "That oddball. What's-his-name—Wendell Urth.''

"Exactly, an oddball who is a brilliant man in his way. An oddball who's acted as a consultant for the Bureau on several occasions and given perfect satisfaction every time. An oddball I was going to suggest we consult this time and then noticed that this card was *telling* us to do so. An arrow pointing to the symbol for the Earth. A rebus that couldn't mean more clearly 'Go to Urth,' written by a man who was once a student of Urth and would know him."

Ashley stared at the card, "by God, it's possible. But what could Urth tell us about the card that we can't see for ourselves?"

Davenport said, with polite patience, "I suggest we ask him, sir."

Ashley looked about curiously, half wincing as he turned from one direction to another. He felt as though he had found himself in some arcane curiosity shop, darkened and dangerous, from which at any moment some demon might hurtle forth squealing.

The lighting was poor and the shadows many. The walls seemed distant, and dismally alive with book-films from floor to ceiling. There was a Galactic Lens in soft three-dimensionality in one corner and behind it were star charts that could dimly be made out. A map of the Moon in another corner might, however, possibly be a map of Mars.

Only the desk in the center of the room was brilliantly lit by a tight-beamed lamp. It was littered with papers and opened printed books. A small viewer was threaded with film, and a clock with an old-fashioned round-faced dial hummed with subdued merriment.

Ashley found himself unable to recall that it was late afternoon outside and that the sun was quite definitely in the sky. Here, within, was a place of eternal night. There was no sign of any window, and the clear presence of circulating air did not spare him a claustrophobic sensation.

He found himself moving closer to Davenport, who seemed insensible to the unpleasantness of the situation.

Davenport said in a low voice, "He'll be here in a moment, sir."

"Is it always like this?" asked Ashley.

"Always. He never leaves this place, as far as I know, except to trot across the campus and attend his classes."

"Gentlemen! Gentlemen!" came a reedy, tenor voice. "I am so glad to see you. It is good of you to come."

234

A round figure of a man bustled in from another room, shedding shadow and emerging into the light.

He beamed at them, adjusting round, thick-lensed glasses upward so that he might look through them. As his fingers moved away, the glasses slipped downward at once to a precarious perch upon the round nubbin of his snub nose. "I am Wendell Urth," he said.

The scraggly gray Van Dyke on his pudgy, round chin did not in the least add to the dignity which the smiling face and the stubby ellipsoidal torso so noticeably lacked.

"Gentlemen! It is good of you to come," Urth repeated, as he jerked himself backward into a chair from which his legs dangled with the toes of his shoes a full inch above the floor. "Mr. Davenport remembers, perhaps, that it is a matter of—uh—some importance to me to remain here. I do not like to travel, except to walk, of course, and a walk across the campus is quite enough for me."

Ashley looked baffled as he remained standing, and Urth stared at him with a growing bafflement of his own. He pulled a handkerchief out and wiped his glasses, then replaced them, and said, "Oh, I see the difficulty. You want chairs. Yes. Well, just take some. If there are things on them, just push them off. Push them off. Sit down, please."

Davenport removed the books from one chair and placed them carefully on the floor. He pushed the chair toward Ashley. Then he took a human skull off a second chair and placed the skull even more carefully on Urth's desk. Its mandible, insecurely wired, unhinged as he transferred it, and it sat there with jaw askew.

"Never mind," said Urth, affably, "it will not hurt. Now tell me what is on your mind, gentlemen?"

Davenport waited a moment for Ashley to speak, then, rather gladly, took over. "Dr. Urth, do you remember a student of yours named Jennings? Karl Jennings?"

Urth's smile vanished momentarily with the effort of recall. His somewhat protuberant eyes blinked. "No," he said at last. "Not at the moment."

"A geology major. He took your extraterrology course some years ago. I have his photograph here, if that will help."

Urth studied the photograph handed him with nearsighted concentration, but still looked doubtful.

Davenport drove on. "He left a cryptic message which is the key to a matter of great importance. We have so far failed to interpret it satisfactorily, but this much we see—it indicates we are to come to you."

"Indeed? How interesting! For what purpose are you to come to me?"

"Presumably for your advice on interpreting the message."

"May I see it?"

Silently Ashley passed the slip of paper to Wendell Urth. The extraterrologist looked at it casually, turned it over, and stared for a moment at the blank back. He said, "Where does it say to ask me?"

Ashley looked startled, but Davenport forestalled him by saying, "The arrow pointing to the symbol the Earth. It seems clear."

"It is clearly an arrow pointing to the symbol for the planet Earth. I suppose it might literally mean 'go to Earth' if this were found on some other world.

"It was found on the Moon, Dr. Urth, and it could, I suppose, mean that. However, the reference to you seemed clear once we realized that Jennings had been a student of yours."

"He took a course in extraterrology here at the University?"

"That's right."

"In what year, Mr. Davenport?"

"In '18."

"Ah. The puzzle is solved."

"You mean the significance of the message?" said Davenport.

"No, no. The message has no meaning to me. I mean the puzzle of why it is that I did not remember him, for I remember him now. He was a very quiet fellow, anxious, shy, self-effacing—not at all the sort of person anyone would remember. Without this"—and he tapped the message—"I might never have remembered him."

"Why does the card change things?" asked Davenport.

"The reference to me is a play on words. Earth—Urth. Not very subtle, of course, but that is Jennings. His unattainable delight was the pun. My only clear memory of him is his occasional attempts to perpetrate puns. I enjoy puns, I adore puns, but Jennings—yes, I remember him well now—was atrocious at it. Either that, or distressingly obvious at it, as in this case. He lacked all talent for puns, yet craved them so much—"

Ashley suddenly broke in. "This message consists entirely of a kind of wordplay, Dr. Urth. At least, we believe so, and that fits in with what you say."

"Ah!" Urth adjusted his glasses and peered through them once more at the card and the symbols it carried. He pursed his plump lips, then said cheerfully, "I make nothing of it."

"In that case—" began Ashley, his hands balling into fists.

"But if you tell me what it's all about," Urth went on, "then perhaps it might mean something."

Davenport said quickly, "May I, sir? I am confident that this man can be relied on—and it may help."

"Go ahead," muttered Ashley. "At this point, what can it hurt?"

Davenport condensed the tale, giving it in crisp, telegraphic sentences, while Urth listened carefully, moving his stubby fingers over the shining milk-white desktop as though he were sweeping up invisible cigar ashes. Toward the end of the recital, he hitched up his legs and sat with them crossed like an amiable Buddha.

When Davenport was done, Urth thought a moment, then said, "Do you happen to have a transcript of the conversation reconstructed by Ferrant?"

"We do," said Davenport. "Would you like to see it?"

"Please."

Urth placed the strip of microfilm in a scanner and worked his way rapidly through it, his lips moving unintelligibly at some points. Then he tapped the reproduction of the cryptic message. "And this, you say, is the key to the entire matter? The crucial clue?"

"We think it is, Dr. Urth."

"But it is not the original. It is a reproduction."

"That is correct."

"The original has gone with this man, Ferrant, and you believe it to be in the hands of the Ultras."

"Quite possibly."

Urth shook his head and looked troubled. "Everyone knows my sympathies are not with the Ultras. I would fight them by all means, so I don't want to seem to be hanging back, but—what is there to say that this mind-affecting object exists at all? You have only the ravings of a psychotic and your dubious deductions from the reproduction of a mysterious set of marks that may mean nothing at all."

"Yes, Dr. Urth, but we can't take chances."

"How certain are you that this copy is accurate? What if the original has something on it that this lacks, something that makes the message quite clear, something without which the message must remain impenetrable?"

"We are certain the copy is accurate."

"What about the reverse side? There is nothing on the back of this reproduction. What about the reverse of the original?"

"The agent who made the reproduction tells us that the back of the original was blank."

"Men can make mistakes."

"We have no reason to think he did, and we must work on the assumption that he didn't. At least until such time as the original is regained."

"Then you assure me," said Urth, "that any interpretation to be made of this message must be made on the basis of exactly what one sees here."

"We think so. We are virtually certain," said Davenport with a sense of ebbing confidence.

Urth continued to look troubled. He said, "Why not leave the instrument where it is? If neither group finds it, so much the better. I disapprove of any tampering with minds and would not contribute to making it possible."

Davenport placed a restraining hand on Ashley's arm, sensing the other was about to speak. Davenport said, "Let me put it to you, Dr. Urth, that the mind-tampering aspect is not the whole of the Device. Suppose an Earth expedition to a distant primitive planet had dropped an old-fashioned radio there, and suppose the native population had discovered electric current but had not yet developed the vacuum tube.

"The population might discover that if the radio was hooked up to a current, certain glass objects within it would grow warm and would glow, but of course they would receive no intelligible sound, merely, at best, some buzzes and crackles. However, if they dropped the radio into a bathtub while it was plugged in, a person in that tub might be electrocuted. Should the people of this hypothetical planet therefore conclude that the device they were studying was designed solely for the purpose of killing people?"

"I see your analogy," said Urth. "You think that the mind-tampering property is merely an incidental function of the Device?"

"I'm sure of it," said Davenport earnestly. "If we can puzzle out its real purpose, earthly technology may leap ahead centuries."

"Then you agree with Jennings when he said"—here Urth consulted the microfilm—" 'It might be the key to—to who knows what? It might be the clue to an unimaginable scientific revolution.' "

"Exactly!"

"And yet the mind-tampering aspect is there and is infinitely dangerous. Whatever the radio's purpose, it *does* electrocute."

"Which is why we can't let the Ultras get it."

"Or the government either, perhaps?"

"But I must point out that there is a reasonable limit to caution. Consider that men have always held danger in their hands. The first flint knife in the old Stone Age; the first wooden club before that could kill. They could be used to bend weaker men to the will of stronger ones under threat of force and that, too, is a form of mind-tampering. What counts, Dr. Urth, is not the Device itself, however dangerous it may be in the abstract, but the intention of the men who make use of the Device. The Ultras have the declared intention of killing off more than 99.9 percent of humanity. The government, whatever the faults of the men composing it, would have no such intention.''

"What *would* the government intend?"

"A scientific study of the Device. Even the mind-tampering aspect itself could yield infinite good. Put to enlightened use, it could educate us concerning the physical basis of mental function. We might learn to correct mental disorders or cure the Ultras. Mankind might learn to develop greater intelligence generally.''

"How can I believe that such idealism will be put into practice?"

"*I* believe so. Consider that you face a possible turn to evil by the government if you help us, but you risk the certain and declared evil purpose of the Ultras if you don't.''

Urth nodded thoughtfully. "Perhaps you're right. And yet I have a favor to ask of you. I have a niece who is, I believe, quite fond of me. She is constantly upset over the fact that I steadfastly refuse to indulge in the lunacy of travel. She states that she will not rest content until someday I accompany her to Europe or North Carolina or some other outlandish place—"

Ashley leaned forward earnestly, brushing Davenport's restraining gesture to one side. "Dr. Urth, if you help us find the Device and if it can be made to work, then I assure you that we will be glad to help you free yourself of your phobia against travel and make it possible for you to go with your niece anywhere you wish.''

Urth's bulging eyes widened and he seemed to shrink within himself. For a moment he looked wildly about as though he were already trapped. *"No!"* he gasped. "Not at all! Never!"

His voice dropped to an earnest, hoarse whisper. "Let me explain the nature of my fee. If I help you, if you retrieve the Device and learn its use, if the fact of my help becomes public, then my niece will be on the government like a fury. She is a terribly headstrong and shrill-voiced woman who will raise public subscriptions and organize demonstrations. She will stop at nothing. And yet you must not give in to her. You must *not*! You must resist all pressures. I wish to be left alone exactly as I am now. That is my absolute and minimum fee."

Ashley flushed. "Yes, of course, since that is your wish."

"I have your word?"

"You have my word."

"Please remember. I rely on you too, Mr. Davenport."

"It will be as you wish," soothed Davenport. "And now, I presume, you can interpret the items?"

"The items?" asked Urth, seeming to focus his attention with difficulty on the card. "You mean these markings, XY^2 and so on?"

"Yes. What do they mean?"

"I don't know. Your interpretations are as good as any, I suppose."

Ashley exploded. "Do you mean that all this talk about helping us is nonsense? What was this maundering about a fee, then?"

Wendell Urth looked confused and taken aback. "I would like to help you."

"But you don't know what these items mean."

"I—I don't. But I know what this message means."

"You do?" cried Davenport.

"Of course. Its meaning is transparent. I suspected it half-way through your story. And I was sure of it once I read the reconstruction of the conversations between Strauss and Jennings. You would understand it yourself, gentlemen, if you would only stop to think."

"See here," said Ashley in exasperation, "you said you don't know what the items mean."

"I don't. I said I know what the *message* means."

241

"What is the message if it is not the items? Is it the paper, for Heaven's sake?"

"Yes, in a way."

"You mean invisible ink or something like that?"

"No! Why is it so hard for you to understand, when you yourself stand on the brink?"

Davenport leaned toward Ashley and said in a low voice, "Sir, will you let me handle it, please?"

Ashley snorted, then said in a stifled manner, "Go ahead."

"Dr. Urth," said Davenport, "will you give us your analysis?"

"Ah! Well, all right." The little extraterrologist settled back in his chair and mopped his damp forehead on his sleeve. "Let's consider the message. If you accept the quartered circle and the arrow as directing you to me, that leaves seven items. If these indeed refer to seven craters, six of them, at least, must be designed merely to distract, since the Device surely cannot be in more than one place. It contained no movable or detachable parts—it was all one piece.

"Then, too, none of the items are straightforward. SU might, by your interpretation, mean any place on the other side of the Moon, which is an area the size of South America. Again PC/2 can mean 'Tycho,' as Mr. Ashley says, or it can mean 'halfway between Ptolemaeus and Copernicus,' as Mr. Davenport thought, or for that matter 'halfway between Plato and Cassini.' To be sure, XY^2 could mean 'Alfonsus'—very ingenious interpretation, that—but it could refer to some coordinate system in which the Y coordinate was the square of the X coordinate. Similarly C-C would mean 'Bond' or it could mean 'halfway between Cassini and Copernicus.' F/A could mean 'Newton' or it could mean 'between Fabricius and Archimedes.'

"In short, the items have so many meanings that they are meaningless. Even if one of them had meaning, it could not be selected from among the others, so that it is only sensible to suppose that all the items are merely red herrings.

"It is necessary, then, to determine what about the message is completely unambiguous, what is perfectly clear. The answer to that can only be that it *is* a message, that it *is* a clue to a hiding place. That is the one thing we are certain about, isn't it?''

Davenport nodded, then said cautiously, ''At least, we think we are certain of it.''

''Well, you have referred to this message as the key to the whole matter. You have acted as though it were the crucial clue. Jennings himself referred to the Device as a key or a clue. If we combine this serious view of the matter with Jennings's penchant for puns, a penchant which may have been heightened by the mind-tampering Device he was carrying—So let me tell you a story.

''In the last half of the sixteenth century, there lived a German Jesuit in Rome. He was a mathematician and astronomer of note and helped Pope Gregory XIII reform the calendar in 1582, performing all the enormous calculations required. This astronomer admired Copernicus but he did not accept the heliocentric view of the Solar System. He clung to the older belief that the Earth was the center of the Universe.

''In 1650, nearly forty years after the death of this mathematician, the Moon was mapped by another Jesuit, the Italian astronomer, Giovanni Battista Riccioli. He named the craters after astronomers of the past and since he too rejected Copernicus, he selected the largest and most spectacular craters for those who placed the Earth at the center of the Universe—for Ptolemy, Hipparchus, Alfonso X, Tycho Brahe. The biggest crater Riccioli could find he reserved for his German Jesuit predecessor.

''This crater is actually only the second largest of the craters visible from Earth. The only larger crater is Bailly, which is right on the Moon's limb and is therefore very difficult to see from the Earth. Riccioli ignored it, and it was named for an astronomer who lived a century after his time and who was guillotined during the French Revolution.''

Ashley was listening to all this restlessly. ''But what has this to do with the message?''

''Why, everything,'' said Urth, with some surprise. ''Did

you not call this message the key to the whole business? Isn't it the crucial clue?"

"Yes, of course."

"Is there any doubt that we are dealing with something that is a clue or key to something else?"

"No, there isn't," said Ashley.

"Well, then— The name of the German Jesuit I have been speaking of is Christoph Klau—pronounced 'klow'. Don't you see the pun? Klau—clue?"

Ashley's entire body seemed to grow flabby with disappointment. "Farfetched," he muttered.

Davenport said anxiously, "Dr. Urth, there is no feature on the Moon named Klau as far as I know."

"Of course not," said Urth excitedly. "That is the whole point. At this period of history, the last half of the sixteenth century, European scholars were Latinizing their names. Klau did so. In the place of the German 'u,' he made use of the equivalent letter, the Latin 'v'. He then added an 'ius' ending typical of Latin names and Christoph Klau became Christopher Clavius, and I suppose you are all aware of the giant crater we call Clavius."

"But—" began Davenport.

"Don't 'but' me," said Urth. "Just let me point out that the Latin word 'clavis' means 'key.' *Now* do you see the double and bilingual pun? Klau—clue, Clavius—clavis—key. In his whole life, Jennings could never have made a double, bilingual pun, without the Device. Now he could, and I wonder if death might not have been almost triumphant under the circumstances. And he directed you to me because he knew I would remember his penchant for puns and because he knew I loved them too."

The two men of the Bureau were looking at him wide-eyed.

Urth said solemnly, "I would suggest you search the shaded rim of Clavius, at that point where the Earth is nearest the zenith."

Ashley rose. "Where is your videophone?"

"In the next room."

Ashley dashed. Davenport lingered behind. "Are you sure, Dr. Urth?"

"Quite sure. But even if I am wrong, I suspect it doesn't matter."

"What doesn't matter?"

"Whether you find it or not. For if the Ultras find the Device, they will probably be unable to use it."

"Why do you say that?"

"You asked me if Jennings had ever been a student of mine, but you never asked me about Strauss, who was also a geologist. He was a student of mine a year or so after Jennings. I remember him well."

"Oh?"

"An unpleasant man. Very cold. It is the hallmark of the Ultras, I think. They are all very cold, very rigid, very sure of themselves. They can't empathize, or they wouldn't speak of killing off billions of human beings. What emotions they possess are icy ones, self-absorbed ones, feelings incapable of spanning the distance between two human beings."

"I think I see."

"I'm sure you do. The conversation reconstructed from Strauss's ravings showed us he could not manipulate the Device. He lacked the emotional intensity, or the type of necessary emotion. I imagine all Ultras would. Jennings, who was not an Ultra, could manipulate it. Anyone who could use the Device would, I suspect, be incapable of deliberate cold-blooded cruelty. He might strike out of panic or fear as Jennings stuck at Strauss, but never out of calculation, as Strauss tried to strike at Jennings. In short, to put it tritely, I think the Device can be actuated by love, but never by hate, and the Ultras are nothing if not haters."

Davenport nodded. "I hope you're right. But then—why were you so suspicious of the government's motives if you felt the wrong men could not manipulate the Device?"

Urth shrugged. "I wanted to make sure you could bluff and rationalize on your feet and make yourself convincingly persuasive at a moment's notice. After all, you may have to face my niece."

About the Editor

MARTIN GREENBERG has compiled over two hundred anthologies, including nine in Fawcett's Best of the West series. He is a noted scholar and teaches at the University of Wisconsin in Green Bay.